Crossroads

John Doriot

Crossroads

This is a work of fiction. All of the characters, organizations, and events portrayed are either products of the author's imagination or are used fictitiously.

Copyright © 2020 John Doriot

ISBN 978-1-7332528-6-7

Dedication

For my wife who never stopped believing in me,
For my son who inspired me,
For the little black and white dog who stayed by
my side as I wrote every word,
And for my closest of friends, "Briney" – Tell
Stevie I said Hello.

About the Author:

A lover of horror stories since he was a very young boy, John began pursuing his dream of becoming a writer after he retired. The stories were always there, waiting for a chance to get out, and now that the door has opened, he hopes they will find an audience. Other than the psychiatrists. Transferring his nightmares onto paper has become, and remains so to this day, a very therapeutic process.

John lives in Georgia with his wife and dog in a secure facility. Feel free to contact him at madcow26@comcast.net and let him know your opinion about the book. He welcomes your feedback.

Table of Contents

Virginia Avenue 1

Maxwell Street 16

Furys Ferry 35

6th Street 63

Clinch Avenue.. 94

Whitney Place 120

Shoemaker Street.. 139

421 171

The Alleys 209

I-75 221

Virginia Avenue

It was 11 a.m., but she had only gotten up about an hour ago. She was sleeping a lot longer these days. She told herself it was just one of those things that happened with age. Her morning routine was the same every day. Stretch for fifteen minutes. Drink a cup of coffee and a glass of orange juice and eat a bran muffin and one banana. She believed this breakfast combination had enabled her to live such a long life.

After getting dressed, she checked the weather by looking out the bay window in the front of the house which also allowed her to see if she recognized anyone that might be out there. She hoped her daughter might visit with her later today. It was her birthday but it might as well have been any other day. No one ever came to see her on her birthday anymore. She didn't receive any birthday cards or 'Happy Birthday' phone calls. There was no acknowledgment from anyone. And as she sat there staring out the window, she understood her loneliness was no one's fault but her own.

She walked out onto her porch, sat down in her favorite chair, and wondered if this would be her last birthday. She couldn't remember if she was seventy-one or seventy-two. Hours were like days and days like years for her now. The timeline blurred a little more each day. She asked herself if her daughter might come by today, forgetting that she had a similar thought just a few minutes ago. She then reminded herself, like she always did, that her daughter was probably busy with her own family and just didn't have the time to stop in as much as she wanted. It had been that way with her mother after she had gotten married and had a family.

Then the memories she didn't like to think about would fill her mind; how she and her daughter used to argue a lot but she couldn't recall what they were arguing about. She tried to convince herself she didn't know why, but if she dwelled on it for any length of time, she would remember the reasons.

"I hate you!" her daughter screamed as she slammed the door and stormed out of the house. Sometimes, she could even see a shadow of her daughter walking away until it disappeared as if the sun had gone behind some clouds. Those words would echo in her ears over and over. "I hate you." The words were not unfamiliar. Her husband also uttered the same thing years ago. Just like her daughter's absence from her life, she didn't know how long her husband had been gone. She did remember that her husband's final comments were somewhat different from her daughter's. "I fucking hate you," he had said as he slammed the door. That one adverb cost him a lot of money.

When her husband left, she told her friends she didn't care that he was gone, but that was a lie. It was true she didn't care that he was actually gone, but she did care about the embarrassment it caused her. In fact, that one aspect of the entire event was what she cared about the most.

She claimed that her husband had been cheating on her. "That's why I kicked him out of the house," she would say. But those who knew her husband did not believe her. They weren't sure he would ever be with another woman after what he had endured with her.

She announced that she didn't need a man to help raise her daughter. The people she referred to as friends noticed that she always said 'her' daughter and not 'their' daughter, but they never mentioned it. She told them that she didn't even like having sex with him. "Fuck him," she always said after a few gin and tonics and then would pause before adding, "if you want, but you will be disappointed." Everyone laughed the first twenty or so times she made that same joke but she soon realized the humor had dissipated just like her influence among her friends within the country club circle.

Though she didn't want to admit it, those people she called friends had become friends with a married couple - not with her. If not for her husband, it was doubtful she would have had anyone she could call a friend at all. Not at the country club. Not anywhere really. And even if none of them ever said it to her face, the lack of invitations, the whispers, and glances of intolerance became very apparent to her.

"Fuck him," she told herself whenever she drove home from the country club, though she made those trips less and less over time. "You made me very rich. So, good riddance, you bastard. You didn't do a damn thing around the house. You went to work, played golf, and watched sports all the time. Who the hell watches bowling? You didn't like the kind of movies I liked or the books that I read. I don't even know why I married you. You had bad taste in just about everything. My friends even said you had bad taste in women." When she realized what she had just said the anger would rumble within her stomach until the words "Fuck them too," came flying out of her mouth as if someone had just performed the Heimlich maneuver on her.

After the divorce, she changed her name from Plank, which she had always hated, to Pemberton, even though that wasn't even her maiden name. She had hated taking the name Plank as her own when she got married. It sounded so common and unsophisticated. She liked the idea of Ms.

3

Pemberton. She thought it sounded important. Affluent. Influential. Rich. Almost mysterious. The beautiful Ms. Pemberton. That sounded like a character in a James Bond movie. But she was just fooling herself. No one would tell her that though. No one except Tish.

Tish was her housekeeper. Her real name was Laquithia. Long ago, her employer had known her name but over time her memory became so bad that she couldn't even remember how to pronounce it. She just started calling her Tish and wondered how odd it was that her housekeeper shared the same name as her mother's housekeeper. The name change never bothered Laquithia. She had been called worse. A lot worse.

Tish never called her employer Ms. Pemberton. She called her Miss Rose even though her real name was Rosalyn. She told Miss Rose that Pemberton was a made-up name and she wasn't ever going to use it. For some reason, it didn't matter to Rosalyn. Perhaps it was because she knew she couldn't afford to alienate anyone else that she cared about and enjoyed being around.

In the past, Rosalyn had been called Rose as a compliment to her love and passion for those flowers. At least that's what Rosalyn believed. Hearing them call her Rose was some sort of a divine edict, she thought, because she was sharing her name with the prettiest of flowers. All of the roses that she grew in her yard were beautiful and reflected the caring and thoughtful manner in which she tended them. She was right that people called her Rose because of the beautiful flowers, but she failed to realize that they were also referring to the prickly nature of the plant which could cut open the flesh of someone's unobservant hand, just like the person who was capable of tearing open an emotional wound with words as sharp as thorns.

Tish had worked for Rose for a very long time. At first, she came every day of the week, but as they both grew older,

4

it had dwindled to only Wednesdays. Rose wouldn't admit it but she looked forward to that day more than any other day of the week. It gave her a chance to show her friend some of the roses that were in bloom, and an opportunity to talk to someone who genuinely seemed interested in what she had to say.

Tish always asked the same question as soon as she walked in the door.

"What's new, Miss Rose?" and Rose would smile and hand her a cup of coffee and tell her to follow her outside. Out in the garden, Rose would point out the latest hybrid that was in full bloom, or the newest shrub rose, or the climbing rose, or tea rose, or carpet rose, or "knock-out" rose. To Tish, the varieties seemed infinite whether in shape, form, or scent.

And after seeing them, Tish always had the same response, regardless of what type of rose she had just examined. "They're very beautiful, Miss Rose. When God gave you a green thumb, he sure knew what he was doing."

And Rose would smile. Divine edict reinforced.

Once back inside, Rose would ask Tish about her family and Tish would talk while she cleaned the countertops or wiped away the dust that had accumulated around the house. She would also inspect the refrigerator for items that were no longer safe to eat or drink. Rose failed to notice the rotten items which grew in volume over time. Then Tish would prepare several meals for later in the week because she knew when she left that Rose probably wouldn't eat very much, if at all. Sometimes when she came back the following Wednesday, she would have to throw out several of the meals she had made for her the previous week or find ones she had placed in the freezer untouched. She would just shake her head and say a little prayer and make some more.

Tish always brought a new set of family pictures to share with her boss and, over the years, Rose watched as children were replaced with grandchildren and she envied Tish. Her pictures were much more interesting than her roses, though she wouldn't ever come right out and say that. As Tish showed Rose her pictures, she would mention something special about each family member. Rose enjoyed hearing all of the stories, but she was particularly interested in hearing about Eleanor.

Eleanor had cerebral palsy but the strength she possessed always amazed Rose. She wanted Eleanor to succeed and overcome the obstacles she had encountered at such a young age because, in some way, she reminded Rose of her own daughter. She didn't know why, because Marie had been born healthy and had succeeded at everything she did. Perhaps in some distorted way of thinking, she thought Eleanor's ability to overcome her difficulties provided hope that she and her daughter could conquer their issues. In any case, she was always fascinated to hear Tish talk about Eleanor.

"How long have you worked for me, Tish?" Rose asked.

"Sixty years," Tish replied. She didn't mind answering that question when it came up and over the past twenty years, it came up a lot.

"That's a very long time."

"Yes ma'am, it is."

"In all of that time, have we ever talked about politics?"

"Oh, my goodness, Miss Rose. Some days, that's all we talk about. Of course, that's only after we talk about the flowers and the family for a bit."

When Rose heard that she smiled, though the fact she couldn't remember what they talked about bothered her a little. "Have you seen what those idiots in Washington have done now?"

"You'll have to be more specific, Miss Rose. There's a bunch of those idiots up there."

They both laughed as they sat down at the kitchen table and had another cup of coffee.

6

"They think that Washington is their own damn house."

"Yes ma'am, I believe they do."

"I regret voting for the people that I put there. They never do a damn thing they say they are going to do."

Tish was amused when she heard Rose refer to herself as if she was the sole person responsible for placing someone into Congress or the Presidency.

"I feel the same way. It seems like we would all learn but it never seems like we do."

"We shouldn't have to learn. They need to learn. That's the damn problem. They have forgotten or chosen not to listen to the people that sent them into that seat of power. I hate every damn one of them. Republican, Democrat. Can't seem to see the difference anymore. Bunch of incompetent nincompoops."

Tish smiled when she heard Rose say "nincompoops." That was an 'old person' word that she remembered her grandmother using, but knew if she said that to Miss Rose she would be insulted. So, she just shook her head and continued the conversation.

"I understand, Miss Rose. I understand. But I don't hate them. I don't use that word. That word has been used way too much. My preacher tells the congregation every week not to hate and I believe he's right. Reverend King said the same thing. Not to hate. Though I will tell you - but only you - I wouldn't want to invite some of them over to my house for dinner."

They laughed and Tish could see the sparkle in Miss Rose's eye. She didn't get to see that shimmer enough she thought.

"You are such a kind soul, Tish. A kind and caring soul. I am very lucky to have you with me."

Tish smiled and patted Rose's hand. She took another sip of coffee as she thought about what she had just heard. She prayed for strength, knowing what she needed to tell Rose. She hoped she wouldn't start crying.

"Have we ever talked about God in those sixty years, Tish?"

"No, ma'am. Not directly."

"What do you mean not directly?"

"I mean, we talk about things that certainly reflect the influence religion has on our life, but we have never really talked about God."

"You believe in God, don't you, Tish?"

"Yes, ma'am. Very much so."

Rose looked at Tish and wished she had the strong convictions that were reflected in her voice, but she knew she didn't. She struggled with her beliefs. And she knew why. She felt like God had abandoned her. Like her husband and daughter. Like everyone else in the world except that one person who sat across the table from her.

"If there is a God, why do bad things happen to good people? And with everything that is so bad in the country and the world right now, why doesn't God do something?"

"I don't know for certain the answer to that first question, Miss Rose, except to say that there is evil in this world. And sometimes evil just gets the best of people. I know it doesn't make sense sometimes. But I have faith and I know sometimes you just have to cover yourself up in your faith and ask for guidance and strength and the power of hope. Hope is a powerful word, Miss Rose. A powerful word.

"And considering everything that is going on around the world, I believe He is doing something. If he wasn't, things would be even worse. There are miracles every day. You just have to have faith, Miss Rose. If you have faith, you can see those miracles. If you don't, you only see the bad things in life. My faith allows me to see the good this world has to offer every day I wake up. In something as simple as a cold glass of sweet tea on a hot day, or in the beautiful flowers that

8

surround us. I see it in the face of my family; especially when I look in the eyes of Eleanor."

At the mention of Eleanor, Rose realized Tish was right, but her belief was fleeting. Within moments, the doubts resurfaced and, like clouds, obstructed her view and confused her. Tish saw the look of bewilderment on Rose's face and continued talking.

"If I didn't have faith and a strong belief system within myself and my family, I wouldn't be able to sleep at night."

"Maybe that's why I don't sleep at night."

"Yes, ma'am. That's one reason."

"One reason?"

"There's that and your daughter."

If anyone other than Tish had said that, Rose would have shut down the conversation but she wanted to hear what her companion of sixty years had to say.

"You and your daughter haven't been good for the longest time. Twenty years now. I know how that loss hurts."

The words made Rose feel like she had grabbed one of her favorite roses by the stem without acknowledging the angry nature of its composition. And instead of releasing the imaginary plant, she tightened her grip around it and embraced the pain that radiated from the palm of her hand. She then thought about her neighbor and how, just like Tish, she had a big family too. She could see them as they walked by her window. And like Tish, they were black.

They were all like that she thought. All the black people she knew had big families. She had never taken the time to get to know her neighbor who had moved in a long time ago. She resented her neighbor and the close-knit family; just as she was jealous of Tish and her family too, but she would never say that to her. She didn't want to hurt Tish's feelings.

"Do you think black people and white people should get married?"

Tish wanted to chastise Miss Rose for asking her the same question that she always seemed to ask but she sighed and answered her.

"Actually, Miss Rose, I don't think it matters. Yes, I know you and I are old enough to know the days when it did matter, but I truly feel like those days are gone."

"Yes, maybe you are right. You're always right it seems. There have been so many changes that I can't remember them all."

Tish watched as the gleam left Miss Rose's eyes and exhaled. She regretted what she had to say next, but she knew she couldn't delay it any longer.

"I have something to tell you, Miss Rose, and though I dread doing it, I have to. I need to tell you I'm leaving. I've gotten too old it seems. My son, Josiah, is taking me back to North Carolina where I was born. I won't be coming here anymore after today."

Rose's hands began to tremble and her first instinct was to shout an obscenity at Tish but she restrained herself. Tears trickled down her face and though she wasn't sure she could find her voice, she found enough of it to ask why.

"My family has been asking me the same thing for years, Miss Rose. Why? Why do I keep coming by here and I tell them every time they ask, that I come here because you need me."

Rose shook her head and knew she should be thankful for the time she had with Tish, but just like her resolve with a belief in a higher power, her ability to say thank you was ephemeral.

"I sure am sorry you and Marie could never put your differences behind you, Rose. I know she wanted to do that and, deep down, I think you wanted that too."

Rose sat there silently. She wanted to admit to Tish she was right but her pride and ignorance wouldn't allow it.

"I wanted you to know that there will be someone to come in my place, Miss Rose. She'll be here tomorrow to introduce herself and set up a schedule with you. Her name is Abby. I waited as long as I could to tell you, Miss Rose, but I couldn't wait anymore. I am sorry. I will pray for you Miss Rose, and I hope you can find forgiveness and hope in your heart."

Rose tried to hold onto Tish's hand to keep her from leaving, but she couldn't. She didn't have the strength. She watched as Tish walked away and the tears in her eyes wouldn't even allow her to see her friend walk through the door for the last time. She wasn't sure how long she sat there at the kitchen table, but when she looked out the window the sky had turned dark. She got up and went to bed. She hadn't eaten anything all day but she wasn't hungry. She lay down, closed her eyes and went to sleep.

She was at the window looking outside the next morning when she heard someone knocking. She opened the door and found a thin middle-aged woman with brown hair and bloodshot eyes, smoking a cigarette.

The wisps of smoke made Rose remember how much she used to enjoy her cigarettes but the advanced COPD prevented her from smoking now and she didn't like to be around it. It tempted her and made her sick at the same time. She wondered what this person wanted.

"Name's Abby. Tish sent me. Where do you want me to start?" she asked as she flipped the cigarette into a flower bed.

Why would Tish send this person here? I don't like her, Rose thought. Not at all.

"The first thing you can do is pick up that cigarette butt. The second thing you can do is never smoke around me again and the third thing you can do is get the hell off of my front porch," Rose said and slammed the door.

As she stepped back into the kitchen, that same woman was sitting at the kitchen table, smoking a cigarette and drinking a cup of coffee.

"How in the hell did you get in here?" Rose demanded.

"I walked. Not that hard. Considering no one else is going to come by here, I figured you'd be happy to see me."

"Well, your intelligence must be equivalent to your hearing. Neither one of them is worth a damn. I don't want you here, so get the hell out. I wish Tish was here. She would know what to do."

"Tish is gone, Rose. Finished. Sayonara. Kaput. Lights out. Dust. She's never coming back."

"Don't talk about her that way! You don't know that. You are rude, hateful, and vile. You don't even know me and I doubt you even know Tish. Put that damn cigarette out. It makes me ill to smell it. And you stink worse than the cigarette. Do you even know what soap and water are?"

Abby threw the cigarette on the floor and put it out with her shoeless foot.

"Ah, but you are wrong, Rosalyn. Or should I say, Ms. Pemberton? I do know Tish and I know you very well. I know Tish's son, Josiah too. You know, the housekeeper's son? The young man that married your daughter, Marie. You remember that Rose, don't you? I saw your daughter's wedding, unlike you. You told your daughter she couldn't marry the housekeeper's son because people like you and she didn't marry the son of a housekeeper. But Marie wasn't like you. She didn't see a housekeeper's son. She saw a kind and loving man. Very much like his mother in a lot of aspects. Very handsome and smart too. But you should know that. Her mother told you that he graduated from Georgia Tech with a degree in computer science, didn't she?

"Your daughter was very smart too. She knew the only reason you didn't want her to marry Josiah was that he was black. It had nothing to do with him being a housekeeper's son. She walked out of your life the day they married and if it had been up to Josiah, she would have never come back. But her mother-in-law kept hoping and trying to heal the rift between you two and finally, after twenty years, she got Marie to meet you at one of your favorite restaurants.

"Do you remember that, Rose? Meeting your daughter that day at Chesapeake's? After an awkward ten minutes or so, she began telling you about her family. When she showed you the picture of Eleanor, sitting in a wheelchair, with a smile that brightened up every room she entered, you started crying. The little girl that shared your middle name. That little girl had a smile that jumped off the picture and into your heart. When that happened, you had your daughter back.

"You both had lobster and she had several glasses of wine while you had your favorite gin and tonic. You had a lot of gin and tonics that day. You both laughed and enjoyed each other's company. For several hours it was like time had stopped and neither one of you wanted the day to end. But it ended. You wanted to take her home and see her house. If she had just refused that last glass of wine you ordered for her, she might have seen that it was not a good idea to get in the car with you. You were both killed instantly when you hit that tree going seventy miles an hour."

"What the hell are you talking about? I have been right here in my house. Tish; she comes by and sees me. I see the neighbors walking by my house every morning. I get up in the morning and I stretch. Then I have orange juice and coffee and Tish comes by. One day a week, Tuesday, I think. No - Wednesday. Yes, she comes on Wednesdays."

"Well, let's just stop this Tish nonsense right now. Her name is Laquithia, not Tish, but your convenient dementia prevents you from remembering. Because you know if you remember her name, you have to remember other things. Yes, she came by every Wednesday for the past twenty years. She came to your grave every week and prayed for you. She was

13

the only one of the family that stopped by to tell you how your daughter's family was doing. Those people you see walking by your window are Josiah's family, his children, and their children. Two of them are your great-granddaughters. The girl in the wheelchair is Eleanor. They are walking to Marie's gravesite. It's right next to yours."

Rose covered her eyes with her hands and shook her head. When she opened them, the middle-aged woman was gone and in her place was someone glowing like a strange Christmas decoration with blues and greens that flickered on and off. Her face was difficult to describe because what should be parts of a face moved around and even disappeared at times, only to be replaced with something that looked depraved and inhuman.

"Who the hell are you?"

"My name is Abaddon. But I know you have a problem with remembering names so you can just call me Abby. Or Tish, if you want."

"No! You are not Tish. Now, get the hell out of my house you crazy bitch!"

"You are stubborn. I'll give you that. Do you know why you didn't talk about God much? You do remember that conversation, don't you? You just had it yesterday."

Rose sat down as she started to remember that conversation.

"You damned him along with everyone else in your life and in doing so, damned yourself. Yet, you still had a chance. For twenty years you had a chance as you were in the presence of the Lord every Wednesday when Laquithia visited your grave. She was an angelic soul with an undying belief and faith in mercy and forgiveness but you failed to recognize it.

"For a moment there, I thought she had turned things around but then good old Mrs. Plank showed up and you missed your chance to acknowledge the presence of God and

14

ask for his forgiveness. Your anger and prejudice just wouldn't allow you to do that. Anger is a bitterness that over time changes the way you see things, feel things, and taste things, and even embitters your soul.

"Laquithia knew that and tried to save you. It was her love and faith and hope that stopped me from getting my hands on you, but she is gone now. She died yesterday. Your son-in-law Josiah is taking her ashes back to Blowing Rock where she was born."

All of Rose's memories came rushing back into focus and pelted her body like the shards of glass she felt as her daughter's head went through the windshield of the car. She screamed and fell to her knees as she heard the laughter from the person that called herself Abby, wrap around her body like a large python choking the breath out of her. She looked up and saw the blue and green colors flicker and she thought they looked very un-Christmas-like.

She sat alone and looked out the window. It was 11 a.m. She had just gotten up about an hour ago. She was sleeping a lot longer these days. She told herself it was just one of those things that happened with age. She tried stretching but it hurt too much so she didn't. She didn't eat the bran muffin either because she thought she saw something inside of it move. The banana peel was black and mushy and smelled bad so she threw it and the muffin in the trash. The orange juice had a bad taste. It appeared that it had soured. Her coffee didn't taste right either.

And then she remembered. She remembered and thought how bitter the coffee tasted. She feared it would taste like that for a very long time as she looked out the window at the dead roses.

Maxwell Street

The thought of getting on a plane again made him nauseous. He had spent most of the early morning hours before the flight in the bathroom as the anxiety he had about flying exited his body with loud grunts and moans. He was unable to contain his sickness even with pills that usually worked because his intestinal tract knew where he was going. His gut knew the human in which it resided was flying to a place that it and the brain dreaded. And feeling threatened, it reacted in a way that reminded both who was really in charge.

He had lived in Tennessee his entire life, just at the base of the Smoky Mountains. His home was a custom-built cabin with a view of the mountains that very few people who lived there, or rented space there, ever saw. He felt it gave him a glimpse of Heaven, and there would be few Tennesseans that would argue with him. Especially when the blue haze of the mountains drifted among the trees as if they were so tall they grew up into the clouds, or clung to the edge of the mountains, changing their outline for just a moment while it lingered there. No matter how many times he saw it, that phenomenon was always mesmerizing to him. The child-like wonder that he maintained enabled him to capture those images on canvas every day.

His professor friend at the University of Tennessee had explained to him the scientific reason why that blue haze existed. It was, according to him, "due to the diverse plant life within the mountains, which emit chemicals known as volatile organic compounds in addition to oxygen. Those compounds allow you to smell the plants as well as create the blue fog because of the molecule's ability to scatter the blue light from the sky, thus creating the bluish tint that is encapsulated within those vapors."

Shit, he thought as soon as his friend told him the science behind what he saw.

"Bill, I understand your need to have things explained. It's what makes you who you are and one of the best at what you do. But don't explain things to me ever again. I don't need to know the science behind everything. I prefer to live in another world. A world where the implausible is plausible. When I go into the woods, I not only see nature, I see where shadows could suggest Sasquatch exists. Where the synchronicity of fireflies might suggest that you have stumbled upon a realm of fairies. Where a tree is not a combination of carbon, hydrogen, oxygen, and nitrogen, but a sentinel that provides a safe haven for those with the ability to rest within its arms, or a landmark for those that dared to venture into that forest hundreds of years ago. I know that is anathema to a scientist but I am not a scientist, nor a madman. I just prefer to see nature in a different manner."

Bill nodded his head at his friend James and smiled. He understood why he said what he did and honored his request from that point forward. It made him who he was and one of the best artists in the world.

The Cherokees considered the mountains sacred and referred to them as Sha-Kon-O-Hey; the land of the blue smoke. James always thought the smokey mist looked like the spirits of the forest that had not learned from ghostwriters or paranormal investigators that ghostly apparitions shunned the sunlight and were not supposed to be there during the day.

Yes, they might disappear in one place, but given time, they would slowly reappear, perhaps in the same place or somewhere close by. It was as if the Indian spirits knew it was their duty to remind you they were always there, watching and guarding that which was hallowed ground. And when he painted, that belief was transferred onto the canvas. There had been more than one review of his paintings that shared that same feeling.

"James Marshall's paintings capture the Smoky Mountains as very few artists can. His work makes you feel as if you are standing beside him looking at ancient Indian spirits that arise from the trees and guard the sacred land. It's as if you had been hiking along a trail and happened upon him sitting there with his brush and paints, sharing his amazement and knowing why he had stopped."

He had saved that review. He liked the way the critic had used the phrase "standing beside him looking at ancient Indian spirits that arise from the trees and guard the sacred land." *He understands*, he told himself.

But that was not all he loved about the mountains. He loved painting the many streams found just off the paved road or miles off a trail that took on different characteristics depending upon the time of day or the day of the year. He loved the magic that was created by the spring and summer flowers that demonstrated their brilliant resilience growing in an area of little sunlight or emerging from the tiniest crack of a rock in a defiant manner. He loved finding a field of Fire Pink flowers that were so red against the green grass that he wasn't even sure he had the ability to mimic it. How could something so common within the forest be so beautiful he wondered?

He enjoyed hiking to the waterfalls and sitting there while the water poured down in strong surges or leaked out of the rocks in small trickles, watching and listening to them for a while before he ever started to paint them. And then there was autumn. Breathtaking autumn. A Crayola box of colors that was one of his favorite times of the year. He always left home before sunrise during that time of the year to find a trail to hike, knowing that as the day progressed the traffic would become so dense that he always wondered how any of the tourists saw anything. But he had to admire their tenacity. Beauty like that was worth seeing even if you only saw a small part of it.

And tomorrow he would be leaving all of that. The flight he would be getting on in the morning would be taking him to their new home. She had bought it for them when she had visited her sister in New York. She was already there waiting for him. He had asked his professor friend to come over and share a bottle of their favorite whiskey with him before he got on the plane. And knowing his friend as he did, the professor brought an extra bottle of their favorite whiskey and knew he would not be going home that evening.

"Why are you leaving?" Bill asked as they sat on the porch and looked at the mountains. "You love this place. You have lived here your entire life. I think Abrams Creek runs through your veins in lieu of blood."

"My wife bought us a house in New York," James replied.

"So? Can't you afford two houses?"

"I could have, provided the new house that she bought didn't cost three and a half million dollars."

"Holy shit. You never told me it cost that much."

"No, I didn't. I've been trying to figure out how I can get out of it ever since I found out about it. But I can't think of any way except maybe to kill her."

Bill looked at James with the eyes of an owl when he heard him say that.

"You do know the police consult me when they find skeletons in the ground? I study bones, early man, you know,

19

that type of thing. I'm considered an expert in my field. And as one of your best friends, they will ask me if I heard you say anything strange or gave any indication about killing his wife. And I would have to say, 'No, I can't think of anything but there was that last night when we were drinking right before he went to New York where he said something about not wanting to move and, oh yeah, maybe he did say the only way out was to kill her.'"

"Bill, you know deep down I couldn't kill her. I'm not sure I could kill anything. I don't even take a gun into the woods with me and you know I have encountered black bears eleven times in the forest. But each time they just stared at me as if they knew that the odd-looking thing in front of it wasn't something that would harm it. And each time, the bears have always walked away."

"Yes, I have been meaning to say something about that."

"Oh, here it comes. Some other scientific explanation that I don't want to hear."

"It will probably surprise you, but I was going to say something very unscientific."

James looked puzzled at his good friend.

"I have a friend at the university in the Anthropology department who studies Indian cultures. I was telling her about all your encounters with the black bears and she told me how the black bear was a reflection of the Great Spirit on Earth. The fact that you have encountered them so many times without incident tells her with 100% certainty that the Bear is your spirit guide. You would have been considered a great shaman four hundred and fifty years ago."

"Four hundred and fifty years ago, huh? Well, it's apparent that my shaman abilities have waned a bit over the years. Otherwise, I would have gotten that university you are associated with to remember how to play football."

"Perhaps you aren't burning enough sage at the games."

"I stopped burning sage in the 70s."

Bill laughed and refilled their glasses with Gentleman Jack.

"Are you leaving your furniture here?"

"Some of it. We haven't actually put our house on the market yet."

"But…"

"Yes, I know I said I couldn't afford two houses but I'm trying to see how much I can get for all the originals in the house that I didn't plan on selling."

"James - the pictures in the house - I thought you would never sell them."

"Me too. But things change. Would you be interested in purchasing the one over the fireplace? I can get you a good deal on it. I want $100,000, but for you, I will let it go for half that."

"50,000? Hell, I can't get rid of all the James Marshall originals I have now in my office. What am I going to do with another one that costs that much?"

"Asshole."

"An asshole with a lot of original James Marshall paintings, thank you very much."

"Come down into my studio. I have three new ones that are in various stages of completion and I would like your esteemed opinion regarding them."

Bill followed his friend into the studio and shook his head as he began to speak.

"Spectacular, James. Just stunning. That first one there - the field of red, blue, yellow, and white wildflowers amongst the rocks and green and brown grasses - it looks like it's a digital image photograph. The other picture of the stream meandering through the woods with slivers of sunlight coming through the forest canopy; it seems as if the light is some divine signal to those that happen upon it. And the last one - the waterfall - is incredible. The water comes bursting over the rocks only to turn into some sort of fine misty veil toward the bottom. How you capture that type of thing, I'll never understand."

Bill walked over to the picture of the waterfall and stared at it. As he did, he thought he saw two eyes from behind the thin watery curtain at the bottom of the falls, looking back at him.

"This is some of your best work," Bill said as he took a drink of the Gentleman Jack. "That field of flowers is lifelike. The stream is a moment in time where one realizes how spiritual nature truly is. And the waterfall is a mirror, isn't it?"

James smiled.

"Finally, after all these years, you are beginning to see what I see. I was starting to think I should find another friend. In fact, I am still giving that careful consideration, but about the waterfall, you are right. I saw it as sort of a mirror, but those eyes you see are those of a black bear."

"You saw a bear behind the falls?"

"I thought I did. Though as I went behind the falls, I saw nothing but a few fireflies in the cave. I did see a few bear paw prints in the mud but I can't say how old they were."

"Shit. Don't you get it? The black bear is a reflection of you. Your spirit."

"Yes, with enough whiskey inside of me I can agree with you tonight. But once the alcohol lessens its ability to influence my opinion, I will tell you in the morning that it was only the shadows of the forest that made me see a bear that day."

"You say what you want, but the ancestral bones never lie and my friend is very smart. There is more to this than you think."

Bill walked over and put his arm around his friend's shoulder.

"Let's finish that bottle we opened and then call it a night. You've got a plane to catch in the morning and I'm hoping you will let me know how well those barf bags truly work."

"Asshole."

"Indeed," Bill replied and laughed as they walked up the stairs.

Because he had emptied most of the contents of his stomach and colon at his house and in the airport bathroom before getting on the plane, he didn't get a chance to see how well the airline's sick bags worked. That and the fact he took several Xanax allowed him to sleep for most of the flight. His wife was waiting when he arrived and, knowing how anxious he would be, had a cooler of ice and a bottle of his favorite whiskey ready for him in the car.

His wife was the type of woman that people noticed wherever she went. She was that beautiful. She attended the University of Tennessee on a cheerleader scholarship and she stayed in good shape after college. He knew when she was walking anywhere with him, men and women were looking at his wife and all the well-rounded firm shapes she still possessed. In college her hair was blonde but as she got older, she dyed it red. He didn't believe it was possible, but she was even more beautiful with her reddish-brown hair.

"I was going to ask how your flight was but I can tell by that drink you're pouring, I have my answer," she said as she leaned over to kiss him. "Wow. Did you brush your teeth or bathe this morning?"

"Bill came over last night. We had a steak and a few glasses of Gentleman Jack."

"A few bottles is more like it. How is Bill?"

"I suspect he's hurting a lot right now which gives me some comfort," James said as he looked down at his watch. It was almost 3 p.m.

"Well, it will take us about four hours to get to our house in Elizabethtown, but the drive is amazing. You'll love it. We can stop along the way and get something to eat if you want, or we can drive straight through. I'd love for you to see the house while there is still light. Its view of the mountains is magnificent."

He wanted to say that he left behind a magnificent view of the mountains but he kept quiet. He put a few more pieces of ice in his drink and looked out the window as she drove. Once they were out of the city, he had to admit the landscape of upstate New York was very scenic. A good place for artists, she told him many times, and he nodded his head as she talked. He promised himself each time she said that, regardless of what it looked like, he wasn't going to admit she was right for as long as they lived there.

Perhaps if she had consulted him before she bought the house, it wouldn't have been as bad he told himself. But as he poured himself another drink, he realized he was only trying to rationalize the move. To justify what she had done like some mathematical theorem that had yet to be proven and he suspected he would never find the answer. He knew he would never be happy in New York even if he had a beautiful wife, a beautiful home, and a beautiful view of the mountains. The Adirondacks are not the Smoky Mountains. But silently, he noticed the difference begin to diminish the more they drove into the pastoral country setting and the more he drank.

He thought about what he told Bill after they had gone upstairs to finish that bottle last night. How his wife had stopped consulting him after she heard him say, "I do," and they had both laughed. But there was an honesty in that statement that he didn't want to admit to his friend. As he had become more introspective through the years, he realized that was the type of woman he was destined to marry. One that wouldn't interfere with his work. The solitary life he had come to love out there in the mountains; alone with nature and alone with his art.

24

His wife's sister lived in the same place they were moving to – Elizabethtown - which was a small town at the base of the Adirondacks. She was a psychiatrist, and though he tried, he never really understood how she made a living, considering the size of the town. He had done some research on the internet regarding Elizabethtown. It had a population of a little over 1,000 which was only fourteen people per square mile. He had enjoyed learning about that aspect of the town, provided they weren't all patients of his wife's sister. The thought of that bothered him.

His wife looked over at her husband as they drove but she didn't try and start a conversation. She knew better than to do that, considering the mood he was in. She just allowed her husband to enjoy the scenery and drink because she hoped that both would alter his demeanor and opinion of her decisions. She was very aware that he hated this move because he had told her that many times. But with her sister's encouragement, she was positive it was the right thing to do. She had been talking to her sister a lot over the past year about their marriage.

She talked to her about the chasm that was growing between them. She told her she was still very attracted to James, but she wasn't sure he shared the same feelings toward her. She looked at him as she thought about her conversations with her sister. Though he didn't exercise with intent, all the hiking he did through the mountains carrying his art supplies kept him very fit. He always had a 3 or 4-day-old beard that matched his thick brown hair and dark brown eyes. If you had seen him walking along without his art supplies, you would have thought he had just come down from somewhere deep in the mountains, with his clothes and old boots covered in paint, like one of those Tennesseans prone to using the words "yonder" and "over air" to mean "in the distance" and "over there." She smiled at that thought because she knew he was nothing like that. He was articulate, well-studied, and an exceptional artist with a rare God-given talent.

She knew he was extremely talented the first time he showed her his sketches and she told him that. At first, she loved hiking in the woods with him and soaking up everything he told her about the plant life and animals that were present in the mountains. He had an encyclopedic mind where those mountains were concerned and she thought it was fascinating. The view, whether it was the mountains or him, always made her smile.

She enjoyed the picnics they had and how, at first, he was easily distracted with the descriptive language she used to tell him what she wanted to do to him or what she wanted him to do to her right then and right there, wherever they were in the mountains. She loved controlling him in that manner but that changed over time. As he became more well-known for his art, the commissions and subsequent volume of work made him more focused on what he was doing and less inclined to become distracted, no matter what she said or showed him. And though she told herself it would be all right to be his mistress, she came to resent the other two women in his life: the mountains and his art.

"Elizabethtown city limits," James said as they drove into the little town by the river.

"Don't you just love the look of this place, James? Nestled by the river. That's the Boquet River by the way. There's brown and brook trout upstream and salmon in the lower part. Everything is just so picturesque, don't you think?" Susan asked.

James wasn't sure how to answer the question. The amount of liquor in his body usually acted as a truth serum, but he was able to subdue the first complimentary thought that came to mind and replaced it with another one that was more restrained and sarcastic.

"Which house is Ichabod Crane's? And when was the last time you saw me go fishing?"

"Oh, James. How can you say that? Look at the cute shops and the river surrounded by the mountains. We are in the mountains, James. And just wait, just wait till you see the house."

They drove about another twenty minutes and came to a gate attached to two large brick pillars.

Fuck no, he thought as he watched her open the gate from a switch in the car. Behind the gate was a cobblestone entrance lined with different kinds of large maple trees, some of which had limbs reaching over the driveway. Between the maples were large conifers of different types interspersed with clumps of paperwhite birch trees. He had to admit it was an impressive entry and, for some reason, it felt familiar. *Perhaps it was in one of those pictures he had seen from her trips with her sister,* he thought.

When she pulled in front of the house, he no longer questioned the cost of the home. Without a doubt, the large estate house and the mountain that could be seen rising from behind it told any observer that this house cost a large sum of money. He thought it looked more like a hotel that had been restored and was now operating as a spa and resort than someone's home.

"Where's the butler and domestic staff? Shouldn't they be out here all lined up for me to inspect them before we enter the house?"

"I gave them a day off, jackass. Quit being such a dick. The house is stunning and don't tell me you can't see that mountain with the sun on its shoulder. Everything looks like a postcard."

"I hate fucking postcards. And if there is a garden maze on the property I'm out of here. Bill was just talking to me the other night about spirit guides and I'm afraid I may be stepping into a place that might awaken 'The Shining' within me."

"I am glad you brought that up. It was going to be awkward otherwise. The house would be historically viewed as Edwardian because it was built in 1910, but I consider it Victorian, even though I am sure with your vast intellect you realize that age officially ended in 1901. The home has been fully restored and all the parts of the living room floor where the blood wouldn't come out were ripped up and replaced with reclaimed heart pine floors. You would never know there was a double murder-suicide here."

"How nice. Was the insane asylum not available?"

"Character, James. The house has character."

"Yes, it sounds like at least three ghostly ones. Well, let's get this over with. The mountain is nice, by the way," he said begrudgingly as he got out of the car.

"That's a start," she said as she opened the large oak double doors and took him by the hand.

"Aren't we going to stop and look at each room?" he asked as she marched him by each one of them.

When he saw the studio, he knew why she didn't stop to show him the other rooms. She wanted him to see his studio just before the sunset. The studio used to be a sunroom and there were three walls of glass with a glass roof that angled down from the house and connected to the other glass panes that made up the walls. No matter where you looked, you saw the mountain just before it became a very large shadow as the sun disappeared behind it.

"That glass is hurricane glass. It's a good thing too because you are looking at Hurricane Mountain."

"Okay. It's not a bad view. Like I said earlier, it's rather nice."

"You are going to be like this for some time, aren't you?"

"I am not sure what you are referring to."

28

"Yes, I know you don't. Why don't I take you up to the bedroom? You've had a long day."

"That's a good idea."

When he woke up the next morning, he found a note on the dresser that said: "Gone to town to do some shopping. Figured you needed to sleep. See you later, Susan."

She was right. He was still a little groggy from all he had to drink the day before. When he walked out of his bedroom he saw several people working there, cleaning the house and carrying bed linen from the room next to him. *Must have been where Susan slept.*

"Who are you?"

"We work here. My name is William and that lady over there is Jill. Would you like some breakfast?"

Damn. She really did hire staff for the house. She never told me that.

"Yes."

"Follow me, Mr. Marshall," William said. James followed him downstairs to a massive dining room. "Have a seat and I will return with your breakfast."

William came back with a large glass of orange juice, an English muffin, and 3 pieces of bacon.

"How did you know I would want that for breakfast?"

"You always have that for breakfast. Your wife informed us."

"What else did she tell you?"

"That you didn't like to be disturbed while you ate," William said as he turned around and left the room.

Well, she is pulling out all the stops, he thought as he admired the great dining hall. There was oak wainscoting along the walls and the paint on the wall was sky blue. Nice color, he thought, as he finished his breakfast and started exploring the house. As he walked around, he stopped to look at each room. He found a library and then a game room with one of the biggest TV's he'd ever seen. There were multiple

29

tables set up to play a variety of games that were piled on the bookshelves. He came across a large sitting room with couches and comfortable leather chairs and recliners (which he thought was a bit overindulgent). Then he discovered the studio.

It looks even nicer in the daylight, he thought as he smiled and walked into the bright room and over to the easel and blank canvas. His art supplies were in perfect order on several tables to the right of the easel. *All the right stuff and in the perfect place,* he said to himself as he inspected them and then looked at the alp-like mountain and the beautiful garden that comprised the backyard of the house.

"Thank God, no maze," he said out loud as he heard his name and turned around to see his wife's sister standing at the door.

"Hello, James," Katherine said as she walked over and sat down on the couch. "There are no garden mazes out in the yard. This isn't a Stephen King movie set."

"Yeah, I know. Just making a joke."

Katherine smiled. "Yes, I've heard it before. You look like you are ready to start painting."

"Yes. I think I am."

"That would be wonderful."

Weird. I never knew she liked my art that much.

"Susan's not here. She left me a note saying she had gone shopping. I'm not sure when she will be back."

"Are you sure?"

"Are you sure what?"

"That you don't know when she will be back."

James looked at his sister-in-law in a confused manner and felt like he was going to get sick. Katherine got up and helped him over to the couch.

"Lie down, James. You've lost the color in your face. Just rest for a moment. Think about Tennessee."

As he lay there, he closed his eyes and tried to think of his home in Tennessee. He saw his view of the Smoky Mountains and then he saw his friend Bill smiling at him. He saw himself and Bill and Susan walking in the mountains on a trail that he had hiked hundreds of times. It was a very remote trail that only a few people knew about, but the views were worth the trip.

He then saw the two black bear cubs run across the trail in front of him. He stood there frozen as he noticed the large dark shadow in the mountain laurel to the right where Bill and his wife were walking in front of him. He didn't have time to say anything as the four-hundred-pound black bear came charging onto the trail and swatted his friend's head. His wife screamed as she saw Bill's head hanging onto his shoulders before it and his body fell onto the ground, and then the bear jumped on her.

She collapsed and screamed until the cry turned into a gurgle as the bear's jaws ripped open her throat. It jumped up and down on her several times, each time pulling away more of her body until there appeared to be just a human puzzle with a lot of missing pieces. The bear looked in his direction and shook its head and lunged at him before it stopped and held its nose up in the air. It growled once and then went running off into the woods. James suddenly opened his eyes and looked at his sister-in-law.

"How long have I been here?" he asked.

"Ten years. This is the first time you have ever come into the studio that I set up for you. I knew if you were ever going to recover, it would be your art that would help you come back. You were able to see everything today, weren't you?"

James nodded his head as the tears fell down his cheek.

"Tell me what you saw."

"I saw my best friend and wife mauled by a large black bear. A mother that felt her cubs were in danger. I watched the cubs run across the trail but I couldn't do anything. I was frozen as I saw that huge bear come out of the woods and decapitate my best friend. And it mauled my wife. It was horrible. I don't know how I survived."

"You don't believe you should have survived. For ten years you have tried not to remember but each year, we made a little more progress, until today when you finally came into the studio. I knew then you would remember what happened and finally realize you are not to blame. You can come back into the real world now, James, instead of the imaginary one that you have occupied for so long. You lost your best friend and wife but you are alive and it's okay that you are alive. I think in a month or so, we can work out a therapy protocol for you. With the right medication and counseling, I think you can go home. You can go back to Tennessee, James."

Over the next month, James realized where he was for the first time. He now knew how his sister-in-law was able to work as a psychiatrist in such a small town. The Adirondack Institute was a very well-known asylum for those rich enough to go there. He started painting again and he donated the pictures of Hurricane Mountain and the beautiful gardens and estate to the institute.

Katherine gave him the name of a therapist at the University of Tennessee who would see him every week for as long as necessary. When he finally got back to his home, he went out to his patio, poured himself a large glass of Gentleman Jack, and gazed at the mountains. He thought about the first time he found out that his best friend and wife were having an affair. He thought about the volatile organic compounds that his friend told him about and how he had studied and learned how to make them into a pine soap that he always used before going into the woods. He thought about the vanilla extract and anise that he had placed on the trail the day before he took his best friend and wife on the hike.

The bears aren't my spirit guide, Bill. There really was a scientific explanation for why I encountered them twelve times and they never harmed me. They thought I was just a part of the forest. And that anise and vanilla extract; I knew it would attract the cubs. I had seen them around there several days before and knew what would bring them back.

"We all have to be responsible for our own actions, don't we?" he said out loud as he tipped the glass toward the mountain. "My art will probably not be as magical as it once was but I have to accept that now. It's taken me ten years to realize it but thank God I finally did. No one can see or paint nature the way I can and I will show everyone once again."

"I am not sure God is whom you should thank," he heard a voice say from out in the woods and even though he strained to see who was speaking, he saw no one. All he saw was a bunch of blue and green fireflies. *Strange*, he thought. *There shouldn't be that many fireflies at this time of year.*

He then watched as they seemed to form an outline of a woman.

"Shit. This whiskey is kicking my ass. Been ten years though, so what do you expect?" he said out loud.

He watched the glow of the fireflies grow brighter as they approached him until they became so dazzling he had to close his eyes. He heard someone laugh and the sound of it caused him to shake as it spilled over his body like Abrams Falls in the winter. The laughter became a cacophonous symphony, at times sounding like a lunatic in an asylum screaming at tortured and distorted memories, and at other times like hyenas laughing in their unique and unsettling manner and he thought how fucked up all of it seemed. He opened his eyes and the fireflies were hovering, right there, in front of him. He heard their wings flapping as they flew into his eyes and felt a burning pain like a hot poker had been thrust deep into his brain. A peal of inhumane and merciless laughter echoed within his ears as he reached up and touched the blisters around his eyes and felt the scorching, unforgiving agony throughout his entire body. He could see nothing and heard a voice telling him that he was right.

"Everyone has to be responsible for their own actions, James. Perhaps you can ask Vincent about his psychotic episodes and delusions. You two have a lot in common. He also drank a lot and was mentally unstable, but he was still able to paint because he only cut off part of his left ear. I'm not sure how well you'll be able to paint without the ability to see. Perhaps they can help you in your new home," the voice said as the laughter became so loud that the screams from James were only heard by the damned.

Furys Ferry

It was the largest ice storm to hit Augusta, Georgia since they began keeping records of the weather. It happened on February 11, 2014, and looked like an EF4 tornado had ripped through every part of town. Augusta made the national news the day that occurred and for several days afterward. Hundreds of thousands of people were without power for a week; some remote areas for more than a month. People were still cleaning up debris from the storm months after it happened. Its aftereffect, in some cases, was still being felt two years later.

The city was given plenty of warning by all the weather experts, and the power companies and hospitals planned accordingly. I was working in a hospital at the time and I am certain our facility was no different from others in town. Since we knew the storm was coming days ahead of time, our disaster plan was put into operation so that our patients would be safe and our staff could get to and from work. Beds were opened up for employees who might be unable to leave. Administrators and managers planned to stay through the night to handle problems and assure all the equipment was operational and that there was sufficient staffing present to perform the myriad of tasks necessary for the hospital to operate effectively.

The amount of science and skill and logistical planning that is required for a hospital to function is really quite amazing. It's like a hundred different kinds of businesses under one roof working together, performing thousands of different tests and procedures on a daily basis, enabling patients that ask for our help to receive it and, for the most part, leave in much better shape than when they entered our doors. It's not a 100% success story, but it's pretty damn close. Having a killer roaming through your halls, though, hurts those percentages.

I can't tell you which hospital I worked for because of the legal documents I had to sign preventing me from doing so. I also can't reveal the payment I received in order to keep that hospital's name out of the news. But I can tell you the money they paid me was a lot less than it would have cost them if the public were to discover that a nurse chose the ice storm as some sort of apocalyptic sign that she needed to listen to the demon inside of her and carry out some very disturbing acts. Acts that, if known, would forever be associated with that hospital.

Well, maybe not forever. But for a damn long time, and though I've heard there's no such thing as bad publicity, I am willing to wager that a serial killer in a hospital would be called bad publicity by any marketing specialist. A hospital is a place where people go to get better, not preyed upon by some sort of lunatic who heard the demon tell her who needed to die. Being described as the best hospital in town is a lot different from being called the "demon hospital." The only people who ask, "Where's the demon hospital?" are those nuts on TV that advertise themselves as ghost hunters.

Like religious zealots who have no reluctance to kill someone in the name of their God, this lunatic said she heard the voice of an angel tell her to kill innocent people. First of all, what kind of angel does that? And second of all, even though I know there will be plenty of people who will read this story and be skeptical of its content, I can promise you that everything I am referring to is the truth as I remember it.

If I hadn't been there and seen it for myself, believe me, I would be one of those who said it was a load of crap too. You won't find any evidence, even if you search for it, to confirm what I am telling you is the truth. The hospital didn't want the Augusta Chronicle healthcare editor taking the events and turning them into what would surely have been an award-winning article. Most of that information has been hidden in some way or another so that the deaths look like nothing out of the ordinary. I'm pretty sure, however, the family of the elderly woman who was killed by a rattlesnake found sitting in her lap like some misinterpreted Old Testament therapy, got a large sum of money not to sue or discuss the cause of her death.

Hell, if it was just the rattlesnake death, I doubt that anyone would have even been suspicious that something else was going on. After all, it is the south and venomous snakes common to the area don't hibernate, but they do look for a warm place in the winter, like your home or possibly even a hospital. I've seen copperheads and rattlesnakes in my yard. A neighbor came home and found a water moccasin sitting on their kitchen table. It happens. In fact, this wasn't even the first venomous snake that had ever gotten into our hospital. And we were a little preoccupied, being in the middle of an ice storm crisis; so, nobody saw that death as a precursor to something much more sinister. It was just seen as an unfortunate death and everybody continued to go about doing their jobs, unaware that the hospital was about to look like the movie "The Evil Dead."

I realize now as I'm writing this that I need to qualify my previous statement. If I hadn't been there and been part of the management team, I wouldn't have even known about all the unusual deaths. But being aware of the crazy shit that was happening probably saved my life. It made me suspicious and, as I am prone to do sometimes, start seeing demons where others just see something strange or a bit odd. I'll leave it up to you to determine if I am crazy or simply trying to tell everyone the truth.

I also have to admit, I am trying to clear things up before I die. Staring Death in the face has a way of making you realize you need to clear the slate of things that may not look so good on your life resume. You know, remove those skeletons from your closet before it becomes too late and you find yourself doing the Macarena with those bony Halloween ornaments in Hell. (I have a theory that song has to be playing nonstop there, though I would much rather keep that as a hypothesis than to know for certain.) Knowing what I know and not telling anyone, well I think that would be one of those things that guarantee that I have one of those life-size x-ray images as a dance partner for eternity.

So, as the great writer, Snoopy, once said, "It was a dark and stormy night," when everything began. I had volunteered to be a transporter for the hospital as we dealt with the storm because I had an all-wheel-drive car. Of course, all-wheel-drive vehicles will only help you so much on icy roads, but I had become very good at driving in wintry weather while living in Tennessee. I worked in a hospital there too, and since hospitals never close, I once worked 24 hours straight during a bad ice storm because the dayshift couldn't get to work. I was a lot younger then and, to a certain degree, it was exciting to test my capabilities and see what I could accomplish under that level of stress.

But this time was different. I was a lot more concerned about this storm and what it would do to a city that was not used to this type of weather. I was even a bit worried about transporting the employees to and from work. Driving myself to work in bad conditions was one thing, but being responsible for other passengers made me a lot more careful and even a little scared at times.

Luckily though, I never had a problem as I maneuvered through the city and some county back roads that I had never even seen prior to this event. Power lines were on the ground, trees blocked roads, and limbs and ice were falling down all around me as I slowly traveled over the snow and ice-covered roads At times, it felt like I was in some war zone. It was eerie. I was the only one on the road, and entire streets were without light except for the beam coming from the headlights of my car. Occasionally I saw lanterns or candles in the windows that let me know this was the house I was looking for before I heard the "arrived at destination" voice of the GPS.

I never did get tired though I slept very little during that week. We were without power at our house for three days and if not for the wood-burning fireplace, we would have had to look for somewhere else to go. But I knew the hospital needed me, so as long as my wife and I had a way to not freeze to death at home, I figured we could make it. After all, I was doing nothing else but what my staff members were doing. I have never been prouder about working with a group of people than during that week. Their dedication and commitment to get to the hospital and work during one of the worst times in their lives was heroic. It pisses me off that a demonic being is associated with that memory too. Perhaps after enough therapy, I can exorcise that bitch from my hippocampus and then be free to remember just the good.

When I wasn't at the hospital, I was picking up and taking staff to and from the hospital. Every evening I would get home around 8 p.m., eat a sandwich or whatever my wife and I could cook over the fire, and then sit and attempt to read a book by candlelight or with battery-operated lanterns. Then we would try to go to sleep beside the fireplace in as much clothing as we could wear.

39

It was very difficult to sleep while listening to what sounded like bombs going off in the distance, wondering if one of them would be close enough to hit our home. I imagine that's how we all felt, huddled in our houses listening to what was happening all around us. The explosions at night made me wonder what it must be like to live in a land that was ravaged by war. Multiple tree limbs cracked and rhythmically fell to the ground like an aerial assault from the air. The cracking and snapping of the tree limbs mimicked gunfire that was sometimes close by and other times off in the distance. Exploding transformers sounded like bombs and 120-foot trees were uprooted and fell to the ground like buildings hit by tanks.

It seems inappropriate to refer to this time as unbearable considering there are people in other parts of the world that live in this type of environment all the time. But I can say it was indeed a hellish world for days and weeks. Anyone that has gone through a devastating weather event will tell you the same thing. You feel powerless for a time as you cope without power, water, and in this case, the extreme cold temperatures. If you were fortunate, your power was restored in three or four days, but some places were without power or water for weeks. The buildings and cars that were damaged by the falling trees just had to wait, along with the street and yard cleanup that would go on for months, while you dealt with the immediate concern of staying alive. And though we can't fix all the problems in the world, we all should do something to help those less fortunate than us that struggle every day in this type of setting. That's another takeaway from this story. Underline this one as a to-do item for later.

Some people were lucky to be able to just stay home. I say lucky even though when you are looking out the window, wondering if that large tree in your front yard was going to fall onto your house, it doesn't sound fortuitous at all. But, if you could, you stayed home. If you worked for the power company, or disaster relief, or in a hospital, you just went to work. As I said, I didn't sleep much. I might doze off for an hour or so before I woke up as the fire began to weaken, but as soon as it was 3 a.m. I would get up and call the "command post" for the addresses of the staff that needed to come to work.

Over those three days, I probably had about ten total hours of sleep, but I wasn't tired. I often felt hot, though, as if I was running a fever. But it would come and go so I didn't give it much thought. I attributed it to stress which I knew caused my body to do a lot of strange things. Sweating was the least of my concerns due to the anxiety that I dealt with daily.

I wasn't sure why I wasn't tired until I looked up what a constant state of fear and concern does to your body. The fight or flight response causes the body's sympathetic nervous system to release stress hormones such as cortisol. These hormones can boost blood sugar levels and triglycerides which can be used by the body for fuel. No wonder I ate so many donuts and cookies and drank so much Powerade during this event. I was just stoking the fire like I did every night at my house. The cold-water sink baths helped me too. I learned that if you need to wake up and feel alive very quickly, using ice-cold water to clean off your private parts will do it every time.

I met her on the first night I became a transporter. There was nothing at first to suggest she was anyone except a night nurse trying to get to work. She worked PRN. I realize as I start to use "hospital speak" as we go along in this story, I will need to explain what those medical terms and abbreviations mean. Acronyms are abundant in our industry and create what sounds like a foreign language. We don't mean it to be that way but with all the sophisticated equipment and the procedures that the staff perform, and the disease processes that the doctors and nurses manage, it just happens.

The fact that you understand that language is something that I call transient hospitability. This process conveys a compendium of medical knowledge to the person who works in a hospital that they were not aware that they possessed. They don't think they possess it, but their family does. That's why a family member calls you when they are having a procedure or someone they know is in the hospital and asks you for advice; not realizing you have no definitive idea as to what all that problem or procedure entails. But unlike your family member, you usually know just *enough* and can explain to them to a certain degree what is going on, thereby reaffirming their belief that you possess knowledge about all things regarding all diseases and the care that will be needed to help them.

It doesn't matter that you tell your family members you are not a doctor because they will just say, "well you've worked in a hospital for so many years - you are just *like* a doctor." And though you will protest once again, you realize that your denial will continue to fall on deaf ears and they will call you back the next time they encounter "hospital speak." So, bear with me as we go along in the story. I will make things as clear as I can. After all, I realize I am burdened with transient hospitability.

So, having said that, let me explain what PRN means. PRN means "as needed," so those employees that are denoted as PRN, work without obtaining hospital benefits and usually for a higher wage. It gives the employee flexibility to determine their schedule and it helps the hospital fill in holes. If you see the words with regard to your medicine, it means "take the medicine as needed."

She said her name was Sara when I picked her up that night and that she had just begun working at the hospital. I asked her where she was from and she said Florida, which gave me the opportunity to make a stupid comment about the weather. Something like, "Cold enough for you?" Now most normal folks, regardless of where they are from (unless they live in International Falls, Minnesota or Deadhorse, Alaska), would simply say, "Yes." But her response, considering she was from Florida, should have told me right then and there that something was wrong with this person.

"I love this weather!" she exclaimed as I looked over at her and saw her smile. She was a pretty young woman but that smile and the look in her eyes kind of creeped me out. Though all she said was, "I love this weather," after seeing those predatory eyes and Joker-esque smile, my mind interpreted her words as, "I love this weather and I love to dance around naked in it while making a blood sacrifice to the moon." I know all that makes me sound like the crazy one, but give me time. Everything will become clear as we progress.

I asked where she worked in the hospital and she told me she worked wherever she was needed. She loved being assigned to different areas and was capable of working in every unit, including the ICU and ED (intensive care unit and emergency department). I was impressed. Most nurses, once they work in the ICU or ED don't like working on a medical or surgical unit, but she said she didn't care; she just enjoyed helping people. At that point, I began to rethink my first impression of her and told her that I had worked at the hospital for a long time and I thought she would like it there. She said she was sure she would.

I picked up two other night nurses before we headed toward the hospital. One of them was an emergency room nurse and the other one worked on the 5th floor. I introduced Sara to both of them, who were friends of mine, and they also welcomed her to the staff. We made it to the hospital without any problems that first night.

It was the next morning and the subsequent nights that became much more dangerous.

With the disaster protocol in place, all the managers were required to meet with administration every morning at 7 a.m. and discuss any problems that had arisen with staffing, equipment or any other weather-related issues. It was at our very first meeting that we heard about the rattlesnake that was found coiled up in the woman's bed on the 2nd floor. She was an elderly lady, eighty-one years old, and had hip surgery the night before. She was too weak to survive the rattlesnake bite. I can remember all of us looking at each other, shaking our heads in disbelief as we listened to the engineering director explain how snakes seek out warm places in the winter and that this was a terrible event but not something completely out of the ordinary, considering where we lived and worked. He said the snake had probably been prompted to leave where it was because of the weather and was just seeking out the next warmest environment.

We were all reassured that snake repellant had been placed in any access points and that the engineering and security staff would be increasing their oversight as the storm progressed. As everyone started to leave, I asked if the snake had been killed and was told that it had been euthanized. I wanted to say the snake deserved a worse fate than euthanization, but I didn't. I later found out they threw the snake into the trash compactor and crushed it in such a manner that it was close to being defined on the molecular level. I decided that particular definition of euthanization was more than appropriate.

I spent the remainder of that morning taking night nurses home and picking up other employees as needed to staff the dayshift. Sara was one of the nurses I took home. We made some small talk and she told me her night went smoothly, with no problems. I asked her where she worked and she said the 2nd floor, not mentioning at all the death of a woman due to a rattlesnake that was found in her lap.

I started to say something but then realized that perhaps not everyone knew about the rattlesnake; even many of those working on the 2nd floor may not have known. Administration told us to refrain from discussing the incident so I stopped myself from asking her about it. So, we all just talked about the weather and how it was impacting our normal routines. Everyone got home safely and I picked up the other staff members before returning to the hospital to check on my departments and complete my regular daily work.

Around 6 p.m., I started taking some employees home and picking up others for the night shift. The roads were much icier than before and large tree limbs blocked some roads and driveways. Sometimes I even had to get out and walk the staff member to their house. I called the "command center" and reported that I had finally gotten everyone home and they gave me the names of three staff nurses who needed rides to work for the night shift.

When I heard that one of them was Sara, I began to wonder if she was requesting me, since I had picked her up for work the previous night and then taken her home earlier that morning. Before I could answer my own question, the nursing supervisor laughed and said I had made quite an impression on Sara. She told me Sara had asked if I was driving and requested me specifically when she heard that I was. She informed the nursing supervisor that I was a very good driver and she felt safe when she was in my car. I could hear the other people in the room snickering and I just ignored them, knowing that if I said anything, it would just make things worse.

This time when I arrived at Sara's home, I noticed more about it as I waited outside for her. It was a small ranch style house, probably built in the '70s with a covered carport and small front porch. The front door was painted a deep purple with a stained-glass transom. There was also some sort of strange-looking glass ornament hanging on the door. It resembled a lightning bolt of some kind. That same symbol was also in her front yard holding up a birdhouse. As I looked at the both of them together, I felt that creepy feeling all over again.

I was thinking about leaving when she came out and opened the car door. She smiled at me and the creepy feeling dissipated like the misty cloud we see for a second when we breathe in cold weather. That night her smile made me feel more at ease than weird, even though she didn't hide the fact that she requested me as her driver.

"Hello, Joshua. I asked the nursing supervisor if you were transporting again this evening and she said you were and would have you pick me up. You made me feel safe. I know that isn't easy to do in this type of situation. It probably has something to do with your name. Do you know what your name means?"

I felt hypnotized by the way she looked at me, so I didn't say anything. I just nodded my head yes.

"Then you know your name means 'The Lord is my salvation.' That's a good name. You were meant to be here in this weather helping people. I don't believe people's names are just random occurrences. They are meant to define who and what that person will be. That's why I asked for you. I knew you would get me safely to the hospital."

"I'll do my best."

"Yes. That's all you can do. Fate will allow you to do nothing else."

Okay. It just got creepy again, I thought. As I drove away, Sara continued talking without any prompting from me. She told me her mother and grandmother were Japanese and that her grandmother had been in an internment camp during World War II. She said her grandmother was 94 now and still very active. She told me how she, her mother, and grandmother had gone to Japan last year and spent a year over there. She asked me if I had ever been there and I told her no, but I did like bonsai trees and from that point forward, all we did was talk about bonsai trees.

I picked up two other nurses that night and Sara introduced herself as soon as they got in the car, learned they worked in L&D (labor and delivery) and the NICU (neonatal intensive care unit) and then proceeded to tell them how I made bonsai trees and we talked about them until we got to the hospital. I began to wonder if she was on drugs because she was so talkative and I looked at her pupils to see if they looked enlarged, but they were normal.

As I dropped them off at the hospital entrance, I told them that I hoped they all had a good night and just before Sara closed the door, she winked at me with a smile and said she was certain she would.

I realized that was not a creepy smile or a friendly smile. It was a seductive smile and it made me quite nervous as I drove home. I even ran a red light although, luckily, it wasn't working at the time. Thank goodness the roads were nearly empty as the conditions had worsened. I couldn't even make it to the top of my own driveway. I parked at the bottom and walked up to my house.

That entire evening I thought about that smile and I not only saw Sara's face, I saw her body as if I was still in the car sitting next to her. She was wearing a hooded jacket and I didn't know how someone could wear a hooded jacket and still look sensual, but she did. The jacket clung to her body like a plastic grocery bag wrapped around two very well shaped oranges. The scrubs she was wearing didn't look like they were just cotton stitched together in an amorphous manner as they did on everyone else. They hugged her bottom, and I realized as I looked at her it was wrong, but there was nothing I could do about it. That evening I didn't sleep much at all as Sara kept walking by my eyelids like they were thin curtains and seeing her each time made me restless and uncomfortable. I had to get up several times to wipe the sweat off my face as I lay there in front of the fire.

I got up about 2 a.m. and went out to my car and turned it on to charge my phone. I listened to the weather reports, but there was nothing new. The roads were still treacherous and they urged people to stay in and away from downed power lines. After the phone had fully charged, I went inside and added more wood to the fire. Sleep was out of the question so I decided to cook something for breakfast. I found some hotdogs in the refrigerator and started cooking them over the fire. The smell of the food woke my wife and she smiled at me as she shook her head.

"Hotdogs for breakfast? You really know how to treat a woman."

"Not just hotdogs. I have a can of pork and beans that is almost ready and some barbecue potato chips, too. I am fairly certain that we would be able to survive the zombie apocalypse now." She laughed. We had become big fans of the show "The Walking Dead" since it had come on and never missed an episode.

After eating, I went into the bathroom and took a sink bath by candlelight. It was about 3:30 a.m. when I called in and got the addresses of two nurses and one lab tech who needed a ride to work. The roads were so bad, it took me three hours to make the pickups and get them to the hospital. I didn't get to the management meeting until a little after 7:00 and the CEO was already going around the room asking the directors for updates. The director of the 5th floor commended a new PRN nurse for noticing a change in the mental status of one of the patients. She immediately called the physician and got a CT of the head, thinking that her patient was having a stroke. (CT is computed tomography and is called a cat scan for short. It is a sophisticated x-ray that takes very small slices of the human body and allows the radiologist to see tiny, almost microscopic, changes and disease states within what is being scanned, which in this case was the patient's brain.)

Everyone smiled and nodded their heads until they heard that the scan revealed the patient had primary amebic meningoencephalitis and that the patient's outcome wasn't very good. The parasite in the brain, Naegleria fowleri, was extremely rare. The CT scan showed multiple lesions, necrosis, and hemorrhagic infarcts, which were probably all contributing to the stroke symptoms that the nurse detected.

I stayed quiet but I knew about that parasite and the nursing director was right about it being rare. You could probably count on one hand the number of people who would get the disease in a year in the entire United States. So, this wasn't normal in any way, shape, or form. It was scary shit. What she failed to add was that fucking bug was something out of a horror show. Once that parasite got in the brain, it hooked itself into the tissue and began eating away at the brain with a sucking apparatus, piece by piece. Yeah, no joke.

It gets even better because the 5th-floor nursing director wasn't finished telling us all of her horror stories. No, she went on to say that a nursing home patient who came in with a UTI (urinary tract infection) had become septic and died last night. Unfortunately, hospitals often get patients from nursing homes with UTIs. By the time we get them, they are very sick, sometimes even septic, which means that the bacteria causing the urinary tract infection has gotten into the blood. When that happens, it begins to affect other organs in the body.

But, the director went on to say, that's not what killed her. The patient actually died from anaphylactic shock due to multiple wasp stings. When she said that, everyone looked around the room at each other in disbelief. You could've heard a pin drop. Finally, the engineering director spoke up to inform us that a wasp nest had fallen onto the floor in one of the older mechanical rooms and the wasps had flown up into a vent that had, unfortunately, funneled them into that one room.

He said they weren't aware of the wasp problem beforehand because so much construction had taken place over the years, but that they would make sure that all the mechanical rooms were checked and the air ducts repaired that had allowed this type of thing to happen. That's when the Administrative team began telling us how this was simply one of those freak accidents and we just needed to go forward with what we were doing as we had a lot of patients counting on us.

I wanted to suggest that perhaps we call a priest because what I was hearing sounded like we had some sort of demonic shit happening. Only one person's name popped into my mind: Sara. As soon as the meeting was over, I went over to the director and told her how sorry I was about everything and asked if that PRN nurse she was talking about was possibly named Sara. She looked at me oddly and asked how I knew that and I said I just had a hunch. That I thought she seemed like a really sharp nurse and she told me she was working on the 5th floor last night when I dropped her off.

Now that I knew it was Sara, I went to the nursing director and asked if anyone needed a ride home, and guess what? Sara was already there waiting for me along with several other nurses who needed a ride. I made sure that I dropped the other two nurses off first that morning before I took Sara home. I wanted to talk to her because I knew I was right the first time I met her. There was something strange about her.

I asked her how her night went and she told me about the patient with the parasite infection.

"Do you know how rare the parasite in that patient's brain is, Sara? You could count on one hand how many people in the country get that infection and then cut off all the fingers and most of the thumb to realize how many survive."

50

"Yes, I do. Sexy analogy, by the way. I suspect you could go an entire career in healthcare and never see that."

There's nothing sexy about it. What a fucking weird thing to say! What kind of sick person are you? "Yeah. I've been in healthcare for almost forty years and have never seen it. And I would have thought he would have shown symptoms much earlier. It's progressed to the point now that he will never recover."

She just looked at me and smiled. This time the creepiness exuded from the edges of her lips like drool and I reached down under my seat to make sure I had my gun. Even though I felt its presence, the look in Sara's eyes made me shiver. At that point, I didn't give a damn what the administration wanted me to discuss or not discuss. She and I were going to talk.

"Did you know about the woman that was killed by the rattlesnake the other night?"

"I did. Awful, wasn't it?"

"And how about the woman who was killed by the wasps?"

"Yes. I heard about that too. Very bizarre, don't you think?"

"Yeah, 'The Conjuring' or 'Insidious' type of bizarre."

"I *knew* you liked horror movies! I could sense that about you. Would you like to come in for a moment and have a beer? Watch a movie? I've got some really interesting adult movies."

So, I am guessing on the empathy scale, you are about a negative 100? As she said that she reached over and placed her hand on my leg. I looked down at her hand and watched her as she leaned over and started to unzip my pants. It was then that I saw the tattoo on her neck and I grabbed her shoulder and pushed her back.

"So, uh, you have electricity?"

"Wow. You can't wait, can you? Already with the dirty talk!"

I knew what I said was stupid but what she was doing and what I saw on her neck startled me. I didn't know what to say or what the hell I was getting myself into, but I felt like I needed more proof that she was something more than what other people saw. That inside of her was something not pure and certainly not innocent. I know this sounds crazy, but I was pretty sure that what was sitting in my car was something demonic. A demon in a Nissan Rogue. Yeah, I know, you don't hear those words every day.

"What is that symbol on your door? It looks like the same symbol that your birdhouse rests on."

"Yes, they are the same symbols. They are 7's. They're my lucky numbers."

Well at least they aren't sixes, I thought. *But still, strange.*

"You know you have an upside-down cross on the back of your neck? What does that mean?"

"Yes. But it's not upside-down when I am on my knees in front of someone going down on them."

Are you fucking kidding me? Who in the hell would think of something like that?

I knew I still needed some answers but I also realized that if I went into that house with her, I wouldn't ever come out of it. I would end up as just another head in her freezer. So, I started to come up with a plan that would reveal Sara's true nature.

"Sara, you're not like anyone I have ever met. Your name means 'princess,' doesn't it?"

"Yes, it does. I'm impressed. You have been thinking about me, haven't you?"

"Yes, a lot. I couldn't get you off my mind last night. I need to get back to the hospital right now, but tonight, I could come by and take you to work. Then I could drop by your floor at around 1 a.m. or whenever you take your break, and we could, I don't know, go somewhere and talk about bonsai trees. Or more about your trip to Japan with your mother and grandmother."

Sara laughed. "I'd like that. I'm sure Nihasa and Naamah would like that too."

"Who are they?"

"My mother and grandmother."

"Oh, shit. They aren't actually here, are they?"

Sara laughed again. "No, silly. I was just playing along with you. See you tonight, Joshua. I'm pretty sure your mind will be blown, among other things," she said as she leaned over and kissed me on my cheek. "And 1 is the exact time I take my break. You must have the ability to read minds," she said as she got out of the car and walked into her house.

I drove back to the hospital as quickly as possible. My anxiety level was at a DEFCON 1 and my colon was getting ready to demonstrate what that meant. I just made it back to the hospital and onto the toilet before the irritable bowel dispersed the hotdogs and bean breakfast from my body like a grenade launcher.

As I walked around my departments, I couldn't help but think about Sara. It was hard to concentrate on the staff's concerns and I had to continue to force myself to focus on what they were telling me. Many people in the lab wanted to know about the Naegleria and I talked with them as much as the hospital confidentiality protocols would allow. I reassured them it wasn't contagious and that they could not catch it unless they sprayed spinal fluid up their nose. Some of them had already checked with the microbiology department and my confirmation of what they had heard quelled that concern fairly quickly.

As far as I could tell, no one knew anything about the rattlesnake or wasp deaths yet. If they did, I would surely have been questioned and no one even mentioned either of those incidents once. We talked a lot about the weather and about getting supplies. I spent a lot of time on the phone talking with our main distributors and the supply chain director to make sure we would have the necessary materials for the laboratory.

Throughout the day I thought about those symbols I had seen at Sara's house and on her neck. I searched the internet and found that an inverted cross had two meanings. The first one signified a Christian symbol of humility, often referred to as the Petrine cross in honor of St. Peter. The second one and the most recent meaning was that of designating a devotion to Satan. Considering how Sara referred to it as she was discussing oral sex, I had a really good feeling that she was in the group that would suggest she migrated toward the latter meaning.

I also researched satanic symbols and found that symbol on her door and in her yard. It was three 7's stacked on top of one another that made it look like a lightning bolt. The three 7's also referred to a person by the name of Aleister Crowley. He said he used the three 7's to identify himself because the three 6's were already taken. Sounded like a real nice fellow, especially considering he wrote the "Guide to Witchcraft and Satanic Worship."

I got up and closed my office door and put my head in my hands and tried to think about what I needed to do that night. My whole face was sweating and I wiped it off with some tissues I had on my desk and then went to find something cold to drink. I came back to my office and closed the door so I could think about her mother and grandmother. Perhaps they didn't know what Sara was truly like. Maybe she had fooled a lot of people for a long time. I remembered their names and I don't know why, but I entered them into the computer, spelling them as best I could considering how she pronounced their names. What I found wasn't very encouraging.

Nihasa was an American Indian devil and/or succubus. I wasn't sure what succubus meant so I looked it up. A succubus is a demon in female form that appears in dreams and takes the form of women to seduce men. And then I read about the other name; Naamah. When Sara said it, it sounded like a nice grandmotherly name, like Memaw or Nana; but no, it wasn't anything like that at all. Good old Naamah was another demon who seduces men and strangles sleeping babies.

I hoped Sara was telling the truth about one thing and that was that her mother and grandmother weren't here with her. I wasn't sure how in the hell I was going to deal with Sara, much less the three of them. And then I began wondering if Sara was her real name. But after a few minutes of thinking about that, I realized it didn't matter. What mattered was - how was I going to destroy her?

My mind was reeling. How do you kill a demon? Unfortunately, the internet wasn't too helpful on that subject. The best advice I could find was to reject the demon and pray for help. So, I didn't have much of a plan except I knew I needed to get her to admit to what she had done, and somehow I needed to kill her before she did any more harm. For the rest of the day, I thought about what I could do and though I had a plan, I wasn't sure it would work. When I looked up at the clock it was 6 p.m. and I knew I had very little time to come up with anything else.

I went to the nursing supervisor and asked who needed rides to work and got the name of Sara and two others. I picked them up and when I saw those 7's in Sara's yard I felt my intestinal tract twisting itself into a jumbo pretzel shape as if the creature from the "Alien" movie was going to pop through my stomach at any minute. As a matter of fact, I would have preferred that to have occurred than to have another episode of diarrhea. Thank goodness my colon settled down as soon as Sara got in the car because the likelihood of me having a heart attack or stroke removed any concern of an intestinal event.

I smiled at her when she got in the car and though she said hello to me, I could tell she knew I was nervous. I felt hot all over. I could feel the sweat on my forehead and wiped it off with the sleeve of my jacket. I think because of that she didn't do or say anything to me. She just talked to the other nurses and we soon arrived at the hospital. She acted like she was putting her backpack together to allow the other nurses to get out of the car and when they left, she turned to me and smiled. And when she smiled, my body shivered as if I was lying naked out there in the ice and snow.

"I'll see you around one, right?"

"I was thinking, Sara. Why don't you "get sick" about that time and tell the nursing supervisor you need to go home? That way we could go back to my house. My wife went to stay with a friend that has heat and electricity. You don't mind candlelight and a fire, do you?"

"I love candles and I love fire. Like I said you must be able to read my mind. I'll see you at one," she said as she reached over and grabbed my crotch. I'd be surprised if she felt anything though because my penis and my testicles retracted into my body at her touch like the witch's feet in the Wizard of Oz when the wicked witch of the west tried to take the ruby slippers off of her sister and they appeared on Dorothy's feet. On the drive home I checked the road close to my house. It was very icy and I knew it would get even icier later tonight as I thought about what I was going to do.

At home, I managed to eat a cold sandwich with my wife and even though I didn't think I could eat anything, I was able to keep my emotions and intestinal tract in check as I thought about what was ahead of me. We both laid down around 10 that night. and though my wife went to sleep, I did not. I made sure there was plenty of wood on the fire and on the back porch and I checked my .38 revolver to make sure it was fully loaded. I didn't take any additional ammunition. If I couldn't kill her with what I was planning, I knew it wouldn't matter how much ammunition I had. At that point, all I would need was one bullet.

I was back at the hospital by 1 a.m. and Sara acted like she was sick until we drove away from the hospital. I had taped my phone under my car seat so it wouldn't come sliding out and put it on "record" as soon as I drove into the parking lot. My gun was next to my seat and I hoped all the prayers I had made on my way to the hospital would help.

"So, how was your night?"

"Perfect. I couldn't have asked for a better night. But the best part is coming later. You will be surprised to see how long my tongue is."

No, I won't. I'm sure I've seen it a hundred times on Nat Geo on a Burmese python, I wanted to say but I didn't. I knew I had to react to that comment in a much different way so she wouldn't become suspicious.

"Is it longer than Gene Simmons' of Kiss?"

"I don't know. You tell me," she said as she stuck it out and licked my face.

I ran off the road and stopped the car and looked at her. "That's fucking impressive. There's certainly a career for you in the adult movie industry but you can't do that while I'm driving. You'll get us killed."

"Yeah, I guess you're right. I don't want to kill you. I've already taken care of that craving earlier."

"What do you mean?"

I knew when I asked that she would either say nothing or tell me everything. If she told me everything, I knew that she would try and kill me later. She began to tell me everything.

"I had one of my patients go down to HBO (hyperbaric oxygen therapy –high oxygen environment that promotes wound healing) and I have to admit she had a lot more hair spray in her hair than should have been there. And a lot of

57

oils that I covered up with bandages. I heard that created a spark in the chamber and she burst into flames."

I didn't know whether to curse or pray so I did both. *Holy shit. Oh God, help me.*

"That created quite the turmoil within the hospital, so I was able to go upstairs to the rehab unit and do something that your idiotic management team would finally have to admit wasn't an accident."

"What did you do?"

"I placed scalpels in the eyes, ears, and nose of a patient. It's a new rehab therapy I wanted to try out. I took a picture of it to show in my church. I think they'll be as excited as I was when I did it. I would love to hear what your risk management team says about that."

I realized I didn't have very much time. We were just at the corner of Furys Ferry and North Belair and I sped up knowing that corner was very icy. As I did, I turned the car into the utility pole and toward the Wife Saver restaurant sign that sat there on the corner. The car clipped the pole on the driver's side and the passenger side was crushed against the sign.

I had turned off the airbags before I left home that evening so they didn't deploy. Sara was thrown through the windshield and my head bounced off the window and I blacked out for a moment. I don't know how long it was before I heard several female voices whispering to me telling me that I needed to wake up and destroy the female shell that something called Abaddon occupied.

When I opened my eyes, three women with wings and serpents wrapped around their bodies were helping me out of the car. The hair on their heads was moving and I realized it wasn't hair but snakes. Blood dripped from their eyes. I knew I must be hallucinating when I heard Sara's voice yelling out my name. I looked up and saw her standing in the Wife Saver parking lot. Much of her face was no longer where it should be. It hung down toward her neck, exposing the muscle and bone it once covered. She now looked like the monster I knew was inside of her.

"Those three bitches that are with you won't save you. I am too strong for them now. I have done what my master asked of me and I am filled with her power. You know that, Alecto, don't you? I know how that pisses you off. Your sister Megaera's jealous nature won't allow her to do much except get in the way. The only one that I am worried about is Tisiphone. Tisiphone the avenger. But even she cannot take me on her own," that thing growled in a guttural manner.

"Wake up, Joshua. Now you must do what you have been put in this world to do. You must trust us."

"Who are you?"

Before they could answer, Sara rushed at me and two of the winged women went flying toward her, grabbed her arms, and flew up into the air before dropping her onto the ground. I heard her body crack and saw her arms and legs twisted around in ways that weren't physically possible.

"My name is Tisiphone. The ancient Greeks called me and my sisters, Alecto and Megaera, the Furies. We are guardians of the law and innocent and that demon over there has harmed many innocents. Those that are weak and seek help should not be preyed upon and she has summoned us by her actions. This road, this place, is a crossroad and is sacred land. Somehow you sensed that. But we can only do so much. You must kill the thing known as Sara and then we will transport Abaddon back to the netherworld.

"We are both immortal beings, but Abaddon derives her power from the weak and the wretched nature of man. We derive our power from hope and justice which is meted out to those who succumb to evil. Neither of us is ever without power because of the broken promise made so long ago and which continues to haunt man today. Abaddon is a demon, but she cannot kill us any more than we can kill her. We can

59

stop her from doing any more harm though. At least for a while."

I got my gun and limped toward Sara who was lying on the ground and I shot her six times in the head., Her body burst into flames. I fell back, but the one who called herself Tisiphone caught me and laid me softly onto the ground. I watched as something dark arose from Sara's body and though I knew it was not human, it had a human form outlined by a blue and green aura.

The winged creatures attacked that form and though it struggled, it could not escape their grasp. I watched as they flew up into the sky and then disappeared. I felt the ice on my back and realized how good it felt. I looked over at the utility pole that rested atop the broken sign and saw the words "We Save" and smiled. I realized for the first time in three days how tired I was and I closed my eyes and went to sleep.

Joshua's wife was in the ICU when they removed him from the ventilator and began to administer oxygen through a nasal cannula. She watched as the respiratory therapist told the physician standing beside her that the oxygen percentage was at 98 on three liters of oxygen.

"That's very good, Mrs. Daniel. Your husband is a medical miracle. We have no other way to explain it. The fact that he had primary amebic meningoencephalitis caused by Naegleria fowleri and survived, well, that just doesn't happen. He had less than a five percent chance of surviving considering the condition he was in when we got him. I personally believe he didn't die because his body temperature was so low from laying out there in the ice and snow after he wrecked. I think that the extreme cold killed the parasite and saved his life.

"His body temperature was only 55 degrees when he got to the hospital, which is close to a record for survival in itself. We saw the parasite on the brain scan and watched as it just disappeared with the antibiotics that we pumped into him and now he's here, off the ventilator. I still don't know how he had the awareness to kill the wolf that attacked him. God only knows what he saw in his fevered mind for those days, considering how sick he was, but I suspect it was not of heaven or earth. All I can say is your husband has a strong will to survive."

"What about brain damage, doctor? Will his brain be okay?"

"We are not sure, Mrs. Daniel, but I wouldn't rule out anything at this point. He shouldn't even be alive, so I just don't know. We'll simply have to take one day at a time and hope for the best."

His wife sat by his side hoping he would open his eyes but he never did. He lay there breathing comfortably though and the nurses kept reassuring her that he was improving every hour. The night nurse came in and said that she would be taking her husband down for an MRI and suggested that she might want to use that time to go and get something to eat since he would be gone for about an hour.

"What exactly is an MRI?" she asked.

"It's a type of picture that uses a strong magnetic current and sound to produce very precise images. The doctors will continue to use that image to watch how his brain does. It gives a much more detailed image than the CT. From what I hear, the doctors are just amazed at how the parasite appears to be dead and the damage it caused seems to be disappearing more and more each day. It's quite something of a miracle."

"That's what I keep hearing and I keep praying that it's true. I think I will go and get something to eat. I'll be back in an hour. You'll take good care of him, won't you?"

"I absolutely will."

Joshua heard the voice of the night nurse talking to his wife and the voice sounded familiar to him. He opened his eyes and saw the nurse smiling at him.

"Hello, Mr. Daniel. My name is Sara. I'll be taking you for your MRI so they can get a picture of your brain. I sure hope they know what they're doing down there with the oxygen cylinders. I heard about a hospital once where someone took the wrong oxygen cylinder into the MRI suite and the magnet's strength was so strong it pulled it toward the patient and crushed his head. I'll be sure to check that when we get there so nothing bad like that happens to you."

As the nurse reached over him to adjust one of his IVs he saw the cross tattoo on her wrist. Due to the abrasive nature of the ventilator tubing that had been in his throat, he could only manage a whisper, but he grabbed Sara's hand and made sure she heard him utter, "Tisiphone" before they left the room.

6th Street

It was advertised as The Peculiarity Museum on the large glass window panes of the empty building downtown months before it opened. The pictures depicted a sword swallower and a woman called the Voodoo Python Princess from the Amazon, who had a large snake wrapped around her body. The bold red, white, and blue block lettering reminded those who were old enough to remember what it looked like when the circus would advertise it was coming to town.

The signs displayed pictures of animals and descriptions of the strange and marvelous, promising feats of magic, strength, agility, and a glimpse into the world of the fantastic. Those who read the words "world of the fantastic" knew they actually meant something else. Something that would be unusual and meant to shock the senses; a collection of oddities or, as it was once known, a freak show, often associated with the early versions of the traveling circus. There was a time when that type of advertisement generated excitement but its capacity to do that had faded away as entertainment choices increased. The ability to shock and astound had morphed into virtual reality and the modern circus had become an act on the Las Vegas strip.

In fact, in today's world, very few "tented" and traveling circuses exist. Ringling Brothers, the largest circus in the world, shut down operations in 2017 after entertaining millions beneath the "big top." A few regional circuses still eke out a living within the US and Europe but for the most part, the circus of yesterday evolved into Cirque Du Soleil-type shows which exist in Las Vegas hotels, with smaller traveling versions performing around the country. Their shows display amazing acrobatic feats and, indeed, feats of strength and agility that can shock the senses of those who are watching. But the sideshow that used to accompany the circus - the freak show - died a long time ago because of the increased sensitivity to the frailty of the human condition and the empathy that generated declining interest in that form of entertainment.

Yes, humanity evolved. At least the majority of it did. Regardless of the evolution and contempt society showed to others who would use someone's deformity to extract a living, there was always a certain portion of the population that remained immune to compassion. There would always be people who would continue to pay money to see the two-headed snake in the jar of formaldehyde or the bones of the dwarf that, when alive, was dressed up to look like a large doll.

And now, there it was on the large window for everyone to see. An announcement to the city that the "freak show" was coming back to town. Given sufficient time and with just the right amount of peculiarity to tweak the inquisitive nature of man; the sensitivity of the general public can be suspended, provided the attraction didn't transcend the obscene or profane. Advertisers of the peculiarity museum were not interested in being politically correct but they did meet all the other criteria as noted above, and so, they were successful in generating interest as to its arrival.

Advertising a sword swallower, a fire-eater, a snake lady, and other peculiarities of nature and man prevented a public backlash that the pictures of a real wolfman, a two-headed farm animal, or horned Siamese twins would have generated had they been advertised along with the others. Therefore, the words "other peculiarities of nature and man" only made the city buzz with anticipation because the proprietor was smart. And what was once a freak show, was now The Peculiarity Museum.

The proprietor of the museum had been fascinated with "freak shows" from a very early age. His own genetic mutations attracted him to the concept and he sought to learn as much as he could about them as he grew up. At first, his parents tried sending him to public school, but their child's appearance subjected him to derision and even frightened some of his classmates. His propensity for scaring the other students didn't help him assimilate into the classroom so he became home-schooled and alienated from society as he grew up.

His name was Jameson Pastriano and he suffered from a rare genetic disorder known as "wolfman disease" by the general public. The scientific name for his appearance was congenital hypertrichosis terminalis. His abnormal hair growth began at birth and covered his entire body. It was long and thick and instead of trying to cut it back or keep it in check, he allowed it to grow as a way to let others know he didn't care what they thought; though, when he was young, he really did. But as he grew up, he began to understand that he would always be on the perimeter of society looking in and he acted in ways that ensured he would retain that position throughout his entire life.

His parents tried to keep him from going out on Halloween at first, but they soon realized that was the one day of the year their son could be seen as normal and so they encouraged him to participate in the activities. At least until the deaths occurred. Jameson, or Jimmy, as he was called then, was seventeen years old and going through the neighborhoods as he always did, finding different ways to scare people. Without them knowing, he followed a group of teenagers who ventured out onto the train trestle. They had consumed a sufficient number of beers, gathering enough stupidity masquerading as courage, to dare each other to walk across it.

If a train came while they were in the middle of the trestle, they would only have two options - try and outrun the train or jump, neither of which were good ideas in their condition. The bridge stood 160 feet over the river and it would have been close to certain death if someone jumped from the trestle into the water. A couple of them had ventured about thirty feet onto the bridge, when Jimmy jumped out from the dark, howling as he ran toward them. He only meant to scare them, and though he was very successful in doing that, he didn't anticipate that both of them would fall headfirst into the water.

The police ruled them accidental deaths, knowing that the teenagers were doing two things that were illegal: drinking and being out there on the train tracks. Jimmy had never stepped onto the bridge and even though many people felt he was at fault for what he did, the court saw differently and did not prosecute. However, his status within the community was destroyed and he watched as his family became ostracized and isolated. He cleaned enough eggs and dog shit off the windows of their house to know how people felt. He didn't understand, and probably wouldn't have cared if he had known, that it was only a small, albeit vocal and active minority that treated them this way. The lack of action by the silent majority to stop the cruelty was just as telling and helped further shape his growing distrust and animus.

When Jimmy turned twenty, his parents were killed while sitting on their back porch. A lightning bolt struck a large metal structure that he had made and given to his parents as an anniversary gift. He was very talented at creating metal trees with limbs full of leaves that moved with the slightest amount of wind in opposite directions without ever hitting one another. He had turned the garage into his workshop and he heard and felt the lightning hit the house that night.

He found them sitting on the porch with their hands black and burned, still gripping the armrests of their chairs that had been charred as the lightning exited their body. The bottoms of their shoes were gone, exposing the scorched soles of their feet. They both died from cardiac arrest resulting from the amount of electricity that surged through their bodies.

Jimmy became Jameson after their death and left the town in which he had lived his entire life. He knew he had to leave because almost everyone in the community now believed he was cursed and he, for the first time, had a similar feeling. His parents left him enough money to do whatever he wanted, and for the first several years he lived in a cabin in the Blue Ridge Mountains overlooking the Shenandoah Valley.

He only left the cabin to get groceries or to go hiking as he spent his time immersed in the beauty that surrounded him. He hiked through the valley and mountains hundreds of times, and as he did, he began to notice that even within the beauty, nature had created other less appealing elements: insects that stung, bit, emitted an unpleasant smell or looked like they had come from an alien planet, plants that were full of thorns or smelled rotten as they decayed, foul pools of water that were overrun with algae and parasites from an excess of animal feces, or dead carcasses of animals swimming in a sea of maggots, and covered with frenzied ants that carried specks of flesh along with a determination and an ill temper when disturbed. From the road or even from the trail, the scenery overwhelmed the senses. But when he looked deeper into the woods and the shadows, there was an ugliness that he always saw despite the beauty.

He tried to avoid interactions with other people, but there were times that he came across them or they encountered him by chance. He didn't know why at first, but he always ran away when this occurred. Because of his reticent behavior, rumors of Sasquatch sightings began to surface in the local newspapers. The solitude that he enjoyed disappeared as more people became interested in glimpsing the Sasquatch being and getting a picture of it on their phones. Some even took beef jerky with them into the woods, hoping they could get a "selfie" with it, reckless and unaware that what they were pursuing may cause them harm.

Two events changed Jameson's image of himself forever within those mountains. They both occurred at night during the height of the Sasquatch sightings. Because of his reluctance to meet others on the trail, Jameson began going on moonlit hikes; unaware of how the full moon, paired with his appearance, might make the more ignorant within those woods believe they were seeing a mythical being.

He came across a drunken moonshiner who, upon seeing Jameson, tried to pick up his shotgun. In doing so, it slipped from his hands. When the stock hit the ground, the gun discharged and blew the moonshiner's face off. He was killed instantly and lay there on the ground for several days until one of his family members discovered him. They didn't report the death to the police but they believed he had been killed by the Shenandoah Sasquatch.

The second incident involved the dead man's brother, who was considered less bright by the other family members and was even more inclined to be drunk at any given time of the day. He saw Jameson on the bank of a stream and tried shooting him with the same shotgun that killed his brother. He missed Jameson and the buckshot ricocheted off the rocks. Four of the pellets entered his eyes and forehead, killing him.

As Jameson stood there, he thought about how they had both tried to kill him just because he was different. Yes, he admitted to himself, he was different in appearance, but that was all. It didn't help that he remembered the teacher's comments to his parents describing him as disruptive and abnormal. The thought of that made him angry as he walked back to his cabin.

All those words that he had heard and held in check until this point came flowing over the mental dam he had created and flooded his mind. Abnormal, different, weird, strange, odd-looking, monstrous, ugly, and deformed, were words that flashed before his eyes like a moving carousel. He realized his parents had never tried to deny any of it as they had heard the same words when he had been confronted with them. He felt a loss from their death, but he now recognized he had never really felt loved by them. Lacking a comparative role model, he hadn't understood what the word family truly meant. He had a mother and father and he was their son, but it was never a family.

Yes, they provided him food and shelter, but only because they had to, he told himself. He could now see their indifference and the distant way they interacted with him. He felt their shame and he was right in sensing that behavior. He would learn later in his life that their shame arose from guilt, but for a long time, it was just another memory that haunted him.

People would always fail to see the beauty around them, he said to himself, or ignore it and seek out the ugliness that was invariably hidden beneath the surface. He knew he had become what many had called him since he was old enough to understand the words - a monster. He felt no remorse for those who died trying to humiliate or kill him. Even though he didn't grab them by the neck and strangle them, or shoot them, or stab them, or kill them in a hundred other different ways, he nevertheless believed he was the cause of their death. Death was a bounty hunter that pursued him like a fugitive and he embraced it. He now knew his destiny and was convinced that the curse he had to tried to ignore was indeed very real and not going away.

Sitting in his cabin that night, he looked at his shadow. He didn't see the playful figure that was often mentioned in children's storybooks. Rather, he saw something sinister. Though he could feel it try, he would not allow it to consume or overwhelm him. Whatever was there in the shadow would have to succumb to his will, not his to it. And if it was why people died within his presence, so be it. It would just be something that happened and he would ignore it as he had learned to ignore the stares that his appearance always provoked.

From that resolute moment, Jameson realized what he was meant to do in life. He would collect those things that were different, or odd, or ugly because, like him, they were unique. He would bring them all together. If they had a strange talent, they would perform. Whether that meant they ate glass, swallowed car axles, or drove nails into their nose, he knew people would like to see them up close and in an intimate manner. If they were alive but dangerous, or dead and preserved, he would place them in a display case for all to see. And it would be beautiful. Nature had created everything and regardless of what others said, he knew strange was beautiful, strange was scary, and strange was alluring. He would become an expert on all things unique and different, not only in this country but from all around the world.

He would feel no guilt for taking others' money in return for revealing to them that they all had a dark cellar within their souls too. Most of the time, people were able to keep the cellar door closed, but at times, they opened it and went down those steps to see what the creaking noise was. They enjoyed the scare and the rush of adrenaline and then came back up and shut the door. He also understood there would be others who embraced their dark cellar and ended up burying things down there that they wanted to hide. Things that, when found, would illustrate their true dark nature. He accepted the fact that he would attract both and it didn't bother him. Thus, was born the Peculiarity Museum, which was now being advertised on the large glass planes and had awakened the city to the arrival of something strange, unique, and beautiful.

The Peculiarity Museum was sold out for the first two months of shows and was all anyone talked about when they visited downtown. It was written about in the arts and entertainment section of the newspaper several times and Jameson explained how he had amassed the amazing acts and displays. Jameson always conducted those interviews by phone and only those who worked for him knew what he looked like. Everyone else came to know him as just another museum performer; a very popular performer that scared the shit out of those who walked by, thinking they were looking at a wax model of the wolfman dressed up in ragged clothes to resemble the transformed Lon Chaney of Wolfman movie fame. The eviscerated body, with real animal intestines hanging out of its chest that lay at the feet of Jameson's statuesque pose, looked real, and when Jameson leapt toward the crowd, the screams could be heard throughout the museum.

Because of his life experiences, Jameson had become very intuitive about human nature. He knew people were afraid of the unknown and most had a fear of snakes and insects. So, he made sure they walked beside the cases with the venomous snakes and preserved and live insects before they came to his exhibit. First, they saw the two-headed snake in a jar of formaldehyde. Next, they would come to the live venomous snakes. There were twelve of the most dangerous snakes in the world lined up in cases with descriptions of them and how quickly they could kill a human being. He always made sure to include information about the effect the venomous exhibits had on a human being if bitten or stung.

There was a black mamba, eastern brown snake, tiger snake, death adder, boomslang, Gaboon viper, king cobra, western diamondback rattlesnake, copperhead, coral snake, water moccasin, and the inland taipan. Next to the snakes, he lined up the cases of the strangest, largest, and most dangerous bugs in the world. There was a black widow, the Arizona bark scorpion, brown recluse, the funnel-web spider, the titan beetle with mandibles that could snap through a pencil, the rhinoceros beetle, the Madagascar hissing beetle, the giant huntsman spider that was as big as a dinner plate, the goliath bird-eating tarantula, and many colonies of different kinds of ants including fire ants, bullet ants with a sting that felt like being shot, and the bulldog ant, which had been known to kill a human within fifteen minutes.

By the time they reached his exhibit, the adrenaline was flowing and when they saw him standing there unmoving like a wax figure, they allowed themselves to relax because they believed what they were looking at was not real. On the exhibit sign, Jameson suggested that were many alien things on this planet and their existence was not dependent on whether you had actually seen them. Just like the wolfman. "Was it a monster that truly existed?" the sign asked. "You decide," were the last two words on the sign and as soon as he had given them time to read that part, he jumped out toward them, provoking their adrenal glands to inject an extra shot of adrenaline into their bloodstream that caused them to jump back and react in fear. He delighted in that look on their faces each time.

Unfortunately, the excitement for the museum died very quickly when the dismembered body parts were discovered in the display case, followed soon by the corpse of the female sword swallower, who was found dead in a back alley with a spear placed through her body as if she was some sort of animal on a roasting spit. The museum became a crime scene and the familiar looks that Jameson had lived with his entire life returned. The plastic sheets covering the glass windows and doors were like clouds of suspicion hovering around the familiar form now known as a strange-looking proprietor, who had hidden in plain sight as just another, but very popular, oddity within the museum.

The murders were publicized throughout the area and the police stated that four women had been killed. What they didn't tell the public was that they believed there were even more, but they didn't want to throw gasoline onto a fire. The knowledge of four victims should be sufficient impetus to stay on alert should you fit the profile of those who were killed. The information was relayed numerous ways and numerous times, with the police being aware they needed to balance the panic that knowledge would create with the information the public needed.

The investigation lasted several months, and The Peculiarity Museum, which had been used in conversations as a destination point, became a subject associated with other horrible murders that had occurred within the area. People were now quoted as saying they had often felt something "cold" when they walked through the museum that caused them to shiver and that they had felt an evil presence watching them during their visits.

Jameson knew it would be impossible to overcome this perception and recapture the interest of the people in that town. As soon as the police were sure he was not involved and had cleared everyone who worked with him, he was allowed to start packing up his curiosities and unique artifacts and begin looking for a new location for the museum.

The ghostly feelings inside the empty building and the unsolved murders soon attracted a group of paranormal investigators who reached out to Jameson and asked permission to film their popular cable TV show, "The Ghost

Rustlers," in the museum before they left town. Jameson quickly understood how helpful having them there would be for the long-term success of his museum. As they talked, he was already thinking about how the "museum murders" would be some sort of tagline for The Peculiarity Museum. It even prompted him to think about using the newspaper articles about the Shenandoah Sasquatch, which until then, he had not even considered.

The dark cellar within the subconscious and death; it was there. It was something he could take advantage of because he knew what people truly wanted to see. He knew the paranormal investigators were just an extension of that desire. They were popular not because they were truly able to find ghosts or communicate with the dead. They were popular because they opened the cellar door and provided people with something that they wanted to peek at for a moment before they ran back upstairs. He wasn't frightened by the real killer who had ventured into his museum. He felt emboldened by the curse and told himself that the killer should be afraid of him. So, he agreed to show the Ghost Rustlers around the museum with the caveats that his face would be obscured when he was interviewed and that he would be present at all times during the filming; conditions which the lead investigator agreed to without hesitation.

Aaron Hubbard was the lead investigator, and according to his bio, he could determine whether a building was haunted or not the moment that he entered it. He had "confirmed" famous and well-known haunted sites in Savannah, Georgia, and the Bell Witch of Tennessee, and had what he called audio and video proof of the existence of paranormal beings. Aaron claimed he had never been to a supposedly supernatural site where he didn't experience something that was "not of this world."

The photographer and paranormal equipment professional was a young man named Chris Farmacie. He loved to tell the audience about the digital voice recorder, the camera with night vision, the EMF or electromagnetic field detector, and all of the other tools they used. He explained what each device was and how it worked and was always excited when one of the machines beeped, flashed, or caught a hazy shadow in the dark. Though he always looked surprised when the people they visited said he looked like Egon Spengler in the movie "Ghostbusters," his appearance was purposeful. It was Aaron's idea when he first met Chris and Chris loved the recognition and the notoriety it provided him.

The third member of the team was considered a psychic. Her name was Anna Nimmus and she claimed, at four years of age, to have been visited by her grandmother when "she passed over to the other side." She let the viewing public know she had felt the presence of many restless spirits within the buildings they examined. Although she was only 25 years old, her hair was platinum white, a fact that she attributed to the evil presence she had experienced in a psychiatric hospital five years ago. Loyal viewers of the show knew about that transformation, and every so often, Chris would find a reason to ask, "Were you a patient there or what?" and together they would laugh as she winked at the camera.

The team announced on their show at the Oakwood Cemetery in Greenville, South Carolina that they would be visiting the haunted Peculiarity Museum in Macon, Georgia next. Unofficially named "Hell's Gate," the Oakwood Cemetery was known as one of the most active haunted locations in South Carolina. Though others had not been able to get electronic equipment to work in this location, Chris had been successful on numerous occasions. Those who watched the show heard the captured voices that led all of them to the graves of those who were speaking to them. At the end of that show, Anna announced to everyone that she was glad they were leaving this cemetery, as the convenient ground-hugging mist began to rise over her feet and caused her to shiver and run back to their van.

Jameson and his group of artists met the Ghost Rustlers on a Friday evening around 5:00. Aaron introduced himself to everyone and told Jameson his team would like to do a walk-through and some preliminary readings right away. They would set up their equipment on Saturday night to begin filming the show. Jameson once again reinforced his position that he wanted to be there during the entire process and Aaron agreed to all of his wishes.

Jameson was not prepared for the reaction that his artists had when they saw the Ghost Rustlers van pull up in front of the building. They were still upset about the death of their friend, but he could feel their excitement about this visit. It was as if they were aware that they would be able to provide knowledge of what happened and show them something that they had not ever seen before.

Nor was he ready for the Ghost Rustlers' reaction when they met him. They acted like there was nothing odd or unusual about his appearance. He had never had that experience before when meeting strangers. He had always considered what these paranormal investigators did as simply capitalizing on people's fears, but he began to think there was something more to them. He sensed that they truly had witnessed the strange and unusual in their travels and that, perhaps, they had indeed been exposed to evil. They all felt like tomorrow's night show would be something very special. Jameson agreed but failed to say it was for an entirely different reason.

They hadn't been there long before Anna stated that she felt something cold around her and then walked out the door of the building. Everyone followed her for several blocks before she turned into the alley where the sword swallower had been found. She walked right over to the exact spot the body was discovered and said she could hear the gasps of the woman as she died. Jameson watched Chris pull out a machine and begin taking readings and reported that the EMF meter was going crazy.

The location of his dead friend was never revealed in the papers and Jameson's friends saw the perplexed look on his face. Aaron noticed his look of concern and walked over and put his hand on his shoulder. "I've never seen it happen this quickly before," he said. "We never know what to expect and can never control what happens. We just document everything. That's all we can do."

Jameson wasn't sure what to believe. As he looked at his troupe, they seemed amazed and a little frightened. He understood why. Everything seemed real, but he maintained a sliver of skepticism, knowing what he did about people in general.

Careful, Jameson, he told himself. *They could have gotten this information with a little probing. Maybe they have a friend on the police force or found someone who would talk. A person who would place their ethical standards into their pocket along with a hundred-dollar bill if given a chance.*

"She is telling me to go back inside. To look in the back where the jars are. Something is there that reveals the evil which still remains in the building."

"Grab your camera, Chris," Aaron said as they all turned and began to follow Anna. Jameson lagged behind, watching the reactions of Aaron and his team. Aaron waited for a moment for Jameson to catch up to him. "Is it true they didn't find any blood or DNA in the building?" he asked

Jameson looked at Aaron and smiled. *He knows someone on the police force. He tipped off Anna.*

"I have no idea. They didn't tell me what they found or didn't find. I found the body parts in the jar and called the police. They only allowed me to see my friend in order to identify her. I'm sure I'm still under suspicion even though there is nothing there to link me to anything that was found. But I've learned that I am always under suspicion."

Aaron nodded his head. "Your appearance. It makes people suspicious. You're nothing but a monster to most everyone that meets you, aren't you?"

No stranger had ever been so honest with him and Jameson was taken aback for a moment by the frank comment. "I have to admit that I was surprised by you and your team's reaction to my appearance. The lack of stares and their friendly demeanor was unusual."

"To be honest with you, Jameson, a lot of this stuff we do is just for show. I have friends in the police department and the newspaper industry and they feed me information all the time. There are indeed times when we have been truly mystified by what we heard or saw, but none of us are timid about encountering something unusual or not even of this world. Just last week when we were in the Oakwood Cemetery in Greenville, we all felt something very evil upon those grounds. So, meeting you - that was nothing scary. You're just a unique human being. I consider myself very lucky to have met you. I don't think there are many of you around."

Jameson smiled. "One in a billion is the estimate. And to tell you the truth, I'm not surprised that your show is so successful. We're alike, my museum and your show. We show the public what they want to see, even when they think or say they don't want to see it. They want that thrill, the adrenaline rush. It's interesting what you said about the Oakwood Cemetery. I may have to go there myself. I'm not sure I've ever been in the presence of true evil."

At least, none I wish to discuss. Even those moonshiners that tried to kill me. I don't think they were truly evil. Just stupid, drunk, and ignorant. And thank God, more drunks than hunters.

"Most people haven't. But I can tell you when people reach out to us, I already know they are ready to believe whatever we tell them. Just by the fact they called. If you look at our shows, you'll see a blip or flash or a shadow that we captured. I don't think most of it is anything. But to the people who are there where we are filming, that sound or flash of light or shadow is a confirmation of what they already believed. I honestly don't think it would even matter if I said we found nothing."

"Yeah, I agree. I doubt it would matter at all," Jameson said as he and Aaron followed everyone back into the museum. As Anna started walking past the stage, Jameson told her to stop. The live animal displays had not been moved yet as they were in a controlled environment and would only be moved when another place was found and made ready for them.

"Anna, stop!" he called out. "Before you go through that door, you need to understand there are very dangerous animals in there that can kill you. They are in reinforced glass displays, but they can still break, and depending on what gets out, we may or may not have another 'ghost' to haunt this place."

Chris and Aaron laughed. Jameson's statement was intentional to gauge their reactions. He saw how all the performers looked at each other nervously, and how Chris and Aaron soon realized their laughter was inappropriate. Anna didn't laugh. She turned around and looked at Jameson as if she was in some sort of hypnotic state. She heard him but her eyes suggested she didn't see him. She simply stared at him, unblinking and unmoving, before finally starting to speak. "That's why he put the jars there. Among the serpents and the spiders and scorpions. To let you know he was more evil than what you had on display."

Jameson looked over at Chris and Aaron. Chris had a big smile on his face as he checked his meter. "Off the fucking chain, man," he said to Aaron and Jameson could tell by the expression on Aaron's face, this was not something that he had planned. *If it was, then Chris and Aaron are very good actors,* Jameson thought.

Anna turned around and opened the door. The lights came on automatically, illuminating the preserved animal remains in jars and the live serpents and spiders in the glass displays. She walked over to the Gaboon viper and the black mamba and stopped. "There, on top of those snakes, were found four jars. The evil is still here. Watching us. Waiting. The restless spirits are here too. Tell me: Are you someone who was killed?" Anna asked.

The apparatus Chris was holding flashed green multiple times. "Look at this shit, Aaron. The binary response device. The green light flashed not once but 6 times. And the EMF is going crazy! Holy shit. Hell, there's a spirit conference going on in here. Tomorrow night is going to be like the fucking Fourth of July!"

Aaron glanced at Jameson and could see that he seemed confused about what was happening. "The green flash of light means yes. The spirits can harness the energy in the machine and use it to respond. Green for yes, red for no. Usually, it only blinks once, meaning one spirit. The six flashes suggest there are multiple spirits here or one spirit that is very eager to make its presence known."

Jameson nodded his head. The device was right. There were four jars on the top of the snake display case. But only he and the police knew that. And then he remembered what Aaron told him. He had friends on the police force. The smug appearance on Aaron's face suggested he wasn't surprised by the response. If fact, he almost looked excited by what was occurring.

Big ratings tomorrow night, huh, Aaron? Yes, I understand. I truly understand.

"I think that's enough for right now," Aaron said as he went over and hugged Anna. At his touch, she blinked her eyes and started looking around as if she wasn't sure where she was.

"What happened?" she asked.

"You made contact."

"I'm scared, Aaron. I've never felt this way before. The presence here is overwhelming. Look at my skin. It feels like it's going to shake off my bones. And I'm very cold. The dead want justice and there is something very forbidding here."

"It will be okay, Anna," Aaron said as he hugged her. "Chris - turn off the camera for right now. Anna, you need to leave and get some rest. I think you're still feeling the effects of the Oakwood Cemetery. You just need to take it easy. You'll be better tomorrow. Right?"

Anna nodded her head as she allowed Aaron to escort her out.

"See you tomorrow night at 9," he said to Jameson as he and Anna walked out the door.

"She'll be all right," Chris said as he turned toward Jameson and his troupe. "She's always all right. Don't worry." He took one more reading with the EMF device and then left.

Jameson could tell his performers were scared and he understood why. He had never seen that look in their eyes before. But there it was. The look that other people, normal people, had when they saw him. That frightened look of what is that and will it hurt me? Is it contagious? Is it a monster?

He couldn't fault them for feeling that way because what Anna said was right. There was something evil here. He knew they would all be better off when the museum moved. And perhaps he felt some sympathy for the performers, but he also knew the serial killer's association would only help the museum in the future. However, he understood that right now he needed to talk to them and reassure them that everything would turn out okay.

"What do you think, Jameson?" the Voodoo Python Princess asked.

"I'm not sure yet," he replied.

"Was little girl right about where policeman find Jillian and jars?" the large man known as Gibralto asked.

Jameson wasn't sure if he should tell the truth or not. Just like the police, he struggled with what would be a proper amount of information and what would make the people in front of him even more scared. He had never lied to any of them before and decided he would not start this evening.

"Yes, it is true, but there are things she didn't say or notice that were also true. I spoke with Aaron, the lead investigator, and he told me that he has connections with the police department and the newspapers. He could have easily learned those things and they could have just been doing a "warm-up" for tomorrow night. He admitted as much to me just before Anna walked back here. Most of what they do is just for show. For entertainment, not real pursuit and documented interactions with the spirit world. Now, granted, we know that there really is a murderer out there and for whatever reason, he picked our place to make the sick, perverted statement of his or her presence. But I will be here tomorrow and I am not worried. And I promise you, I will find out who killed Jillian. I am certain I can do that with their help. I feel it."

He didn't tell them about the curse that had followed him his entire life or that because of it, he may have been responsible for Jillian's death. He also couldn't tell them how the notoriety from the show would only help them sell tickets in another city and make all of them even more famous and wealthier. They weren't ready to hear that. Especially Gibralto. Jillian was his girlfriend.

"I wish be here too," Gibralto said. "I protect Jameson."

Jameson had to admit Gibralto was big enough to protect him; he was big enough to protect several of him. He was 6 feet, 8 inches tall and weighed 405 pounds. Jillian had broken cinderblocks on his chest as part of his act; cinderblocks resting on a platform of three-inch nails that covered his body. He could also snap bricks into two pieces with his bare hands or by smashing them on the top of his bald head. He was a brute but Jameson knew that if he was there with him tomorrow, he could die. The curse that followed him didn't discriminate. Just as he started to tell him no, Gibralto looked at him and shook his hands.

"Jameson. No matter what you say. Gibralto be here at 9 p.m. tomorrow to protect you."

Jameson knew he wouldn't win this argument so he nodded his head but he told everyone else to stay away and they all agreed to do as he requested. Before they left, several of them went back to help Jameson feed the animals and hugged him as they said goodbye. He locked the front door and went back to the room where they kept equipment and supplies and pulled out his cot. Some nights he never left. He liked sleeping there. He felt comfortable in that building; normal. He set up the cot, laid down, and closed his eyes.

He thought back to the night that sick bastard decided to leave those trophies in his museum and how he wished he had been there. He now understood that he had probably been watched. The killer was most likely someone who had visited the museum. Someone who had observed him coming and going from the building and knew when it was safe to enter and leave his "gifts" for him to find. As he thought more about that, something began taking form within his mind. A shadow with the outline of a female body. There were no distinct features but he knew it was a female body and he opened his eyes.

He suddenly realized he had never really mourned Jillian's death. He had treated her death like the others who had died around him and he recognized how wrong that was. He didn't want to become that indifferent monster that he knew existed inside the malignant shadow that followed him. It was removing his ability to feel sorrow, and he sat up as he started crying.

"I'm so sorry, Jillian. I'm very sorry you died and I hope I was not responsible. You were a great performer and a good friend. Forgive me for my callous treatment of your death. I should know better. Me, more than anyone else in this world, should know better. God bless you, Jillian. I hope you will soon be able to find peace."

He pulled a beer from the small refrigerator in the supply room and thought about Jillian and Gibralto's acts. He toasted them several times and then laid back down for the night.

The next day, Jameson came to the museum at 6 p.m. and looked around before the Ghost Rustlers arrived. After ensuring everything was in order, he went back to the supply room and lay down on the cot. Though he didn't intend to, he fell asleep and when he opened his eyes, Gibralto was sitting next to him.

"How long have you been here?" Jameson asked.

"One hour, fourteen minutes. Investigators here soon. Almost nine. Boss man ready? Gibralto ready."

"Yes. I am ready," Jameson said as he sat up and smiled at his friend. "Follow me into the back. I want to talk to you about something before they get here."

The Ghost Rustlers team arrived at exactly 9 p.m. and Jameson let them in. He re-introduced them to Gibralto and when Anna shook his hand she stepped back.

"You have lost someone. Someone that you worked with, that was close to you. She is here. Chris, do you have the binary response device with you?"

"Yes. I have it on."

"Let me know if you are here, spirit. Are you here?"

Everyone except Anna looked at the device in Chris's hands and saw it flash green. Chris gave the device to Aaron and started filming.

"Were you someone that was killed recently?"

The device flashed green.

"Are you here to protect us?"

The device flashed red.

"Are you here to warn us?"

The device flashed green.

Anna looked at Aaron and he could see the look of fear in her face.

"I'm not sure I can do this tonight, Aaron. There is something here besides the lost spirit. Something very evil. Who is the person that knows you?" she asked as she looked over at Gibralto.

Gibralto looked at Jameson before answering and Jameson nodded his head, granting permission to tell her.

"Jillian. Girlfriend. Girlfriend killed in alley."

"Over here, Aaron," Chris said as he placed a device behind Gibralto and started filming. "Look at this, Aaron. The infrared thermometer is 60 degrees. You don't keep this room that cool, do you?" he asked as he looked over at Jameson.

"We do keep it cool but not that cool. We usually keep it at 67 degrees. It helps the performers and it makes the crowd a little chilly. We want them to shiver a little."

"Yeah, but, man, a three-degree difference from the rest of the room would be significant. This is reading seven degrees cooler. That's a strong sign of a spirit that has moved on to the other side."

Aaron walked Anna over to the area where Chris was pointing and she froze.

"Oh shit, Aaron. She, this Jillian, was killed by something big…something that was forced down her throat. Oh my god! She died as a spear was shoved down her throat."

The police had never disclosed that to the public. Jameson was certain that even Aaron's police friends wouldn't have told him that. It was too gruesome and critical to their investigation. This was a sick display of horror and he knew Anna was right. Evil was present. They walked back into the room with the animal displays and Anna stopped again. Jameson looked over at Aaron and asked if he could say something. Aaron nodded his head, turned to the camera, and started speaking.

"The owner of this museum is here with us, but because of the ongoing murder investigation has asked us to blur his appearance and mask his voice. You will see a blurred image in a moment and hear a voice that has been altered. This is not an apparition. This is the owner. Chris, will you get the camera ready?"

Chris nodded his head and when he was ready, Aaron again looked at the camera. "What would you like to say?"

In a garbled voice, Jameson asked Anna how many spirits she felt were present.

"Just the one. But she is telling me that there were things that the police didn't find. Things that the murderer left that they failed to find."

"What was that, Anna?" Aaron asked.

"There were four jars symbolizing that four people were killed, but there were also body parts in some other cases. Oh my god! That means there were more than four people killed. There were seven. There are fingers underneath the nests of the spiders. In the cases of the black widow, the brown recluse, and the funnel-web spider."

"There aren't any fingers under the funnel-web spider! There were six green flashes, not seven, you idiot!" Aaron blurted out.

Everyone turned toward Aaron and stared at him.

"How would you know that, Aaron?" Jameson asked. "And don't say some ghost told you. It won't work. Not tonight. I knew as soon as I spoke with you, there was something wrong. And when I met you, I recognized the shadow of evil that followed you. I am all too familiar with that feeling."

Aaron started backing up as he pulled out a long hunter's knife with an eight-inch blade and smiled.

"You were right, Chris. This will be one hell of a show. It will be talked about for a very long time," he said as he lunged at Anna.

Before he could reach her, Gibralto grabbed Aaron by the shoulder. Aaron slashed at him with the knife and Gibralto caught the blade in his hand, oblivious to the pain. He pushed Aaron back onto one of the snake cases which broke as Aaron fell onto it. The startled snake bit him on the wrist and the palm of his hand as it moved away. Jameson quickly grabbed the snake with the snake tongs and placed it into a plastic container that he had hidden behind the spider cases.

"That snake that just bit you, Aaron, is called an inland taipan, or fierce snake. It is the most dangerous snake in the world. One venomous bite can kill up to one hundred people. I suspect since it bit you twice, you have about fifteen minutes to live. Don't bother to try and do anything. Gibralto will make sure you can do nothing but lay there and suffer and die. The ambulance will not be here in time. And everything is on camera. You knew there were six people you killed and where you put the fingers, just as I did.

"I knew you would come back. And I would be ready this time. You are the evil presence that Anna felt. She felt it because I told her about it. I told her that it was you. She came to my rescue again to help me catch you, just like she helped me a long time ago. A time that I had forgotten until I saw her on your show. And then I remembered."

"Fuck you both," Aaron panted. He started to convulse before his breathing became very painful gasps and then stopped.

Chris turned off the camera and they all stood together waiting on the police and ambulance to arrive. When they did, they pronounced Aaron dead and placed the knife in a sealed evidence bag. Jameson removed the fingers that were in the black widow and brown recluse case with gloves and also dropped them into the evidence bags. The EMTs told Gibralto he would need stitches and before he left, he thanked Jameson for helping him.

"Jillian rest now, Jameson. I feel it. Thank you."

The police decided not to press charges against Jameson for withholding evidence because they knew if they did, they would be overwhelmed by a public outcry that had watched on live TV the capture and death of a dangerous serial killer who had haunted the area for over a year. The police asked everyone to come to the station to make a statement about the night's events. Jameson said that he would be there after he made sure his animals were safe.

Just before Anna left, she and Jameson sat down on the bleachers in the stage area and held each other's hand.

"I never thought I would see you again, Em," he said.

"Nor I, you," Anna replied. "When you left town after your parents died, I thought that would be the end of our relationship."

"Yes, I tried to put all of that in the past when I moved away." Jameson looked into her eyes and remembered the first time he saw her. She was there when he jumped out onto the trestle and scared those two teenagers. She had kept his life from becoming a permanent eclipse and shrouded in darkness when they died because she had become his friend soon after that occurred. Like the moon that eventually moves away from the sun, the dark moods that obscured his vision were removed by her friendship. She was the only true friend he had up until the time he began putting together the group of people that became the performers in his Peculiarity Museum.

"Are you okay? You were very brave tonight. I couldn't have done this without you."

"I knew you would protect me, Jimmy. You would never ask me to do anything that would harm me. I was never afraid of you. You are a kind soul and I hope you know just how special you truly are. I know you think I saved you, but you saved me, Jimmy. I never told you that, but you did. I hope years don't go by before we see one another again."

He wanted to see her again, as soon and as many times as possible, but he remembered the curse and just nodded his head. He told her that he would stay in touch, knowing that he wouldn't. And though Anna wasn't a psychic, she knew that too.

"See you later then, ok?"

"Yes, Em. See you later."

He walked her to the front door and watched her leave and then sat back down on the bleachers. He stared at the stage and looked at the shadowy figure that was over in the corner of the room. It glowed blue-green.

"Come on out, Goddammit. I know you're there. Reveal yourself. Aaron is gone but the evil presence that Anna alluded to is still here. I can feel it. Come on and let's get this over with."

The shadow took a female form and came forward but the face was indistinct. It looked like the blurred face of his own when Chris adjusted the camera while filming him.

"What do you mean 'get this over with?' There is nothing to get over. I was waiting for you to deliver Aaron to me and you did just as I expected. You are very good at that."

"What do you mean? Who are you?"

"I am called Abaddon. Sometimes called, Abaddon the Destroyer. Look me up or reference Demonology. I'm there on the internet or in the books of old. I'll always be there. Talked about by some. Worshipped by some. Forgotten by some. Feared by many."

"Why are you here?"

"Because you bring me cellar dwellers."

"I don't understand."

"You said earlier that you doubted whether you had ever been in the presence of true evil, but you have been surrounded by it your entire life. You were not the monster in your family. Your parents were the monsters. Your father harmed young innocents and your mother poisoned them. She was slowly poisoning your father and once he died, she planned to set herself on fire. Your gift to them - that wonderful tree-like design that was the perfect conductor of electricity - ended their life much sooner than expected. And your mother was able to experience what it felt like to be on fire a lot earlier than she anticipated. I could tell you what your father is experiencing now but it's quite horrible. I'm not sure you would want that image in your mind for the rest of your life. They didn't love you because they didn't know what love was. Their shame did not arise from you. Their shame arose from their own unforgivable actions.

"And those young men you frightened and killed. Do you realize they forced themselves on your friend Em numerous times? She was close to committing suicide before you came by and allowed me to have them. Em wasn't the only one they assaulted, and unlike her, several of their other victims did kill themselves. Their wretched proclivities would have gone on for a long time had you not appeared that evening."

"No! Em? Why didn't she tell me? You're lying. Damn you, you are lying," Jameson said as his voice became a whisper and he started to cry.

"She didn't tell you because she knew you were already tortured. She didn't want to burden you with something she wanted to forget. You helped her forget. You were the friend she needed. Someone who didn't judge her."

"She was that for me."

"Yes, she was. But, enough of all this touchy-feely shit. This isn't a pity party. It's a day to celebrate. Let's talk about those two moonshiners who killed themselves while trying to kill you. Filthy drunks. Horrid little creatures. They had raped and killed three women, including their sister. There are a lot of pig-like things where they are now that make them understand how it feels to be torn apart. Over and over. Too bad they only think that they can drink something that tastes like urine. The idiots don't even know it is their own urine.

"And that brings us to Aaron. A serial killer who brutally killed six women and wanted you to know how 'special' he was. But the only thing special about him will be the way he suffers. Again, I can go into detail if you would like, but I wouldn't recommend it."

"But what about the curse? The curse that follows me."

"There is no curse that follows you. You think you are a monster but you are far from it. In reality, you help rid the world of the monsters that live here. You are a natural conduit for evil because of the perverted's ignorance. What others know is a promise, they see as a curse. They are very unbalanced and unfortunately, they see their own reflection in you. A reflection that at times haunts them from the other side of the mirror. It's misguided, true, but these are psychopaths and very twisted individuals. They hear and see things that are much more horrible than you. You just remind them of it in a three-dimensional and non-hallucinogenic manner. No offense."

"None taken."

"But I can leave the shadows if you want. The shadows that follow you. All you need to do is say, 'Be gone,' and I will go away. But even if I leave, you'll never be able to stop the evil that is around you or that gravitates toward you. Evil has a presence and an ability to destroy and always will. Who knows? There's always the chance that you could be that evil person one day. You teeter on the edge at times. But I can tell you now, you didn't kill Jillian. Aaron killed her. As I said, you can't stop evil from doing what it does. But you can stop it from going on for longer than it should for some of those cellar dwellers. You know, the ones that have something to hide and linger there in the darkness."

"You say, all those that die, all those cellar dwellers that seek me out are evil and are headed to hell, or wherever it is you take them?

"Yes, indeed. Some of the most debauched individuals in this world. And yes, you are correct, it is Hell. I can tell you more about it if you so desire. We tailor the experience for each individual. It's like an all-inclusive resort, but instead of sandy beaches, the beaches are made of sulfur, brimstone, and shit. A lot of shit."

Jameson stared at the shadowy figure and realized he had not truly understood what his destiny was until now.

"'Better the devil you know, than the devil you don't.' So, what the hell, stick around."

"What the hell, indeed."

It was advertised as The Peculiarity Museum on the large glass window panes of the empty building downtown in Gate City, a small town in southwest Virginia. The pictures depicted a sword swallower and a woman called the Voodoo Python Princess from the Amazon, who had a large snake wrapped around her body. The art and bold lettering reminded those who were old enough to remember what the advertising looked like when the circus was coming to town. The signs were lettered in bright primary colors with pictures and descriptions of the marvelous and strange, and promised feats of magic, strength, agility, and a glimpse into the world of the fantastic.

Those who read the word fantastic knew it meant something else - a collection of oddities, or as it was once known, a freak show. The fact that it was also now advertised

92

as the "infamous" Murder Museum and had actual hair from the Shenandoah Sasquatch generated a surplus of excitement and gave it the ability to shock and astound, even more than that of the virtual reality world or the circus acts that had become so famous on the Las Vegas strip.

Jameson inspected the letters on the glass panes and smiled. He looked up at the full moon and howled and hoped someone was around with a phone taking his picture there in the dark. He was sure there was someone out there, even though the town was under a curfew due to several murders that had happened over the past year. The newspaper hadn't said so, but he knew that the murders looked similar to the police. He knew his museum would be very successful here but he wasn't sure how long it would be before they had to move on to another city because another person with unique talents would show up and make his presence known. His arrogant ignorance causing him to be unaware that there was a cellar door within the building that would open up when he got there and welcome him into its darkness; where malevolent entities would demonstrate to him how his perverse actions in this world, would become an eternity of torment and agony within the next one.

Clinch Avenue

She got her undergraduate degree in Biology from the University of Tennessee in Knoxville before she was accepted to their school of dentistry in Memphis. After another long and arduous four years, she graduated at the top of her class. She had loved her time in Knoxville and decided to return there to start her practice. The fact that her best friend from high school and college lived there also helped her make that decision.

Her friend had graduated from the University of Tennessee with a B.S. in Interior Architecture and now operated a flourishing company in downtown Knoxville. Her father was a highly successful builder in the area and he helped fund the renovation of the old bank that she designed. His construction company occupied the first floor while her interior design and architecture business occupied the second. When the building was completed, it won several awards for its innovative design and she became very successful despite her father's money and "outdated ideas," as she would say to anyone that asked. Her father didn't mind. He was making a lot of money in building referrals from his daughter's impertinence and independent manner.

When Dr. Keera Donaldson arrived in Knoxville, her friend Chloe Murphy, had a party for her in her downtown office so that she could meet some of the most influential people in the city. Over two hundred people attended and it was covered in the Knoxville News Sentinel as well as by several University of Tennessee publications. Keera was overwhelmed by the response. She had thought it was funny when Chloe told her that she would get close to a hundred business cards that night, but the next morning when they went to breakfast, she grabbed her friend in her arms and told her that she must be some sort of sorceress to have been able to predict the exact number.

They met at the French Market Creperie on Clinch Avenue, which was bustling that morning. "Chloe, I can't thank you enough for last night. It was beyond stupendous. I had no idea."

"You didn't believe me, did you?"

"One hundred business cards, when they don't even know me? No, I thought you were just being Chloe. You have always talked in a grand manner. Always had big ideas. I knew you would be a success but it appears that you have surpassed success and transcended into some sort of world that is usually only reserved for UT's football stars."

"Well, to be honest with you, I have to admit, my father's money and donations to the University did help me. But don't tell him that."

"You think he doesn't know?"

"True. But enough about him, tell me where you are thinking about putting your office. Any ideas?"

"I thought out west. But Knoxville has changed so much in just the four years that I've been gone. Who would have thought a place on Clinch Avenue that doesn't sell beer and cigarettes would be this popular? This food is delicious!"

"That's why I brought you here. There's a house I know, two blocks up, right here on Clinch that I'm sure we can get a great deal on. I mean, not a good deal. A great deal. The owners died and the children don't want to keep the house as

95

a rental property for students. You know how that goes. I think with the right renovation, that house would be perfect for a dental office. There's easy access and the house and property are so big, that we can design it so that you would have plenty of parking. Oh, my gosh! I just realized I never even asked you if that was your plan. I just assumed. Sorry, are you planning to open your own dental practice?"

"When have you ever bothered to ask what people thought?" They both laughed when Keera said that. "But yes, I think I would like to be an independent practitioner. I don't have a lot of school debt due to my grandparent's trust that covered all but one year, so I've been looking at the numbers and that type of setup is exactly what I was thinking. Have you been dabbling in the black arts since I've been gone?"

"Dabbling? I was doing that our entire time in college."

"I thought that was just called pot, beer, and sex?"

"Don't you remember that football player I dated for a while that looked like Denzel? Now that was black art."

Keera laughed. "I do remember him. I think your so-called date with him the night before the Auburn game caused us to lose. He looked very tired in that game."

"Yes, he did, didn't he?"

"Will you ever change?"

"I hope not. I'm having too much fun now. But have you noticed how much harder it is to keep your girlish figure as you get older?"

Keera smiled. Chloe had always struggled with her weight and the perceptions of her self-image. She was a beautiful woman but she was always dieting or doing something to ensure that she didn't become what she considered obese. Though when she used the term, it was done in a medically incorrect and mentally unhealthy manner. Obese to Chloe meant she weighed 130 pounds on her 5-foot 2-inch frame. She never took into account how athletic and how pretty she was, regardless of what the scales indicated or the BMI suggested.

"You're 27, drop-dead gorgeous, have your own successful company, and you are worried about five pounds that no one sees but you. Chloe, you are beautiful. You always have been. You obsess about this too much. It can be unhealthy. It's nothing I haven't said to you before. I love you. You are my best friend and I am telling you that you are one of the most beautiful women I've ever met."

"You're a good friend, Keera. Scratch that. You are my best friend. And thank you. You always know what to say."

Chloe reached over and grabbed her friend's hand. "So, want to look at that property?"

"Yes. Provided you can promise me you can get the pot smell out of the walls."

"Yes, I think I can do that unless you brought some with you." They both grinned as they walked arm in arm out of the restaurant.

Keera loved the building and within two weeks, she had met with the owners and secured a loan for the property and the renovation due to the help of Chloe and her father. And of course, when all the papers were signed, Chloe had a party for Keera. Only this party was much smaller, a dinner at one of her favorite restaurants downtown, with just Keera, Chloe, and Chloe's parents.

"Here's to Keera and a successful new dental business," Chloe said as the waiter brought champagne when they first sat down.

"A successful new dental business in three months," Chloe's father Richard added. "It will take me at least that long to do that renovation and that's pushing it as hard as we can. But I'll get it done, Keera. I can't let you down."

Keera smiled and said, "Thank you," as she held up her glass. She wanted to say something else as she felt the anger growing inside her. But then she remembered what her therapist said about controlling her feelings and that she could only heal when she had put the past into the past. She had never reported the attack to the police and the only person who knew that Richard had forced himself upon her was Chloe. Even then, she had made it seem to Chloe that it was really her own fault for getting so drunk that night. Even telling her that she thought she had placed her hand in his crotch.

In truth, however, she knew she hadn't done that. She only said that to make Chloe accept what had happened and not cause a rift within their family that could not be undone. Being back around him though, seeing him laughing and enjoying himself, didn't help Keera put the past 'into the past'. It just brought everything screaming to the surface again as if someone was drowning and had managed to get their head out of the water before they went under for the last time.

Keera drank her glass of champagne and asked Chloe to hand her the bottle as she filled up her glass again.

"Oh, it's going to be one of those nights, is it?" Chloe asked as she took the bottle from Keera and filled up her glass too. She looked over at her friend and they touched their glasses together in a toast-like fashion and then emptied them.

Alcohol will help. Remember your best friend is here with you, Keera. She is helping to make your dreams come true. Focus on that. Let go of the past. Chloe's mother is like a mother to you. Don't destroy her life. You have turned yours around. Keep moving forward. Remember, you have the power. You control the situation. You control your life. You control your actions.

She repeated that mantra several times before the waiter came by with some bread and she asked him for a Crown Royal on the rocks.

"I'll have a glass of Prosecco, please," Chloe said. "Anything from Napa Valley should be fine. You are not going to outdo me tonight just because this party is for you, Dr. Donaldson. Hey, that's the first time I have used that name. It sounds pretty good. Damn, you are a doctor, aren't you?"

Keera smiled. "I am, Chloe. Thanks to you. I couldn't have done it without having you as my friend."

"Oh Keera, that's so sweet," Chloe's mother said. "And even though my daughter was there for you, and I admit she can be quite a force, you accomplished everything due to your hard work and willpower. Don't ever think otherwise. I am so proud of you."

"Thank you, Cynthia. I only wish my parents were here tonight. You would've liked my mother. You remind me of her in so many ways."

"Cynthia is right," Richard added. "You will be very successful here in Knoxville, Keera."

"It's Dr. Donaldson," Keera said and then smiled as everyone laughed.

No, it's really Dr. Donaldson to you. Don't forget it, she said to herself as she grabbed a piece of bread.

"What's good here?" Keera asked Chloe as she looked over the menu.

"Everything, but the fresh trout with shallots and wine sauce is my favorite."

"Sounds like it could become my favorite too," Keera replied as she put her menu aside.

"Just like in college, you two," Cynthia said. "Always the same no matter what we did or where we went. I don't say this enough Chloe, but I'm very proud of you too."

"Damn, Mom. We would like to at least get a salad out of the way before we all start jogging down memory lane and begin the sob-fest."

I won't cry in front of your father, Chloe. I won't allow that to happen. Never again.

Keera told Chloe the dinner was delicious and complimented her on having such good taste. "A curse I was born with," Chloe replied and everyone laughed. She told her parents that they would be skipping dessert so that she could show her friend the downtown area known as Old City. Her parents looked at Keera and told her to make sure that they didn't stay out too late and to call an Uber when needed. Keera reassured them that they would be fine. She didn't tell them that going out at night in downtown Memphis had enabled her to acquire a skill set that allowed her to feel safe wherever she went.

They left the restaurant and headed to the Old City Wine Bar, a place that Chloe frequented and they ran into some people she knew. They had a few drinks with them and then Chloe suggested they go to another one of her favorite places: The Double S Wine Bar.

"We have to go to The Double S, Keera," Chloe said though her words were become slurred. "It's a double S, you know."

"What does that mean?"

"There are two S's. It's a woman silly. Two S's? Think about it. A sexy little teapot like me."

"Chloe, you're drunk. We should go back to your place. We can go to The Double S another time."

"Just one drink, Keera. Then you can call us an Uber, though I don't think we look like one."

"Look like what?"

"An Uber."

Keera grinned and rolled her eyes as Chloe pointed at her and then herself and started laughing.

"All right, one drink little teapot. Lead on."

Chloe put her arm around Keera as they walked out of the bar and headed left. Chloe was confused as they headed into a dark alley that was taking them further away from Gay Street.

"Are you sure this is right, Chloe?" Keera asked. Before Chloe could reply someone knocked Keera to the ground. The man jumped out of the shadows and hit Chloe in the face and grabbed her shoulders as Keera looked up at both of them.

"Stop, you fucking freak!" Keera yelled as she seized his leg. He reached down and slashed her arms with a knife and told her that if she knew what was good for her, she would stay the fuck away. The next thing Chloe heard was a loud noise and then something wet hitting her face. Keera went over to her friend and asked if she was okay. Chloe nodded her head as she asked, "What happened?"

"I shot the son of a bitch that was trying to hurt you, Chloe. I never told you this but I was mugged in Memphis. Mugged and raped. I said it would never happen again and I learned how to use a gun and got a concealed weapons license so I could always be ready to protect myself."

"What? So, we didn't make it to The Double S?"

Keera nodded her head no, as she wiped Chloe's hair, embedded with blood and small bits of flesh, from her face. Blood from the wounds on Keera's arm dripped down onto Chloe's face and clothes as she sat there holding her confused friend. "Another time, Chloe. Another time."

The police and ambulance arrived within ten minutes. The EMT's examined the girls and told the police that Keera needed some stitches for her wounds. The police wanted to question her before they took her to the hospital. The EMT's said to take five minutes but no more. Chloe was incoherent at that moment so Keera explained to them what happened. She gave them her .38 and showed them her concealed weapons license. When they checked the dead man's prints, they discovered that he had prior arrests for armed robbery and rape and realized they didn't need to check anything else.

The police offered Chloe a ride home but Keera wanted her to stay. The EMTs agreed since it would allow the doctors to do more thorough evaluations of both of them. Keera was glad that the EMTs had placed Chloe in the ambulance with her. She got hit very hard in the face too and she didn't want Chloe's parents to see their daughter like this. Not again. On the way to the hospital, Keera thought about what Chloe's mother had said at dinner. "Just like in college you two; always the same." Those words flashed before her eyes like the flashing lights of the ambulance.

Yes, they were the same in a lot of ways. But this was a similarity that Keera didn't wish to share with her best friend. She doubted Chloe would even remember what she told her tonight about being mugged and sexually assaulted while she was in Memphis. It was hard to put the past in the past when the past kept becoming the present. But this time the outcome was different. Different for both of them. Keera wasn't afraid of the dark anymore; she welcomed it. Whenever she left the house now, she was prepared and ready to send any asshole that fucked with her straight back into the shadows from where they came.

The EMT sitting next to her told Keera it was a good thing that the cuts were on the top of her arms considering how close they were to her wrist. If they had been on the other side, the knife would have probably cut both her radial and ulnar artery and she could have possibly bled to death. She just nodded her head as if that was something she didn't know. She wanted to tell him more, but she knew it would do nothing but belittle him and alienate her so she kept quiet, closed her eyes, and tried to rest.

They were in the emergency room for almost three hours. The police were still unable to question Chloe but the doctor told Keera that she suffered very little physical harm. She would have a bruise on her face and her jaw would probably be sore for about a week, but nothing was broken. He wasn't sure what psychological damage might have occurred though and gave Keera the number of a support group for women who had been assaulted. Keera took the card, thanked him for his help, and placed it in her pocket. She doubted Chloe would use the service and she knew she wouldn't. After all, there was nothing new that they could tell either one of them.

They got back to Chloe's apartment around four in the morning and Keera helped Chloe undress and get into bed. She lay down next to her and fell asleep soon after her head hit the pillow. She woke up five hours later when she heard Chloe moaning beside her.

"What the hell happened last night? I feel like someone hit me in the face with a brick."

"It wasn't a brick but a man tried to mug us, Chloe. He hit you in the face and knocked me down. But he won't bother us anymore."

"The police got him?"

"Yes. He had a record for multiple assaults and rape and they took him to the morgue."

"The morgue?" Chloe shouted as she sat up.

"I shot him. I told you this last night, but I doubt you remember, so I'll tell you again. Like you, I was mugged and raped in Memphis one night. I went through a lot of therapy just like you did, and I knew I needed to empower myself. I needed to take back control so I learned how to use a gun. I never go out anymore unarmed. I will never allow myself to succumb to another sick asshole's fantasy or perverted sense of superiority. He would have probably raped at least one of us, if not both of us. When I warned him to leave, he ignored me. He cut my arms as I tried to get him off of you. I had ten stitches in my left arm and twelve in my right, due to that son of a bitch."

"Oh, my God!" Chloe exclaimed as she got up to look at her face in the mirror. Her cheek was greenish-purple and her jaw hurt as she moved it up and down.

"What did you tell my parents?"

"I haven't told them anything, Chloe. I'll let you decide how you want to handle that."

Chloe walked back to the bed and sat down next to Keera. She looked at the bandages on her arm and shook her head.

"Why didn't you tell me, Keera, when all that happened to you? I would've been there for you."

"In my mind, you were there with me, Chloe. I remember how it affected you. And seeing how you dealt with it and how you moved forward gave me strength. Strength, determination, and motivation. You gave me the ability to acquire those traits. I didn't want to put you through everything again. And I'm okay now."

"Shit, Keera," Chloe said as she hugged her friend and began to cry. "Thank you," she whispered into her ear and then went to take a shower.

When she got out of the bathroom, she suggested that Keera get cleaned up, and then they would call her parents and tell them what happened before they heard about it from someone else. Keera nodded and asked for a trash bag.

"Sure, but why do you need one?" Chloe asked.

"I don't want these clothes that he touched and that have his blood on them to ever be on my body again. You should throw yours away too."

"Good idea," Chloe said as she added her clothes to the bag. "Keera, do you think we have to tell my parents what happened? I could take some vacation time, and we could go to the Caribbean or somewhere down in Florida. My parents have a home on Anna Maria Island in Florida. We could go there and give my face a chance to heal and never have to tell them anything."

"I'm afraid the story of the man getting killed may be in the paper," Keera replied.

"Were the reporters there?"

"No, none that I talked to. But there were a lot of people standing around once the police and ambulance showed up. Someone will talk and some reporters check the police reports every day, searching for a story. I'm sure it will get into the newspaper somehow."

"But those reporters can't use our names without our permission, can they?"

"They're not supposed to, but that doesn't always stop them."

"Let me call my lawyer," Chloe replied as she retrieved her cell phone and walked out onto the balcony. Ten minutes later, she came back into the living room and smiled.

"All fixed, Keera. No one will ever know. Get packed - we're going to Anna Maria Island and it's a long drive. We'll call my parents once we get to Florida. That way they can't say anything except, 'Have a good time.'"

"You are a force of nature, Chloe."

"Fucking right I am! Have to be if you wish to be successful in the old boy's club."

Keera laughed. "Do I need anything but a bathing suit?"

"Not much, just shorts, jeans, t-shirts, sandals, tennis shoes. Anything else, we can buy when we get there. They have a lot of really nice shops. And I think my father will be paying for most of this. I still have a credit card that he gave me when I started my business. He said I could always use it in case of an emergency. And I call this an emergency. Don't you?"

"Yes," Keera replied and she thought how appropriate it was that Richard was paying for everything. He owed her that and she would enjoy spending his money.

They packed their suitcases in Chloe's Audi TT roadster and headed toward Florida. They were already on the other side of Atlanta when Chloe's parents called. She placed the phone on speaker mode and told them they were headed to Florida. Her parents asked if they had heard about the man who was shot and killed in Old City last night. Chloe glanced at Keera wondering how to reply, but Keera spoke up and said they didn't hear about it until today. She added that they were glad they were in a different area from where it happened and got home and went straight to bed as they had a lot to drink.

Her parents thanked Keera for watching out for their daughter and told them to be careful in Florida and to have a good time.

"Don't worry, Mom and Dad. With Keera at my side, I don't have to worry about anything. She'll take care of us." Chloe looked over at Keera and winked as she told her parents that they would see them in about a week and then ended the call. "Do I want to know where you shot him?"

"No," Keera replied.

"Yeah, I didn't think so," Chloe said as she turned up the music. They stopped in Jacksonville and got something to eat before they drove the remaining four hours. They got to the home around 1 a.m. and even though they were very tired, they opened a bottle of Prosecco and went out onto the deck to listen to the waves as they drank.

"Washes away the memories doesn't it, Keera?"

"What - the wine or the ocean?"

"The ocean. The wine is for my jaw."

"Yeah. I could sit out here all night."

"Good idea. Wait right there," Chloe said as she got up. She returned with some blankets and before the bottle was finished, she was asleep. Keera sat and watched her as she finished her glass of wine and then stepped inside and got a small derringer she kept in her purse. The police had kept her .38 for analysis and confirmation that it was the weapon that killed the man.

She placed it under the blanket in her lap and fell asleep as she listened to the waves. But unlike Chloe, the soft, repetitive sound of the waves, provided only a temporary respite from what troubled her sleep. The sound of the waves reminded Keera of the white noise that was always playing in the therapist's waiting room. She never liked it and told the therapist that several times, but her complaints were ignored. The therapist explained that she was fixating on the noise because she didn't like coming to the office. Though Keera agreed with her explanation, she still didn't like hearing it or anything similar.

In her dreams, Keera could see the man pushing himself onto her and could hear herself scream. But as she looked around, she saw nothing but darkness and trash, and the screams only agitated the person who was attacking her. She could see the dirty face of the man pulling on her legs and arms trying to drag her down before she saw his head explode and the gory splatter hitting her in the face. She woke up each time that happened and this time was no different.

The sun was beginning to rise and she could hear the gulls and other shorebirds making their presence known. She saw that Chloe was still asleep and sighed. She closed her eyes and concentrated on the sound of the birds and felt the warm caress of the sun on her face and soon went back to sleep. She didn't wake up until she heard Chloe's voice asking her if she was ever going to get up. She opened her eyes and saw her friend looking down at her.

"Let's go get something to eat, go shopping, pick up some beer and snacks, go lay on the beach, get drunk, get something to eat, go to sleep, and then repeat. Sound okay with you?"

"Sounds wonderful, Chloe."

After showering, they followed Chloe's itinerary in pristine order and enjoyed the day immensely. At the restaurant that evening, Chloe noticed several men watching her and Keera. Keera noticed them too.

"Don't encourage them, Chloe. I don't want to meet any strange men right now."

"After you meet them, they won't be strange, will they?"

"They may be even stranger."

"I suppose. But let's say they come over here and talk to us and you think they are not nut jobs or serial killers. Would it be okay to maybe go out with them for some drinks or ask them back to the house?"

"Chloe. We've been drinking beer on the beach all day. We're having wine with our dinner. Do you honestly think either one of us can make the right decision here?"

"I do. I think you can. You always have that ability."

"Yes, but Chloe...." Keera started to say something but stopped. She didn't want to talk about what happened in Memphis. She knew she had a gun in her purse and she knew she could stop anything bad from occurring with either one of them even though she was probably legally drunk. She knew her friend wouldn't stop anyway so she just nodded her head.

It wasn't long before the two men came over and asked if they could buy them a drink and Chloe agreed. *Of course,* Keera thought. As they talked, Keera realized she really liked the man who seemed interested in Chloe. He was an ER physician in his first year of practice at the local hospital. The other man was a real estate developer and though he was good-looking and seemed nice, Keera wasn't attracted to him. She knew she had more in common with the physician and found herself becoming immersed in her friend's conversation and ignoring the man who was trying to talk to her.

"Happens all the time," she heard Brian say and she turned and oddly looked at him.

"What did you say?"

"Whenever the two of us go out, the women are always more interested in my friend there. Dr. Nolan Robinette. I should leave him at home."

Keera laughed.

"Yeah, I understand what you mean. It happens to me too. If I go anywhere with Chloe, the men flock to her. I used to call her Chloe Bo Peep in college because she herded them in like..."

"Sheep. I understand," Brian interjected.

Keera smiled as she nodded her head.

"So, how long should I sit here before it would be acceptable for me to excuse myself?" Brian asked.

"You don't have to leave, Brian. You seem like a nice guy. I'm sorry for my rudeness, but I have a lot on my mind. Things that don't worry my friend as much. She's always been able to forget the past much easier than me. And I'm sorry, I shouldn't even bring any of that up. Let's just have a drink and talk about anything you want. But please understand, it won't go any further than just this place."

"Okay. You like football?"

"I do. Very much. Chloe and I graduated from UT."

"They still play football up there?"

"Oh, God. Don't tell me. A gator?"

"Chomp, chomp."

"Shit. You don't mind being called all sorts of foul names, do you?"

"Not if you don't."

"Then order up a round. And by the way, we're going to kick your ass this year."

"I wish I had a dollar for every time I heard some deranged UT fan say that."

Keera laughed. "How's your men's basketball team?"

"Good move."

Keera talked with Brian for about an hour before Chloe looked over at her and told her that she and Nolan were going out. Keera knew "out" meant back to the house as she silently acknowledged her friend's statement. She gave her car keys to Keera and Nolan told Chloe he would order an Uber. As they walked out the door, Keera realized the keys to the house were on Chloe's keyring and started to laugh. She told Brian what had just happened and said she would have to go back to the house to let them in. She knew she was too drunk to drive so she just left Chloe's car there at the restaurant and also ordered an Uber. She told Brian it was nice meeting him as she got in the car and left.

Before she got very far, Chloe was calling her and Keera answered the phone telling her she was on her way. She got there within fifteen minutes and smiled at them as she opened the door. She went out on the patio, while Chloe and Nolan went into Chloe's bedroom. She only shut the screen portion of the patio door because she knew very well what were normal moans and groans from her friend and what was something that should worry her. She remembered how it was in college and just shook her head. This type of thing used to make her angry but she had learned to put those feelings in the past too. *Funny how the past keeps repeating itself,* she said to herself as she drank a beer and waited for the noise of the ocean to outlast the noise from the bedroom.

Chloe was with Nolan for the next few evenings until his seven-night shift started and he told her that he wouldn't be able to see her while he was working. Though Keera didn't say it, she was glad that he would no longer be around.

"Well, that was fun, but now that I have that out of my system, we can just be two lesbians, here on vacation."

"Chloe, I'm not a lesbian."

"Well, neither am I. I just meant that if men come up to us in the bars - and they will come up to us," she laughed, "we can just tell them we're lesbians and that will send them on their way. And then we can just concentrate on spending my father's money."

"Sounds like a great idea, Chloe."

The next four days were helpful for the two friends. Both of them healed, but as Keera expected, Chloe always seemed to take less time to do that. Keera still had nightmares which caused her to awaken and required medication and reassurance that her gun was nearby so that she could get back to sleep. She doubted that would ever change.

When they returned to Knoxville, Chloe helped Keera decorate her office. Within a month Keera had ordered her dental equipment and was interviewing candidates for hygienists and clerical staff. Chloe arranged for a large party when Keera's office was ready to open and it did not take very long before she had an active practice.

After about six months, Chloe called Keera and asked her if she could come by before the office closed. She thought she had lost a crown. Keera told her that she would be waiting on her, but if the door was locked to just knock and she would come open it. Chloe said she should get there just after five, but it was closer to seven before she arrived.

"I'm sorry, Keera. I mean - Dr. Donaldson. I got caught up in a big new building being planned in South Knoxville. Which as you know, if you have been driving around there, could really use it. A big multi-use facility. Apartments, movie theater. But get this - it will have an outdoor as well as indoor theater screen, bars, restaurants, gyms, gaming complex. Catering to the students and damn affordable, too."

"And do you mean Chloe-affordable or normal person-affordable?"

"Hissssssss," Chloe said as she swiped at Keera as if she had cat claws.

"Sorry, Chloe. It's just been a long day. Come on in and sit down and let me look at that tooth."

As they walked back to the exam room, Chloe started talking to Keera about her weight and how she wished she could lose about 15 pounds. It wasn't anything that Keera hadn't heard her friend say a hundred times. After she looked in her mouth she told Chloe she had indeed lost a crown and that she would fit her with a temporary one after she took an impression of her bite. As she worked on her tooth, she took

111

the opportunity to try and readdress the self-esteem issues that haunted Chloe like an angry spirit.

"You know, Chloe, maybe you should give therapy a chance again. It can help you."

"No thanks, Dr. Donaldson. I've had enough of therapy. No more for me, thank you very much."

"Okay, I thought you might say that and I understand it. I do. But if you aren't going to do that, perhaps you can try some alternative therapy."

"What do you mean by alternative therapy?"

"In Memphis, I had a little bit of a weight problem. Stress eating. So, I did a lot of research on Chinese herbal supplements and tried some of them. They helped me have more energy, helped control my appetite, and even helped me sleep. Now, I did get a little nauseous at first, but that went away and it's not like you have to keep taking them forever. Take them for as long as you want for the results you want and then quit. If you want me to, I'll even order them for you and have them here by the time your crown comes in."

"You had me as soon as you said alternative. Fix me up, Dr. Donaldson. This will be included in my cost for the crown, won't it?"

"Chloe. Just think of this as a small payment for everything you have done for me. I won't charge you for anything."

"Well, get that damn temporary crown on, and let's go get a steak."

"How about some pasta or fish? Let's not stress the temporary with a steak," she laughed.

"Crab or lobster, ok?"

"Yeah, that'll be fine as long as you don't tear open the shells with your teeth."

"Damn, Keera. I only did that once. I was hungry! Plus. it was spring break. How many beers had I drunk?"

"I stopped counting at twelve," Keera replied as they both laughed.

Within a week, Keera called Chloe to tell her that her crown was ready and that she had those pills for her. They arranged to meet at the office later that evening and she would have a bottle of Prosecco chilling for them. Chloe arrived a little after 6:30, again apologizing for being so late.

"It's not a problem, Chloe. Really. I've been doing a little research on some new dental techniques. Have to keep up even though I just got out of school. Things change so much and so quickly."

"Well, let's get going and pop that crown on! Where are those pills?" Keera handed her the brown glass jar with some language on the label that she didn't understand. "Do I take one now?"

"You can if you want. Would you like a glass of Prosecco with that?"

"Yes, Dr. Donaldson and if you treat all your patients like this, I am beginning to understand why you are becoming so successful."

Keera smiled as she left the room and came back with a glass of wine. Chloe opened the jar and took the pill with a sip of wine.

"Only one a day, Chloe. It will cause you a lot of pain if you try and double them up and it won't make things work any faster. I'm going to give you a little sedative so that you don't feel anything at all while I adjust your crown and you should be awake and ready for another glass of wine in about thirty minutes. Ready?"

"Yes, Doctor. Please administer the anesthetic," and as soon as she said the last word, Chloe was asleep.

Keera replaced the crown, made sure it looked right with ultrasound and tested her bite and then looked at her friend resting peacefully in the chair. She poured herself another glass of wine and waited about ten minutes for Chloe to wake up.

"All done?"

"Yep. Move your jaws up and down and tell me how everything feels."

Chloe did as instructed and said everything felt perfect. "Can you tell I have lost weight yet?"

Keera rolled her eyes. "Don't worry. Just give it time. Now, how about a glass of wine and some fresh fish?"

"I'm going to recommend you to everyone I know, Dr. Donaldson," Chloe said as she toasted Keera and they laughed together.

Over the next couple of weeks, Chloe experienced some nausea but it always went away. After two weeks, she had lost five pounds. She called Keera and told her that she had given her a miracle drug. Keera said it wasn't a miracle and asked her how she felt. Chloe said she had been a bit nauseous at times but otherwise felt very well. She even had more energy and Keera said that was great and was exactly how she had felt when she had taken them the first time.

After three weeks had passed, Keera called Chloe and invited her to go out later that evening. Chloe said she couldn't because she thought she might have the flu. She felt weak and light-headed and had bad cramping, vomiting, and diarrhea. Keera said she would come right over and check on her to make sure she didn't need to go to the hospital. When she knocked on Chloe's door, no one answered. She turned the knob and the door opened, and as soon as she entered the condo, she started calling out Chloe's name. She heard a loud moan come from the couch and she ran over to Chloe. She sat down on the side of the couch and looked at her friend and touched her head to see if she had a fever.

"Chloe, how much weight have you lost?"

"About twenty-five pounds, but I feel awful Keera. I can't eat. My stomach is cramping and I feel like I need to go but

I can't. I had really bad diarrhea earlier in the week but now I wish I could even do that. Should I stop taking the pills and go to the ER?"

"I don't think it will matter."

"I don't understand."

"It's a fish tapeworm. Nasty little creature. That's why I never eat sushi. But you eat it all the time. I suppose that's where the doctors will say you got it."

"What are you talking about?"

"Listen, Chloe. For once in your life, listen. Even better, here. Watch this video on my phone and listen. Look at it, Chloe. It's called Diphyllobothrum latum. It's the name of the tapeworm that's inside your body. I put it in there the other day when I was doing your crown. Look at it, Chloe. Look at the undulating movement, like some creature riding the waves of the ocean. Isn't it magnificent?"

Chloe couldn't say anything as she stared at Keera.

"By now, it's probably about twenty to thirty feet long. They produce proglottids, little parts of themselves, with male and female reproductive systems that are probably clogging up your gall bladder. The worm itself, obstructs your intestinal tract, causing that intense abdominal pain. I knew you would wait until the very last minute to do anything. Thinking to yourself, just one more pound, just one more pound, all the while, the worm inside of you was growing one more foot.

"The fact you haven't gone to the bathroom in several days means you are certainly obstructed. Probably when you had diarrhea earlier in the week, you were shitting about a million eggs into your toilet each time you went to the bathroom. A million eggs! Can you imagine that? I hope Knoxville's water treatment plant is working well. Otherwise, some other people are about to get very sick."

Chloe gagged and tried to vomit but nothing came up.

"You lost weight at such a rapid pace because the worm was depriving you of all your nutrients. Since you aren't eating, it's just eating away your body. You probably have a very severe case of pernicious anemia too caused by a lack of vitamin B-12. You do look very pale. Those pills that I gave you were just vitamins and though they had some B-12 in them, there wasn't enough."

"Why?"

Keera looked at Chloe and shook her head and Chloe could see the look of contempt in her eyes.

"You have the audacity to ask me why after all these years? After your father defiled me and took away my holy virginity? When I was a princess: a Celtic princess? But after your father penetrated me, no man would have me. The people, Chloe, the people must be able to see and touch the divine on earth. But after what your father did to me, I was nothing. Your mother knew that. She knew I was a Celtic princess because of the mystical birthmark behind my ear," Keera said as she lifted her hair and showed Chloe the small dark full moon with two crescent moons extending out from it on each side.

"This proves it," Keera said as she turned back around. "That is the symbol of a goddess. Your mother knew I had that symbol a long time ago. She knew my destiny and how her husband had ruined it for me. She was sorry but your father and you were never sorry. Now I am exacting my revenge. Just as I did on those people that tried to rape me in Memphis. The town you convinced me to go to. All that happened because of you. Everything happens to me because of you.

"You have controlled my life ever since we met. You stole all my boyfriends, even the ER doctor we just met down in Florida. He wanted me, not you. But you seduced him. You probably told him I was no longer a divine entity; a princess here on Earth. You have always told me what I should do in life. When I came back here, you told me where to put my office. You told me how my office should look. You told me who to hire. And God forbid you ever came to a restaurant or my office on time! Oh no! Everyone needs to wait on the wonderful and beautiful Chloe!"

"Keera," Chloe whispered as the tears ran down her face. "My father didn't rape you. He told me how you tried to have sex with him but he stopped it. We discussed that with you. We kept it a secret from my mother and we forgave you. Don't you remember?

"And, you weren't sexually assaulted in Memphis. I was raped here in Knoxville one night - while you were away at dental school. You had a breakdown soon after that. I came to Memphis to help you because I knew it would help me too, but you didn't even recognize me. For the longest time, you didn't even know who I was or even who you were."

"Stop it! You're lying!"

"No, I'm not, Keera," she said as she winced in pain. And for the first time, Chloe felt something moving inside of her and she screamed. Not as much for the pain it caused, but more so because of what she knew was causing her to feel that movement. After the pain stopped for a moment, Chloe tilted her head and pulled her hair back from over her ear.

"Look Keera. Look at the tattoo. I have one just like you. You're right, it is a goddess symbol that we got when we went to Key West. The tattoo parlor was called The Isle of Erin. We did that together, Keera. I am so sorry that I didn't see this. I should have seen this," Chloe said as her voice became a whisper and she closed her eyes.

When Keera saw the same image on Chloe's neck, she almost passed out from the pain within her head. It was a familiar seizure that she had fought for a long time. Only this time it felt like lightning bolts were hitting her face. She had to reach up and grab her head to try and stabilize it from the throbbing torment that threatened to remove it from her

117

shoulders. The image of her friend was blurred and as she stood up and backed away, she saw the homeless man pulling on her pants leg asking for help, and then saw his head explode.

And like bloated corpses that had separated from the weights that held them down under the water, she began to see the faces of the other people she had killed. The other homeless people in the alleys that she ventured into sometimes, unaware that she was drawn to those areas for another reason. The helpless and forgotten were there trying to reach up to her. She was frightened as she thought she saw a knife or gun in their hand, making her think they were trying to harm her, but they weren't. It didn't matter. She killed them because she thought they were trying to hurt her and that was the only way the hallucinations stopped.

Keera wanted to punish Chloe for her father abusing her. For taking away her virginity, for raping her. What Chloe was saying now wasn't true any more than it was when they talked about it years ago. The images twisted inside of her like corkscrews and when she saw Chloe sitting by her hospital bed holding her hand, they penetrated even deeper into her brain and spine. Her entire body felt like it was coming apart at the seams as if some angry child was pulling apart a doll and she screamed.

Keera backed away further from the sofa as she heard Chloe begging for help. But within a few minutes, she realized she didn't know who that person on the couch was and she didn't understand what she was saying. It sounded as if the person was speaking a foreign language. She looked around the room and didn't know where she was.

She backed up until she felt a table in the small of her back and then turned around. There above the table was a beautiful mirror with colorful tiles around the edges. When she looked into the mirror, she smiled but she couldn't see a smile. All she saw was a distorted figure with a nose that was turned upside down and eyes that moved all around the face, stopping for a moment to blink before they moved somewhere else.

She opened her mouth and tried to say something but she couldn't. She saw the beautiful but distorted face surrounded by a blue-green aura looking back at her with arms that reached out from the mirror to grab her neck. She thought she was in the hands of an angel. She felt the fingers of the scaly hand reach down into her throat and pull. It was as if they were pulling out a plug that popped and when it did, she heard the air escape from her lungs and she struggled to breathe. Her knees buckled and she fell to the floor to pray one more time to the dark and glowing angel that had come to take her away, back to the place where she was a princess.

Whitney Place

I remember the exact date and time when the doctors said they had cured cancer. It was 1:39 p.m., Friday, April 26, 2023. I was at school in my history class. Everyone was saying what a great achievement it was. One of the teachers, a Mr. James Edward Cannon, said it was one of the most important days in the history of man. Considering that he was a history teacher, I would have expected him to say something like that. He liked to quote people. I guess if you are a history teacher it comes with the territory. I remember him telling us on the very first day of class that an Edmund Burke once said, "Those that don't know history are doomed to repeat it." I bet Mr. Cannon wasn't thinking about Mr. Burke when he said that this was one of the greatest days in the history of man, but I felt like he should have been. I know I was.

I enjoyed learning about history and I also liked English class when the teacher talked about famous authors and poets. There was another quote I especially appreciated that I learned in English class. It was by C.S. Lewis. He said, "I have learned now that while those who speak about one's miseries usually hurt, those who keep silence hurt more." He was a very famous author who didn't believe in God but over time, recognized he was wrong and came to believe that there was indeed a God.

I liked the idea that there were other people who struggled with the idea of a God. People a lot smarter than me. I think C.S. Lewis was a very smart man when he said that about pain and silence. And like he did when he was younger, I think he would understand why I struggled with a belief in God. I often imagined talking to him, both when he didn't believe and when he did. Those were always interesting discussions regardless of what stage in life Mr. Lewis occupied or how old I had become.

Perhaps for all those who believed in God, curing cancer was another sign that he existed. I could understand why they may think that, but I wasn't sure it was absolute proof. All the teachers and students were screaming and high-fiving or fist-bumping each other. I didn't ask any of them if they believed in God or not or whether this was some sort of divine revelation for them. I just stood there watching them and tried to think of the right word to describe their reaction. I only had to think for a moment about God, church, and the hymnal. "Rejoice" was the word for what I was witnessing.

My initial reaction was much more subdued and uncertain. I tried to think of the right word for what I felt and I found it fairly quickly too. But not in the church or a hymn. No, my word was a lot more common. On the farm, it would just be another word they used as they did their work. But used in another environment, it would be considered coarse and perhaps even swearing. But I liked the word. I used it a lot. It wasn't a surprise to me that it jumped into my mind that day. "Bullshit" was the right word to describe a lot of things and I thought it was very appropriate at this particular time.

Why, out of the millions of words I could have chosen, did I choose bullshit to describe my reaction? Probably because I knew doctors. I had known a lot of them as I grew up. I remembered what each one looked like and all their names too. I even remember the name of the doctor who delivered me. Her name was Dr. Cox. I saw her blue eyes behind her glasses when she cut me right out of my mother's stomach. She was wearing a mask and head covering when she yanked me out. I wish I could have told her she was a little rough with me that day but I never saw her after we left the hospital.

Don't ask me how I remember that because I couldn't tell you. There are just some things that I don't ever forget. The faces of doctors and their names happen to be two of them. My school referred me to a lot of doctors and I saw a few others when my mother took me to the ER. She didn't like doing that and only did it when she thought I was hurt really bad. Regardless, I have never trusted any of them. What they said or what they did. None of them ever fixed a goddamn thing that was wrong with me. None of them even understood what was wrong with me or could see that my body would have healed itself over time. If they had looked closely, they would have seen the evidence of that. None of them ever knew what was wrong with my mother or sister or father either. None of them.

As I think more about everything, I guess I should go and find Dr. Cox one day and thank her for framing my opinion of the world from that very first day. As I said, she was pretty rough in the way she handled me when she hauled me into this world. She handed me over to the nurses like I was just another burden for them to deal with. I suppose she was telling me life was rough and that I needed to be tough in order to survive. That was a good lesson, Dr. Cox. If I do see you later, I will indeed walk up and introduce myself and thank you. After all, you were just laying the groundwork.

So, when they said the doctors cured cancer that day, I think you could see now why I was suspicious of this great achievement. Hell, if I hadn't been there in school and heard Mr. James Edward Cannon mention it, and seen the reactions of the students and teachers, I doubt I would have ever known

122

about it. At least not for some time. I knew that the subject would have never come up at our house. As far as I know, no one in our family ever had cancer. If they did, no one had ever talked about it or told me or my sister. And I would have remembered if they had, as I would have asked a lot of questions about it.

I did that a lot. If there was something that interested me, I asked a lot of questions and did my own research at the library. Knowing that something like cancer killed some relative of ours, I would have wanted to know how it did that. And if you could catch it like the flu. Or if some people got it and others didn't, like sickle cell anemia. I had a good friend named Billy, who had sickle cell anemia and he explained to me that mostly black people got it. "Well, mostly black people," he said, but he added, "there are some other types of sickle cell disease that some Mediterranean people get."

When he told me all of that I looked it up at the library. I didn't tell him, but white people could get sickle cell too even though it was a lot rarer for that to occur. It was more common in blacks, those from Central and South America, and people of Middle Eastern, Asian, Indian and Mediterranean descent. That sickle cell disease he was referring to in Mediterranean people was actually called thalassemia and the severe form of it could lead to death. I didn't tell my friend what I had discovered with my research, because I saw no need to. It was useless information for him. It wouldn't have made him less sick. And if I didn't know better, I would have sworn that he was yanked out of his mother by Dr. Cox too. He had learned to be tough from a very early age just like me. He always reminded me of that C.S. Lewis quote I mentioned earlier. I saw him wince in pain but he never complained. Never.

So there you have it. When they said they had cured cancer, I said, "Bullshit." Then I said, "What's the big deal?"

I knew it wouldn't be that big of a deal for my father. And I was right. He never even mentioned it that day or any day in the future. Not one time. Ever. And I saw no reason to bring it up. As soon as I did, I was sure what my father would say. "Bullshit." He had a way with words. I think I learned that from him.

I remember seeing a bunch of people interviewing doctors on TV after this cure mania started to take hold of everyone. Man, there was a steady flow of bullshit coming out of their mouths every time they got in front of a camera. They talked about how wonderful life would be now for everyone. How a bunch of other diseases other than cancer would be eradicated too. I kept hoping that I would hear them say they would soon have a cure for sickle cell disease but I never heard them say that. I know Billy was listening for that too. I felt sorry for him that he didn't hear those words.

But that didn't stop the doctors from going on and on about how in the very near future no one would ever have to die from a terrible disease. I wish I could have been there when they were conducting some of those interviews. I would have gone over to the stupid prick in the white coat and told them people died of other things besides cancer. Things more terrible than cancer. I know they would have ushered me away, but I would have made sure they heard me before they took me away screaming and hollering. And maybe someone would have heard what I was saying and thought, "You know, he's right." But it didn't happen.

Usher them away. A polite way of saying, "Get them the hell out of here." I heard a doctor tell a nurse, "Give them this prescription and then usher them away," once when we were in the ER. He was talking about me and my mother. I told my mother about it but she told me that they wouldn't have said that. My mother was like that. She didn't realize that's what they were doing to us every time we went into the ER. And if the doctors were wearing white coats, they were inclined to say it even faster. Not sure why it was like that but I could tell my mother each time, as soon as the doctor in the white coat saw us, we would be out of the ER within thirty minutes. I was never wrong.

On the way home, I told my mother that they weren't fixing the real problem when we went to the ER and that we should just stop going. I told her that they didn't want to know what the real problem was. I told her that they were no different from the people we saw on the road; patching the holes. The patch of tar they put down would last a little while and then they would have to do it all over again. Why? Because they never addressed the real problem that created the hole. She just looked at me and said I was a very smart boy and then reached over and brushed my hair back from my face. And though I wanted to tell her more, I couldn't. I never could say anything else after I saw the tears in her eyes. Like Billy learning about thalassemia; what good would it do her for me to keep talking? So, I just looked out the window of the car at the holes in the road.

Just as soon as we got home from the ER each time, we heard the same thing from my father. Only it wasn't stated as a conceptual abstract, as my English teacher would have said. He was a lot more direct, my father. He just said whatever it was they did was "just a waste of time." And he was right. My father was right about a lot of things. He was a major influence in my life and established the way I looked at things from an early age. He was very insightful and observant. I was certain I learned that from him.

Soon after I was born, I remember my father looking down at me in the crib and telling my mother that I was different. I didn't know what he meant by that word and am still trying to figure that out, but I do remember it. You may not believe this, but I can remember the day he said it. It was June 30th, 2005. I was only four days old. Like I said earlier, I remember a lot of things. Not many people remember being born, but I even remember things before that. I know. I can hear what you are saying. Bullshit. But it's the truth.

I remember my mother reading to me when I was in her womb. "One Fish, Two Fish, Red Fish, Blue Fish" by Dr. Seuss. I heard her read that book to me a lot. I started reading it on my own when I was two years old. I read every one of the Dr. Seuss books. He was the only doctor I ever knew that never tried to 'usher me away.' I always felt he wanted me to stay there in the world he created in the pages of his books. I have to admit, there were many days when I thought about doing that.

My mother took my sister and me to the library a lot when we were young. We loved going there. It was always clean and warm in the winter and cool in the summer. My mother read to us or let us pick out our own books to read. I almost always chose Dr. Seuss when I was very little. But as I got older, I started reading Edgar Allen Poe and Arthur Conan Doyle's "Sherlock Holmes" stories. I loved Rudyard Kipling's "Jungle Book" and his short story about Rikki-Tikki-Tavi. I must have read that short story a hundred times. I even read that one to my sister over and over. She loved to hear me read to her.

But she didn't care for the Poe or Sherlock Holmes stories. She preferred Nancy Drew and the Hardy Boys stories and she and my mother loved looking at travel books and always talked about what it would be like to go there, wherever "there" happened to be on that particular day. I didn't enjoy looking at those travel books. I thought it was just a waste of time as I doubted we would ever be able to go to those places. My father also said it was a waste of time to be looking at those kinds of books and even reading so much. He said life wasn't a mystery and that the only book we need to read was the Book of Life. Of course, then he would say you can't read the Book of Life, you just experience it. As I said, he was very intuitive and direct.

126

And somewhere in every conversation, I heard between him and my mother, he would find a way to tell my mother that I was different. Hearing that comment was one of my earliest memories, and though he may have been the first to say it, he just became the first of many. And looking back, I realize he was right about that too.

I always felt different than everyone else around me. Once your own father calls you that less than a week after being born, it makes an impression on you that you never forget. I remember as Dr. Cox jerked me out of my mother's womb I felt some sort of electrical sensation in my body. As if the umbilical cord was plugged into an electrical socket of some kind. Maybe that's why she handled me so roughly. Perhaps I shocked the shit out of her. I hope I did. She probably deserved it.

When I started going to school, well, I heard the word "different" a lot. As if I had the word stamped across my forehead. I learned when people called you different what they really meant was that you were strange. As I got older, I learned there were other people, other famous people, that did strange things and I thought perhaps I shared some of their genius because it was apparent to everyone that I shared some of their strange behavioral traits.

Being labeled as strange made me research "strange" throughout history within the reference books in the library. I found out that Benjamin Franklin started his day with an air bath; half an hour each day in front of an open window, stark naked. He said it got his mental juices flowing. A lot of the people that read Poe's stories thought they were too gory and morbid and unreadable. He also called his cat "Catterina" and thought that she was his literary guardian. Einstein was so aloof as a child that everyone thought he had a learning disability.

Edison made people who applied to work with him eat a bowl of soup. If they added salt to the soup without trying it, he didn't hire them. They made too many assumptions, he reasoned. He didn't go to sleep either. Well, you know, like normal people. He just took naps. Francis Crick (you know - the guy that helped discover DNA?) believed in "directed panspermia." What the hell is that you ask? Good question. It meant that he believed that aliens "seeded" life on earth. Or another way of putting it: we were all sons and daughters of alien life forms. I kinda liked that idea.

Ever heard of Paracelsus? Well, he was a scientist around the 15th or 16th century. Considered the father of modern toxicology and linked chemistry to medicine. Some of what he did led to the chemotherapy practices that they used to treat cancer. Granted, he will become just a footnote, considering that they supposedly cured cancer, but he was still a genius for his time. He also believed that you could create a tiny human being by keeping semen in a warm place and feeding it human blood. If I said crazy stuff like these famous people had done, I would have been locked up and sedated. Hell, everything I did pales in comparison to these guys. So if you wanted to call me different or strange, go ahead. Bring it on. I was good with it. I liked the idea of being on the same short bus as those students.

When I started school in the first grade, I liked going around and shocking the other kids in my class as I rubbed my feet across the floor during the winter. That was the first time I heard a teacher tell my mother and father that I was different. My father just looked at my mother and shook his head and muttered, "I told you so," under his breath. My mother never responded when she heard the teachers or my father use that word. She just took me by the hand and led me away, often to the library. She's the one that first prompted my interest in Benjamin Franklin and Edison and those other people who were considered different. The people at school taught me that the word different meant something was wrong with me. She taught me that the word different meant something uncommon.

I got bored very easily in school. That was one of the reasons why I went around shocking everyone. There wasn't anything else they were doing that was interesting. I was reading books at a sixth-grade level when I was in the first grade. But it didn't matter, because the teacher, a Mrs. Evangeline Sanders, said I needed to be evaluated by a doctor. She said I was different. She said she could see that there was something wrong when she looked in my eyes. Too bad she never bothered to look at my back. Or my legs. Or my arms. I heard her tell another teacher that I was full of demons. If she had bothered to look elsewhere, she could have seen more evidence of demons other than in my eyes.

I didn't like that teacher. Mrs. Evangeline Sanders. She was short and fat. I wasn't sure where her breasts ended and her stomach started. She liked jerking people around by their ears when, as she said, "they acted up." She did that to me one time and I bit her hand. She screamed a lot that day but she never jerked my ear again. After that incident, the principal said I had to see a doctor or I would not be able to come back to school. So, my mother took me to see a doctor.

The doctor that we went to see was a child psychologist. His name was Dr. Robert Milhouse Banks, Ph.D. He had a big fish tank in his waiting room with a lot of tropical fish. I knew the names of every fish because I had seen them in a book I had read at the library. I told my mother what the names of each one of them were and she smiled and said that was amazing. When Dr. Robert Milhouse Banks asked me what I wanted to talk about that day, I told him, "Fish."

I then proceeded to tell Dr. Robert Milhouse Banks about each of the fish in his fish tank. He then asked me one of the stupidest questions I have ever been asked: "Would you like to be a fish?" I told him that seeing how I couldn't breathe underwater that I didn't think that would be a very good idea.

He smiled and asked me a few more questions and then sent me and my mother on our way. I learned later that he told Mrs. Evangeline Sanders and my mother and father that I was different. When we got home that evening, I heard my father tell my mother, "I told you so," again.

Mrs. Evangeline Sanders was very happy to send me on to the second grade but things didn't get any better there. It seemed I was always in some sort of trouble. Whether it was shocking the other children, eating chalk on a dare, standing in front of the window naked; it didn't matter. Every teacher that had me in their class told my mother and father that I was different. The teacher in the sixth grade, a Mr. Brian Lancaster, was the first to suggest to my mother that I had anger issues that needed to be addressed.

That's when I started seeing a lot of social workers and more people that had a Ph.D. at the end of their names. Some of them referred to themselves as "life coaches." What a bunch of douchebags. Though I have to admit, if I am being honest, some of them did seem to care. If I had bothered to listen to everything that they said, maybe they could have helped. But I didn't care. They just stamped me with the same label which made it impossible to wash off. So, I said fuck it and I just accepted that there was nothing I could do about it.

I read one of the reports that they gave my mother. It said that I exhibited "a wide range of anger management issues that need to be addressed. Seems angry with everything and everyone in the world around him. Appears unwilling or unable to resolve anger issues in a constructive manner. Exhibits anti-social behavior. Does not display any interest in changing. Resents authority. Very intelligent." It was signed by a Dr. Frank Littleton, Ph.D.

Dr. Frank Littleton, Ph.D., was very good at describing me. But he missed several things about me. He didn't mention that I had good hygiene or that I hated people who had bad breath or body odor. I wasn't afraid to tell anyone about it either. I mean, how hard is it to brush your teeth every morning or at least eat a Tic-Tac or something? And take a shower every once in a while, for God's sake.

Sometimes it isn't easy to do it, I get it. When you are poor or living on the streets, it's a challenge but it's still doable. I know because I've been there for short periods of time. I ran away many times as I got older, but my mother always came and found me. I think if it had been up to my father, I would still be out there on the streets. But I learned a lot being out there. I felt more at home on the streets than at home. On the street, being different kept you alive. At home or at school, being different just got you sneers and whispered finger-pointing and slapped around.

As I was saying, it isn't easy but you can always find a place that will let you take a shower. Provided you haven't already said, "Screw it," and are carrying around lice or have some disgusting open sores on your face and skin like something out of a horror movie. Then, yeah, I understand why it's a little harder to get people to let you in to clean up. Who wants a stinking zombie in their shower? I sure as hell don't. But all I've got to say is why did you let yourself get like that? Perhaps you will call me a hypocrite for pointing fingers at the crazy and the addicted that begin to look like some extra from a horror movie, but I don't give a shit. Call me what you want. You may sleep where rats live, but you don't have to become one.

Talking to people that aren't there or seeing things that aren't there is no excuse for not staying clean. Take the damn hallucinations into the shower with you. Believe me, that six-foot rabbit that you are talking to all the time will appreciate the fact you brushed your teeth and showered. Be a lot better world out there if all the crazy-ass people walking around the streets didn't smell like they were carrying around a dead animal in their pocket. Why don't the damn politicians or doctors in the white coats focus on something as simple as that? Everybody gets a meal and a shower. Doesn't sound that hard to me. But I see things they don't. Remember? I'm different.

I remember the ER doctor telling my mother that I was different for the first time when I was seven years old. She had taken me to the ER to get some stitches in my head. That was also the first time I had gotten stitches. The doctor said it was going to hurt but it didn't hurt. For some reason, cuts and bruises and even broken bones never really bothered me too much. And I became very familiar with all of those types of injuries as I was growing up. Some of them, my mother never saw. I knew it would have bothered her more than me so I just took care of them myself. Like I said, I was a fast healer. Broken bone one day; several weeks later, as good as new.

"Overcoming adversity makes you stronger," my father used to say. "Everyone gets knocked down. How you get back up is what matters." He was very good at demonstrating those philosophies to me. The son of a bitch was right though. My bones got stronger each time they encountered an adverse break of some kind. Funny how the doctors who patched me up never saw that.

Some of the social workers told my mother that I was just a product of my environment. As if she was supposed to do something about that. Other doctors, like the neurologists Dr. Littleton referred me to, told her that I had something wrong with my head. They told her the EEG suggested the electrical impulses in my head were very irregular and I was probably having seizures, which were not evident to either her or me.

They didn't know what caused them but they told her they knew it probably made me want to do things that so-called "normal" little boys didn't do. They prescribed a bunch of pills for me to take, but I hated taking them so I didn't. They made me feel tired and slow. Made me move around like I was a zombie and I didn't like that feeling. I had to put up with a lot of shit but I wasn't going to feel tired all the time or not have the ability to run away. That would have been dangerous in the house where I lived.

My mother tried to protect my sister and me from the other person that lived in our house but she could only do so much. She did the best she could. She fed and clothed us. She was always looking for things that we could do that didn't cost much money and that we enjoyed doing together. She made us smile. Laugh. Yeah, she did the best she could and made sure that we stayed alive during the years we were growing up, but I don't think my sister thought that being alive was all that wonderful most of the time. I know I didn't.

My sister and I wore a lot of long-sleeved shirts. Even in the summer. We did that to hide the bruises and cigarette burns on our arms. They never lasted long because, like me, my sister was a very fast healer too. But unfortunately, when one went away, there was always another one to take its place.

I never understood until I was much older, why my mother didn't take us away from that world. When you are scared, you don't think rationally. You can even convince yourself that a world of abuse is better than a world of loneliness and poverty. You can convince yourself of that but, in the end, you will always realize that you were wrong.

I asked one of those people with a Ph.D. at the end of their name why a parent could harm a child and he said it was because they were battling their own demons. When I first heard that, I thought it was a lot of bullshit but as I got to thinking about it, I realized it was true. The person with the Ph.D. at the end of his name was referring to demons in a metaphorical manner, but he was right. I didn't feel it was necessary to explain to him that the demons he was referring to were actually very real. He would have just said something like I was different or strange for suggesting demons were real and would have told my mother to stop letting me read

Edgar Allen Poe. He was, after all, one of those doctors that wore a white coat.

That same doctor, a Dr. Michael Doyle, told me that he could tell I was strong and that eventually, I would be a much stronger and better person as a result of these "growing up" pains, as he called them. I almost pulled his lips off of his mouth when I heard him say that. At the time, I thought it was just bullshit. But instead of standing up and making him a ton of money as a real-life phantom of the opera, I just laughed and was quickly 'ushered away.' My mother didn't intervene because she understood laughing was a coping mechanism for me. She taught me how to do that. Laugh. She introduced me to "The Three Stooges" and they were capable of making me laugh each and every time I saw them.

Those doctors with the Ph.D. at the end of their names, or the doctors in the emergency room, would never understand why people who lived in a world of abuse would find humor in what "The Three Stooges" did to one another. But we did. I think it was because we could watch Moe hit Larry in the head with a shovel and not see blood squirt out onto the floor. Larry would just yell and then hit Moe in the face with a two-by-four. And instead of Moe falling to the floor with a broken nose and jaw, he would just get up. And then it would start all over again. No matter how many times they hit each other, they never hurt one another. They lived in a world of abuse but it didn't hurt them. Their world of abuse was funny. It may be a warped way of looking at things but it sure helped me grow up. That's why my mother and I enjoyed The Three Stooges. It was like reading Dr. Seuss. We could escape into another world and not be hurt anymore. We could escape and just laugh.

My sister, however, didn't like "The Three Stooges." She watched them with us, but I could tell she never really enjoyed it. She watched them because she could be with me and my mother, but she usually had her head in a book while she was sitting there with us. Looking at something in Alaska or Hawaii, or maybe all the way around the world in Australia or New Zealand. What my sister really loved to watch was Julie Andrews in "The Sound of Music." As such, I have seen "The Sound of Music" eighty-four times. My sister even told the teachers at her school that her last name was Von Trapp. I could always predict when we would be looking at "The Sound of Music" instead of "The Three Stooges." Whenever I saw my father take my sister down into the basement, I knew the next day, we would see "The Sound of Music."

My father was smart. He did things to me and my sister that could be explained away as just accidents. Kids are always having accidents as they grow up and they have broken bones as a result of those accidents. And when you are on summer vacation or not in school over the holidays, those broken bones or smaller accidents have time to heal. Almost everything could be explained away. Almost everything.

But, if I am being honest, I have to say my father's sadistic nature was helped by the fact that we never saw the same doctor. The ER clinics we went to always had a different doctor. Usually, they were residents learning how to be a doctor. The people working there always looked stressed, especially the doctors and nursing staff. I heard the nurse or technician say something on more than one occasion about poor record-keeping or problems with the computer and how everyone was being overworked and understaffed. I don't think that's a good excuse but I could understand their frustration.

I understood frustration very well and because I did, I never brought up the fact that I had similar injuries a year ago, or the same broken arm four times. They couldn't tell when they looked at our bodies because, like I said earlier, my sister and I healed fast. They couldn't see with their technology that the real problem with our bodies was the

135

foundation. The home. Just like those people that worked on the road. The ground was shifting but they couldn't see it. All they saw was a hole that they needed to fix, so they fixed it.

It's all our fault for not telling them about the cigarette burns. But we were never in the ER with a fresh burn. My father was smart that way. Insightful. He knew not to cause an injury that would take us to the ER when we had fresh cigarette burns. He knew that would create suspicion because children didn't have those types of accidents on their own. I kept quiet about those types of injuries because of my mother and sister.

If I spoke up about them I knew my mother would have suffered and my sister would have been taunted like I was at school. And I couldn't allow either one of those things to happen. So I kept silent. In fact, over time, I didn't even feel any pain. And being taunted at school never bothered me. I think it was because there was something in my genetic makeup that allowed me to ignore the pain and verbal abuse from my classmates. I had a good teacher at home. And, like he had said more than one time, I was different. Plus, I didn't suffer at home to the extent my sister did.

I never spoke to my sister about the sexual abuse she endured and she never spoke to me about it. I think she knows I wish I could have stopped the pain for her many years earlier if I could have. When I turned 18, I think I stopped some of the pain for her. I know I stopped a lot of the pain for me. It happened soon after my sister and I watched my father strangle our mother to death on the kitchen floor.

He had grabbed my sister by her hair and thrown her out on the porch. While I was trying to help her, we heard the backdoor lock. We ran to the kitchen window and though we both screamed and tried to get into the kitchen before he killed her, we couldn't. I was only able to get into the house as I heard the last breath of air escape through her mouth. That last breath. It wasn't an anguished gasp of a dying woman. It sounded more like a sigh of relief, and when I looked down at her face, I think I saw her smile. I think she was telling me with that smile that she may have even prompted that last argument with my father because she knew we were old enough now. Old enough and strong enough. Not old or strong enough to save her; but old and strong enough to save ourselves.

My father saw me out of the corner of his eye and turned around and yelled, "Asshole!" at me before I took away his ability to say anything abusive like that ever again. Unlike the shovel that Moe used to hit Larry in the head, the shovel that I swung at my father took the top of his head off. As he dropped to the floor, his scalp fell onto the tile. Blood didn't come gushing out of his head as I thought it would. It just trickled out like a spilled cup of grape juice that only had a little left in the glass. I sat there and watched as the trickle turned into a small dark reddish-brown pool around his head thinking about what Dr. Littleton said about my inability to resolve anger issues in a constructive manner. Wrong again, Dr. Littleton.

I thought the blow to his head killed my father but it didn't. He was still alive thirty minutes later when my sister came into the kitchen and dropped the white charcoals onto his closed eyes. As soon as he started to scream, she dropped several more hot coals into his mouth, and we held him down as we watched them fall like lava down his throat and open up several holes in his neck. We stared at the charcoals that burned through his eyelids and dissolved into his skull until the green and blueish glow of the fiery embers revealed the demon that we knew existed there beneath his skin. When it was exposed, we knew he was dead. We let loose of his body and watched as the demon hovered for a moment in the air above us before it disappeared.

As my sister pulled our mother up into her arms, she began to sing.

"Do - a deer, a female deer; re - a drop of golden sun; me - a name I call myself; fa - a long, long way to run."

I looked at my sister when she stopped singing. I saw her smile and I knew why. I heard that C.S. Lewis quote in my head and I whispered it to myself. She didn't need to finish the song. She had stopped running that day. We had all stopped running that day.

Shoemaker Street

Monsters come in all shapes and sizes when you are a kid. At least they did in 1962 when I was six years old. There are monsters in fairy tales that somehow manage to emerge from the book during the night and sneak into your closet or under your bed and do things to try and scare you. They make weird noises that moan or creak. Sometimes you can even see them open the closet door just a tiny bit, or make the sheets or bed move, just enough for you to call out to your parents or for you to run into their room and tell them about its presence.

Most parents, mine being in that category, will either let you sleep in the bed with them for a night or two or they take you back into your room and lead you on a monster safari with the deadly monster-killing flashlight. They keep that big flashlight in the drawer next to their bed. It requires a slap or two on your parent's palm in order for its vaporizing light to work. And it's amazing how well that light works. When you and your mom or dad look through the closet the light causes the monster to flee or, as my father said, "disintegrates them." Same thing under the bed. Grab the light, slap to activate the vaporizer (which I found out the next morning actually exists within the D batteries), and the monsters are gone. Destroyed and confined to the pages of the books.

My parents would tuck me back in bed and tell me everything was okay and even though I knew it probably was okay, I always asked them to leave the door open just a tiny bit. They would smile and do as I asked. I would lay there listening for the slightest noise or movement. If I heard none, I would soon fall asleep. If I did hear or feel something, I would just pull the sheet up over my head because everyone knows that monsters are unable to see through white sheets made of cotton. Once they realized there was nothing in the bed, they would leave. My father taught me that trick too and I didn't really care which method worked because I knew the monsters would go away.

As you get older, the monsters that haunt you change. By the fourth grade, they usually changed into the form of a teacher. One who looks old enough that he or she (but in most cases a she) could have been present during some of the history lessons they were teaching. You and your friends would talk about that teacher in the hallways or at recess, wondering and laughing about how it must feel to sleep in a coffin. Then when you got home you'd stare at the pile of homework the old vampire teacher had assigned and wonder if that #2 pencil in your hand would suffice as a stake.

Sometimes you get confronted with two monsters when you are in the fourth grade. There's the old vampire-looking one at the school that must have been over a hundred years old and then there's the mean-looking old man who lives behind you, whose yard backs up to yours and is separated only by a chain-link fence. That's what happened to me. I had the old vampire-looking teacher called Mrs. Arnold and the mean old man living behind me that my friends and I called The Ogre, though we never let him hear us call him that. We were afraid of what he would do if he did.

His real name was Mr. Strauss. He was a very large man with white hair and a white mustache and a face that looked like he hadn't shaved for several days. He spoke with a thick accent which was very hard to understand. It wasn't a southern accent like everyone else in town possessed, or accents like people from up north had, many of whom I met in my father's restaurant where I sometimes worked clearing off tables.

I heard those northerners say we sounded like hicks when they didn't notice that I was listening. When I asked my father what it meant to be called a hick, he just laughed and said it meant that we were strong backwoods men like Daniel Boone and Davy Crockett. I liked knowing that although I had a feeling those people from up north were making fun of us. But I didn't care. There were a lot more of us hicks living in the mountains of southwestern Virginia than there were visitors from New York or Massachusetts.

But Mr. Strauss had a very different accent, the type that let you know he wasn't from anywhere in the United States – north, south, east, or west. No, his accent came from the "old country," or Europe, as Mrs. Arnold would tell us. It was so strong that it made the words he used in English sound just like the European words he used. He never said anything just in English. Probably because he was never talking to any of us. He just yelled at us. He would yell at us in English and then say something in that other language that none of us could understand.

My parents told me that he was from Austria. They told me he had lost his wife and son and his heart was probably broken. When that happens to some people, they just live in the past and do everything they can to avoid interacting with the present. My mother said my friends and I should feel sorry for him and we should do everything we could not to aggravate him.

But that was kind of hard to do, seeing how we walked down the alley by his house every day on our way home from school or from the playground or the store, and without realizing it, we would step into his yard. Mr. Strauss did not like anything or anyone stepping into his yard. It didn't matter if it was just one foot onto his property for just a few seconds or if we ran through his entire yard. If he saw our shoe cross over into just the smallest edge of his property, he would start yelling and waving his fist at us or sometimes even his rake or shovel.

He worked in his garden a lot. And when I say a lot, I mean all the time. All-year-round. It wasn't a useful garden like the others had around town with corn or potatoes or tomatoes growing in it. It only had one thing: roses. Roses of all colors and shapes. No one in town had more roses than Mr. Strauss.

And God forbid if your dog dumped a load or peed in his yard or even just walked into his yard, unaware that he or she was crossing into the "Forbidden Zone" (that's what I called Mr. Strauss's yard). He would yell at the animal and chase it away or if he thought no one was watching, throw rocks at the animal. I suppose if you had asked him, he would have said that getting hit by a rock clears the mind of an animal and makes them remember. And we would have had to agree even if we knew it was wrong to do such a thing to a living creature that didn't deserve that kind of treatment.

But Mr. Strauss didn't care. If the animal didn't get hit by a rock and learn to stay away, he would then yell at you and threaten to do something to your dog or cat if he ever saw them in his yard again. My friends and I thought there should be a law against someone who said or did something like that. We didn't have any evidence of him actually doing any of those things, but we told our parents that we saw him hit dogs or cats with rocks lots of times, even though we never had. We just knew he would do that sort of thing if given a chance.

I think they believed us but said we couldn't do anything about it unless we had proof. Proof that the dog or cat was hurt and bleeding, I guess. I have to give my parents credit though. My father did go over and talk to Mr. Strauss when I told him he threatened our dog, Cindy. But unlike his uncanny ability to vanquish the monsters in my room, my father failed in trying to conquer The Ogre.

I knew it didn't go that well when my father came back from talking to him and slammed the door. I heard him raise his voice as he told my mother about the encounter. He said Mr. Strauss was just an angry old man and he didn't doubt he did any of those things that my friends or I had told him. I could hear my mother telling my father that he needed to calm down and that we would just have to respect the man's property.

He came into my room soon after that and told me to make sure we kept Cindy out of his yard. It would be difficult to win a case in court, seeing how there were leash laws for dogs within the city and it was, after all, his property. I wanted to say this was an injustice (a word I had just learned from Vampire Arnold), but I knew it would be better just to nod my head and agree. I knew he cared and was frustrated but he didn't want to hear anything from me saying it was unfair.

I told my friends at school what my father had said and done about The Ogre when he threatened Cindy. I then told them he said that we didn't have a legal leg to stand on regarding his yard or the way he yelled at us or our animals for going on to his property, even if he did threaten us. That's when my friend Billy told us that his little dog Skipper had been missing for over a week.

Skipper was a beagle who was known to stay out for days at a time in the woods when he was young but he no longer did that now that he was older. Billy asked us if we thought it was possible that Mr. Strauss had done something to Skipper. We looked at each other and then back at Billy and told him it was possible, even though he and his family lived clear across town.

That's when my friend Sammy announced that the two of us would go looking for Skipper after school and that we would search The Ogre's yard and his garage. I looked at

Sammy like he had been hit in the head by a rock; but when I saw the look of relief on Billy's face, I knew it was the right thing to do.

During school that day, I could think of nothing else but venturing into the "Forbidden Zone" later that afternoon. Sammy sat next to me in class and when I looked over at him, he would just smile at me and give me a thumbs up. When he did that, all I could see was him in an army uniform with a parachute looking over at me as we stood at the open door of an airplane.

"Don't worry, if your first parachute doesn't open, you have another one as a backup. If that one doesn't open, you don't have anything to worry about. You'll hit the ground so hard that they will be able to bury your body in a matchbox," he said as he laughed and hit me on the back as I went falling out of the plane.

As we walked by Mr. Strauss' house on the way home that afternoon, we glanced around but didn't see him. When we got to my house, we put our books away and Sammy asked if we had a flashlight and any firecrackers. I told him we did and got them. Though I knew what the flashlight was for, I wasn't sure what he expected to do with the firecrackers. He told me that those would be used as a diversion should The Ogre sneak up on us and we needed to get away. When he said the word diversion, I saw that man in the airplane laughing again and I felt a shiver go up my spine.

We walked back to the alley and started toward Mr. Strauss's garage at the very back of his yard. Once we got behind it and couldn't be seen from his house, Sammy told me to stay at the edge of the garage and watch as he went around and tried to get into the door that was on the far side. He was taking a chance by going through that door because it could be seen by Mr. Strauss if he was in the house and looking out his window.

Sammy told me to whistle once when it was all clear and that he would try and open the door as soon as he heard me. If I saw Mr. Strauss I was supposed to whistle twice and he would get out, using the firecrackers if needed. I went over to the edge of the garage and managed to get one eye around the side of the building and scan the yard and the house. From his house, I knew it would be impossible for him to see my barely visible eye which I was certain looked like just a large spider on the side of the building.

I whistled once and heard Sammy open the garage door. I wasn't sure how long he was inside but I felt the sweat coming off my forehead and I had to move my eye back behind the garage to wipe the sweat out of it so I could see. When I looked back around, I didn't know how it was possible, but I saw Mr. Strauss about ten feet from the garage. I tried to whistle but my throat was so dry that nothing came out. I heard him say something about the garage door being open and then something in the other language he used and though I didn't understand what it meant, it sounded like he was cursing.

I heard what sounded like a bunch of paint cans falling off of the wall onto the garage floor and then heard Sammy yell. I went running into the garage and saw Sammy leaning up against the wall and Mr. Strauss with an ax in his hand getting ready to throw it at him. I couldn't get to Mr. Strauss before I saw the ax leave his hand, so I had to watch as it turned over and over toward my friend like it was in slow motion. I lowered my shoulder and hit Mr. Strauss as hard as I could in his legs, knocking him over onto his knees.

When I looked up, Sammy was frozen against the wall, his eyes as big as saucers, with the ax buried in the wall next to him. Blood covered Sammy's clothes and I heard Mr. Strauss say to come over to him slowly. I couldn't believe Sammy did what Mr. Strauss said but as I looked closer I saw something moving on the ground and I heard that familiar rattle. Sammy was as white as the sheets his mother sometimes put out on the clothesline in his backyard to dry, and I could see the snake's head opening and closing as it tried to find the rest of its body.

The ax that Mr. Strauss threw cut the head off the large rattlesnake just as it reared up to strike Sammy. Mr. Strauss escorted me and Sammy out of the garage and came out with the body of the snake a few minutes later. He was smiling as he held up the wiggling body that was as big as us. He started laughing as we ran back to my house. When we got there, my father saw the blood on Sammy and rushed out of the house before we could even say a word.

My mother didn't try and stop him either. She was too worried about us, asking if we were all right and checking us for injuries. I managed to choke out the word "water" and she handed us both a glass. We guzzled the water and asked for more as my mother peppered us with questions about what happened. Sammy was not able to say anything and I was just starting to explain to my mother what had happened when my father came back and started checking Sammy for injuries all over again.

When he was satisfied Sammy wasn't hurt, he began to tell my mother the story. A large 5-foot eastern diamondback was in Mr. Strauss's garage and it struck out at Sammy but Mr. Strauss killed it with an ax. My mother almost fainted but my father caught her and helped her into a chair next to Sammy. He had to get her a glass of water too.

When my father asked us what we were doing over there in Mr. Strauss's yard, I told him about Billy's dog. Before I could explain any further, Sammy pulled out the dog collar he had found in the garage. You know that voice that's in the back of your mind; the one that some folks call their conscience or their intuition? Well, that voice was telling us it was Skipper's collar and that Mr. Strauss had killed him, but because of everything that was going on right then we

146

just didn't hear it. We didn't hear that voice until several days later, but then it started whispering to us again and when it did this time, we heard it loud and clear.

My father couldn't explain what the collar was doing there in the garage but he told us that snake was certainly big enough to have killed a dog. Sammy and I may have thought differently, but we didn't say anything about it until several days later. We were too busy thanking God that we were alive. And though Sammy was unable to say much, I could see that man in the army uniform smiling and telling me that it was a good thing we had two parachutes.

Billy cried when my father took me over to his house and I showed him the collar. My father explained to him and his father that a big eastern diamondback got hold of him and he was just too slow to get away this time. Billy's father thanked us for letting them know. He bent down and looked at Billy and said he was sorry but Skipper was getting old and he would have had to say goodbye to him one day soon anyway. Billy nodded his head but I knew he didn't really care what his father said right then. I wouldn't have if my father was telling me my dog was dead. So I began to ask him about Skipper and what he was like when he was a puppy and Billy smiled as he started talking about him.

Billy's dad asked my father if he wanted a beer and, together, they walked into the kitchen. I don't know how long I talked to Billy that day but I suppose it was close to an hour because it was almost dinner time before we got home. My mother asked me how Billy was doing and I told her not that good. She said she understood but that over time he would be okay. I just sighed as I looked down at Cindy who was there by the table waiting for some food. I handed her the last of my fried chicken and then asked if I could go watch some TV before I did my homework.

I watched "Batman" and "F-Troop" with my mom before Cindy and I went to my room. I finished my homework and fell asleep with Cindy beside me. My mother didn't even make me get up to brush my teeth. She woke me up the next morning and said that I should be happy because it was Friday and the weekend was almost here. She told me to get showered and come downstairs because we were in the newspaper. I didn't know what she was talking about but got cleaned up and ran downstairs. As soon as I got in the kitchen, she had my bowl of cereal ready for me.

She showed me the article and the picture of Mr. Strauss holding the large snake in his hands. How the paper found out about what happened is something I will never know, but there it was. As I listened to my mother reading the story, I realized that in a small town like the one we lived in, nothing went unnoticed - even if the city newspaper came from a town 40 miles away in another state. My mother read me the story as I ate and I could hear how the story made Mr. Strauss out to be a hero. The story didn't even mention Sammy's name; it just said that a young boy was looking for his dog and that the snake had killed the poor dog.

They even quoted Mr. Strauss. According to the reporter, he said, "I was just doing what anyone would have done if they were faced with that situation. I was lucky to have been brought up on a farm in Austria that made me very comfortable with an ax." The reporter said the humility of Mr. Strauss was refreshing and indicated that he was a hero. I had to ask my mother what humility meant and she explained that it meant modest or humble or shy. Though I didn't say anything to my mother, I thought none of those words described Mr. Strauss. When I looked at his picture all I saw was someone that looked as scared as Sammy did.

Everyone on the block, probably in the entire town, considered Mr. Strauss to be a hero, but he sure didn't act like one that weekend. He acted like the Mr. Strauss all of us kids knew. In fact, his actions were what triggered me and Sammy to hear that voice I was talking about earlier.

That Saturday, we were playing a game of Wiffle ball in Sammy's backyard, which was across the alley and pretty far back from Mr. Strauss's yard. We never figured anyone could hit the Wiffle ball hard enough to land in Mr. Strauss's yard but we were wrong. Sammy must have still had adrenaline pumping through his veins from his encounter with the snake and that ax flying toward him because he really tagged one that day. It went sailing across the alley and into Mr. Strauss' yard, who happened to be out in his garden that afternoon.

As soon as Mr. Strauss saw the Wiffle ball in his yard, he ran over to it and started yelling at us in English and that European language that none of us understood. He picked it up and held it in his hand, waving it at us as he pulled out a lighter, set it on fire, and threw it into a large old rusty barrel. He said something else we didn't understand and waved his fist at us one more time while we all just stood there staring at each other wondering what we should do.

Sammy and I told the other guys that we would have to cancel the rest of the game for the time being and then we ran to tell my mother what had just happened. She acted like she didn't believe us, but when she looked out the window, she saw Mr. Strauss standing next to the trashcan with the smoke billowing out of it.

She poured me and Sammy a glass of grape Kool-Aid and told us both to sit right there and that she would be back in a minute. As soon as she left, we jumped up and went to my room. My bedroom window looked out over Mr. Strauss's backyard and we wanted to see what happened when my mother confronted him.

Sammy and I watched my mother wave to Mr. Strauss as she walked over to him in his garden. We saw her point at the trash barrel and Mr. Strauss nod his head. To me and Sammy, it looked like my mother was lecturing Mr. Strauss, but we found out later she wasn't doing that at all. She was actually apologizing to him for the children bothering him and then turned to his roses and began asking him about them. My mother said that she told him he had the most beautiful roses she had ever seen and she was telling the truth.

We didn't know that's what she said from the window, but we could tell it was something that Mr. Strauss enjoyed hearing because it was the first time we had ever seen him smile. For the next twenty minutes, Mr. Strauss took my mother around his garden and pointed out different flowers for her, and before she left he even cut some and put them in a vase for her.

When my mother came back, she sat us down and told us what they talked about. He told her that we hit a bunch of balls in his yard and he was afraid that we would damage his roses. He didn't dislike kids but he knew they wouldn't be as careful around his roses as they needed to be. She told him she understood why he felt the way he did and complimented him more on his roses. She got him to agree not to burn another ball if one came into his yard provided that we promised to just get the ball and stay away from his rose garden. If the ball went into the rose garden, we would have to come and ask him to get it for us.

She said she expected us to hold up our end of the bargain and we promised her we would. Sammy and I went back to my room and talked about what had just happened. Even though we now knew we were allowed to go in the yard to get the ball, we made a deal that should it go there, the person that had to go get it would be the loser of rock, paper, scissors. Even though my mother made a good deal with The Ogre that day, after we thought about it a little more we both decided that if the ball went into his rose garden, we would just get a new one.

We sat and talked some more, wondering how my mother got Mr. Strauss to agree to do all of that.

"Maybe he was drinking vodka earlier than usual," I said. "I know it isn't Sunday, but maybe he started drinking on Saturday this week."

"No way, man," Sammy replied. "He isn't like that. He's very set in his ways. You've seen it lots of times. He does things a certain way and that's the only way he'll do them. He only drinks on Sunday. I think it maybe had something to do with the fact that your mom is pretty."

That was the first time that I had ever heard someone call my mother pretty. She had always just been my mom. But as I sat there and thought about what Sammy said, I realized that my mom was pretty. She always exercised a lot and I know when I saw her with the other boy's moms she did look different than them. Pretty, I guess, was the word and I just didn't know it.

It was soon after that when Sammy and I began talking about the dog collar he found.

"If that snake killed Skipper like everyone is saying, how did it get the collar off of him?" Sammy asked.

"It didn't. Mr. Strauss did that. He had to. I wouldn't be surprised if he killed the dog and fed it to the snake."

"Really, Bobby? You think he would do something like that?"

"I do. Look at this picture. I cut it out of the Kingsport News-Times. The reporter said he looked humble holding the snake but to me, he looks scared. Don't you think so?"

"Well, it is a 5-foot timber rattler. It scares me just looking at it in a picture."

"That's not what I meant, Sammy. I think he's hiding something. And he was afraid that you or somebody would find it."

"Like what?"

"I don't know yet, but we need to keep an eye out on things. Just because he thinks my mom is pretty, I don't think he would hesitate to hit us in the head with a rock, like he does to other animals."

"Bobby, we've never really seen him do that."

"Just because we haven't, don't mean he doesn't do it."

Sammy shook his head in agreement. We finished off our Kool-Aid and went out riding our bikes for the rest of the day. The next day was Sunday and though I got to sleep a little later, I still had to get up and get ready for Sunday school. When I came down to breakfast that morning, I heard my parents talking about an article in the paper describing a dead body found over in Big Stone Gap. My mother said that was awful and asked my father if they knew who it was.

Dad told her that they didn't but they were treating it as a murder case and would be checking their missing person files. My mother shook her head and said that we all needed to pray for that person and their family in church and she looked at me and told me to make sure I did. I said I would and finished my breakfast and went up to my room to dress.

When I looked out the window, I saw Mr. Strauss on his back porch, just like he was every Sunday. I knew the preacher would have appreciated the faithful manner in which Mr. Strauss approached each Sunday. He sat outside and read the paper, and by the time we got home from church, he was starting to drink his vodka. Smirnoff vodka. Sammy and I saw the bottles in his trash and we saw him out there every Sunday doing the same thing. Some Sundays we saw him fall down the steps a couple of times, but that was always late in the afternoon and he never seemed to hurt himself. He just got up and went over to the garden or the garage and then went back on his porch to finish what he had started earlier that day.

Viktor Gruning had acquired a liking for vodka during World War II. He had to change his name to Otto Strauss in order to emigrate from Austria to the United States in the

1950s, but it wasn't hard to do. As a colonel in the SS, he had acquired a lot of useful tools that helped him to change his identity. Plus, the Austrians and the Americans were stupid. He couldn't understand how they had lost the war to such stupid and inferior people.

That afternoon as he drank the Smirnoff vodka, he thought about the young boy in the garage. He was lucky he wasn't killed by that rattlesnake. He had put it there to keep the dogs, cats, and anything else away. He wasn't scared of it. He knew it was there and it always warned him where it was if it moved around. He kept it fed with rats and he knew the snake wasn't going to attack him and cut off his food source. Snakes were smarter than that.

He smiled as he thought about what was written in the paper – the bravery he displayed and how humble he was after being told he saved that young boy's life. *Stupid reporter*, he thought. *You mistook concern for humility. Humility is an innocent-enough-looking emotion that can conceal other more sinister ones.*

He had learned that a long time ago in Austria when he saved a young boy from being trampled by some horses that he owned, even though he had arranged for that boy to be in the wrong place with the wrong horse at just the right time when there were other people present to witness the event. They talked about how brave he was, but it was all planned. It was a wild horse, true, but he had a way with horses. And if it hadn't reacted the way he wanted it to, he would have shot it. He needed the Austrians to trust him and they did after what he had done. He knew they would.

Most soldiers from World War II drank to forget the bodies that consumed their memories, but Otto Strauss consumed alcohol to remember. He ordered a lot of people into the gas chambers and he enjoyed watching his soldiers bring them out of the chambers and bury them in large pits of dirt. *Dirty degenerates of a lesser race that deserved death,* he thought. *Especially the children.* They would just grow up to make the world a horrible place and he knew he was doing a service to society by ending their lives at an early age.

He didn't want to blur those images with vodka. He wanted to enhance them in his deviant and distorted view of the world. Death was not something he was afraid of; it was something that entertained him. Except for now. His son had started sharing some of his father's proclivities. Every Sunday morning, he went downstairs and found his son on the sofa with a bong and a half-empty bag of marijuana on the table amidst a sea of empty beer cans. And some Sunday mornings he would find a gift from his son in between his aluminum glass door and the back door that led to his kitchen.

The gift was always either a leg or an arm from someone that his son had killed. After he collected all four appendages, he knew his son would rest for a while before he took up the hunt again. He was reckless though and Viktor warned him more than once that he needed to be more careful with his very special appetites. He told him he appreciated them and he could help him perfect them, but his son never listened. He had read about the body that they found in Big Stone Gap earlier and acknowledged his son was responsible. He also understood that this would be the last gift for a while as this was the fourth piece to the severed set that he knew was missing from that body; even though the paper didn't provide any specific details.

And he would do what he did many Sunday mornings: clean up the mess and dispose of the body part. He had become quite adept at disposing of the body part. He ground up the arm or leg in a meat grinder and mixed it with nitrogen-rich mulch and dirt. It made a wonderful fertilizer. Anyone who saw his roses would admit that.

He was never certain what his son did with the heads but he imagined he dropped them into one of the many quarry ponds that existed around the area or threw them down a coal mine that was no longer in use. Even though he would have disposed of them differently, he told his son that he was probably safe in doing that. The police would have a hard time identifying the torso. No one was ever good at identifying torsos. He had learned that in the war.

But that collar, he thought, as he took another drink of vodka. That boy found the collar of the dog. That was a problem. One that he would have to deal with sooner or later and he began to think about what he should do. And then he started laughing. "I don't need to do a damn thing," he said. *The stupid idiots around here have not even concerned themselves with that. They probably think the damn dog just lost his collar somehow trying to get away from the snake.*

"Dummer Amerikaner!" he cried out as he toasted himself with a shot of vodka. He walked down his porch steps to till the ground with his new batch of mulch. He worked in the garden until the sun went down and the bottle of vodka was finished. He went inside and fixed some bratwurst and sauerkraut, ate it, and then fell on his bed and passed out. It was pretty much the same routine every Sunday.

He wasn't sure when his son would show up again or where he went when he left his house. He tried to talk to him about all of that, but his son would never say much to him. He answered a few questions but most of them he ignored. Viktor would tell his son how he was a Hitler youth when he was growing up and how wonderful Germany was as the National socialist party began to grow after World War I.

"Dose were very gut days back den. Everyone vorked. For de cuntree. For de most beautiful cuntree in de vorld. Deutschland. But you know noting of dis. You never vill because you don't listen because you are dumpfbacke. Alvays dumpfbacke." His son just smiled at him and left.

A month later, Viktor found another leg in his doorway on a Sunday morning. He brought it inside and opened the newspaper. There it was on the front page: another murdered body was found in Weber City. The paper didn't reveal that it was found in the same condition as the one in Big Stone Gap a month ago, but Viktor knew it was. He went downstairs and found his son sitting there.

"Dumpfbacke. Why do you do dis? Even dough de American police are stupid and menial, dey vill catch you."

"They haven't yet. And what about you? You killed thousands. They haven't caught you yet."

"Because I know. I know how de human mind tink. I study it for many, many years. See it in de camps wid de men and vemen. Very smart men and vemen dere and I talk to dem. Make dem freund."

"Before you killed them."

"Ja. Before I kill dem. For Deutschland."

"Whatever, old man. You probably need to clean this place up. I'll be back later."

"Wilheim. Aufenthalt. Please stay longer. Please."

"Fuck you, old man. I've got to find where I put those presents for you. Later."

And just like that, William, his son, was gone. And just like he did every other time, Viktor put away the bong and marijuana and cleaned up the beer cans. He put everything in the trash and then went upstairs and took out his meat grinder and the large metal canister he used to capture the ground flesh and bone. Once the leg was ground up, he mixed in the soil and cow manure and took it down the back steps and left it there as he returned to his porch, his paper, and his vodka.

My father put down the newspaper that Sunday morning as I came into the kitchen. I knew something was up by the way my parents were acting. My father told me to come and sit next to him while my mother sat down at the table across from me.

156

"I didn't do anything. Whatever Mr. Strauss said I did, I didn't do it. But I do know who broke out his garage window with a rock. I told him not to, but it was Billy and I thought he had a right to do it. His dog was killed in that awful garage. I'm sorry I didn't tell you about it."

"It's not that, son," my father said. "There's been another murder. This time over in Weber City. And it concerns us."

I just looked at my parents, not sure why they were telling me this.

"We just want you to be careful, Bobby. For a little while, we want you to come straight home from school. And for a little while, we want you to stay inside the house when you come home. You and I can go to the movies some of those days," my mother added.

"You mean go to the movies during the week and not on a weekend?"

"Yes,"

"Can Sammy go with us?"

"Of course. And we can go down to the restaurant and you and Sammy and I can have some of your father's famous cheeseburgers and French fries and a chocolate milkshake."

"Can I have strawberry?"

"Yes, son, you can have strawberry."

"Are you afraid those murders are connected, Dad? I've seen enough Perry Mason shows to know that happens sometimes."

"To be honest with you, son, I don't know. But we just want to be cautious. Is that okay with you?"

"Yeah. But to be honest with you, Dad, I think people should be talking to Mr. Strauss about all of this."

"Now Bobby, don't you and Sammy get all worked up about this and start thinking Mr. Strauss had anything to do with this when we have no reason to think that. He's just a very lonely man who's been worn down by his memories. The memories of the war and the loss of his wife and son."

157

"Are you sure his son is dead? Just because he might have told you he is, that doesn't mean he is."

"Bobby, stop it. Just do as we say and leave Mr. Strauss out of it. You understand?"

"Yes, sir. I understand."

I saw Sammy at Sunday school that morning and just before we went into church, I told him what my parents had talked about earlier.

"You are not going to believe this," Sammy whispered to me. "But Tommy's father is a cop and he overheard him talking to his mother about the body they found. Only it wasn't much of a body. It was missing all its body parts including the head. Just like the one they found in Big Stone Gap a month ago. They're almost positive that the same person did it."

"I knew it! I bet it's Mr. Strauss's son."

"His son? I thought he was dead."

"That's what he *said*. But what if he's not? It sounds like something his son would do, doesn't it?"

"I don't know, Bobby."

"Well, we just have to keep an eye out on things, Sammy. You will help me keep an eye out on things, won't you?"

"Yeah, I will. But it'll have to be from my house. I can use my father's binoculars that he uses to hunt with sometimes."

"Good, and I'll sit up in my room and keep an eye on things too. We'll find out what is going on."

Sammy nodded his head and we headed into the church. I was singing the hymns and opened my Bible as the preacher told us what to read, but my mind was on other things. I knew Mr. Strauss was involved in this somehow and I meant to find out how and why.

Over the next several weeks, me and Sammy observed whatever we could at Mr. Strauss's home to the best of our ability, considering that Sammy was using binoculars and I was looking out from my bedroom window. I suggested that we keep a log of the date and time that we saw anything and Sammy agreed.

Mr. Strauss stuck to his regular routine and on each of the next three Sundays, he got a new gift from his son. He would bring it inside and lay it on old newspapers while he went downstairs and cleaned up the basement from the party that occurred on Saturday evening. His son was always there grinning at him as he cleaned.

"You must feel very guilty, old man, for cleaning up this mess every Sunday morning. Why do you do it?"

"Es ist meine Pflicht. It's my duty. I do my duty. I vill alvays do my duty."

"You are more fucked up than I can ever get off this bong. Oh, by the way, next Sunday, expect an even bigger surprise. See you old man."

And with that, Viktor's son was gone. *What did he mean by a 'bigger surprise'?* he wondered. *"*That dumpfbacke will get himself caught," he said out loud. "But I vill be prepared. I am alvays prepared." He went upstairs and made the special mulch for his beautiful roses.

That next Saturday, I convinced my parents to let me spend the night at Sammy's house. We watched a lot of TV and played with Sammy's electric football game until his parents told us it was time to get some sleep. We went upstairs and got in bed, but we were wide awake and we waited. We waited for his parents to go to bed and then we got up and very quietly put on our shoes and went outside with the binoculars.

"Man, it's hard to see anything at night," Sammy whispered to me as we knelt down behind the hedges that surrounded the back of his house.

"Just look at the light in his windows. Focus on that."

"Hey, I see him, Bobby. He's down in the basement. The light just came on. And he's with somebody."

"Let me see," I said as Sammy handed me the binoculars.

"It looks like a girl. I told you. His son *is* alive! He's got some girl in the basement with him. I bet he's going to kill her!"

"Bobby, you're scaring the crap out of me."

"We have to be brave now, Sammy. We have to be brave."

"What do you expect us to do?"

"We just need to watch what happens. That's all. And if we see him bring the knife up in the air and start stabbing her, then we need to call the police."

"Shit, Bobby. Why did you say that?"

"You said the body parts were missing, didn't you? Well, how do you do that without a knife?"

"It would have to be a really big knife."

"Just watch, Sammy. Just stay here and watch with me."

Sammy and I sat there behind the hedges and watched until it was five in the morning but we never saw a knife. All we saw was the light go out and the two figures that were in the basement disappeared.

"What do you think just happened?"

"I don't know, Bobby. But I ain't going over there to find out. And I ain't letting you go over there either. It's almost time for us to get up so we need to get back to bed. We know something went on; we just don't know what."

"Yeah. But, we're one step closer to finding out," I said as if I was Batman talking to Robin.

We snuck back to the house and got in bed not long before Sammy's mother came in and woke us up and told us breakfast was ready. "Sammy, why do you have your shoes on?" she asked surprisedly.

Before he could answer, I spoke up. "He told me his feet were cold so I told him to put his shoes on, Mrs. Gregory."

Sammy just nodded his head.

"Hmmmmm…well, that's strange," Mrs. Gregory said as she walked out the door, shaking her head.

When Mr. Strauss got up that morning he went out to the kitchen and opened the door. He fell backward and wanted to scream out loud about how stupid his son was but he knew he couldn't. Not now, with that rotting head looking at him. He bent down and picked it up and put it in a bag as he went down to the basement.

The young prostitute was still there asleep on the sofa. He dropped the bag when he saw her and watched the head fall out and bounce in a sickening way off the steps until it lay still on the floor. He heard his son laughing at him and watched as he ran down the steps and stuck the bayonet through the ear of the young girl, twisting with all his force until the end of the blade exited through her other ear.

"I told you there'd be a surprise waiting for you this morning, didn't I?" his son gloated, but Viktor didn't answer. He just looked at what was on his basement floor and then went over and put up a blanket over the windows of the garage door so no one could see inside.

He walked back up to his kitchen and cleaned his hands with a mild acid that he used every Sunday after he received a gift from his son. He grabbed the bottle of vodka from the cabinet and went outside to gaze at his rose garden.

Before we left for church, me and Sammy looked over at Mr. Strauss's yard and saw him sitting on the porch with the bottle of vodka.

"He's starting early today, isn't he? I bet there's a good reason too. There's something down in that basement. Something that his son did."

"Bobby, not now. Please, not now. Let's just go to church and then think about what we need to do."

161

"I'm way ahead of you, Sammy."

When we got back from church, we had lunch with our parents and then met up over in Sammy's backyard.

"He doesn't look like he moved since we left for church several hours ago."

"Can you get those binoculars?"

"Yeah. Hold on a minute." Sammy ran inside and brought the binoculars back out. I looked through them first.

"The bottle of vodka on the table is empty and there is another empty bottle at his feet. No one can drink that much liquor, can they?"

"I don't think so, Bobby. I heard my mother talk about her uncle that turned up a bottle of moonshine one time and died."

"Well, he ain't moving, Sammy. I think he's dead. "

"Then we need to call the police."

"We need to make sure before we call the police."

"How in the heck do you plan on doing that?"

"I'm going over there and seeing if he has a pulse."

"You're crazy, Bobby. Don't do it. Please don't do it."

I handed the binoculars back to Sammy and looked at him and smiled. I saw the young man in the army uniform standing there with me at the back of the plane. And this time, I didn't feel afraid about jumping.

"Be back in a minute," I said as I started toward Mr. Strauss's yard. I picked up a few rocks in the alley and began throwing them at his garage door as I got closer to the back porch. Each time a rock hit the metal door it made a clinking sound but Mr. Strauss didn't move. I threw four more rocks at the door until I was standing at the bottom of the steps looking up at Mr. Strauss. He was slumped over with drool dribbling out of his mouth. It was dripping onto his pants and I thought how gross it looked but I was determined to go up those steps.

162

When I got there on the porch, just in front of Mr. Strauss, I glanced over at Sammy and waved to let him know everything was okay, even though my entire body was shaking. I walked closer and tried to feel for a pulse in his left wrist that hung limply down next to his leg. I couldn't find one and was just about to leave when I felt Mr. Strauss's hand grab my wrist as he lifted his head.

When I looked into his eyes, it was like looking into the eyes of a dragon or a vampire as they burned red.

"Vat are you doing out of de chamber, little boy? How did you get out?"

"Let go of me, you crazy old man. I don't know what chamber you're talking about."

"Ze screams. Can't you hear all da screams? Dey scream and den dey are silent. Silence is gut, no?"

I twisted my hand back and forth but I couldn't get free of the old man's vise-like grip.

"Perhaps ve put you in da oven. Verbrennen die Haut? Ja, perhaps ve do dat."

"I don't know what you're saying old man, but if you don't let me go, I'll start screaming."

"Yes, de screaming. I hear it all de time. It never stops. Do you have nightmares, little boy?"

"No. But I'm sure I will after today."

"Dats gut. Gut to have nightmares. Keep you alert. Ready. Informiert. Need to alvays be ready. Dat vay you stay alive."

I twisted my wrist again and then I remembered something. Something very important I had learned from my mother.

"Those are pretty roses you have, Mr. Strauss. Let's go down and look at them."

He smiled and let go of my wrist.

"Ja. Hubsche Rosen. Very pretty roses. Special mulch. You are Bobby, ja?"

163

I nodded my head a lot of times and tried not to look scared but I probably looked like some big bobblehead.

"Den go enjoy dem, Bobby. Play. Take some roses to your mutter. Mochte die Rosen, your mutter. Take some and go."

After saying that, The Ogre got up and walked back into the kitchen and locked the door. I ran down the steps as fast as I could toward Sammy who was yelling at me that we needed to get our parents.

As Viktor walked inside, he remembered the head that was on his porch earlier that morning. His wife's head, which he had kept with the rest of her remains in the freezer down in the basement, along with his son's body. He had ground their arms and legs up into mulch until all that was left was their bodies and heads, and had disposed of their torsos some time ago.

Viktor could never forgive his wife for producing an imperfect child, so he poisoned them both. It was easy enough to rig the gas lines so they died of carbon monoxide poisoning while he was away on business. It was also very simple to have the funeral director honor his wishes and not open the wooden coffin he had stuffed with blankets and towels to make them feel like they were a mother holding her autistic son. Gold had a way of making people blind to the truth. He had learned that a long time ago in the war.

Because of the racism and prejudice he had embraced his entire life, he could not see God's beauty in the autistic brilliance that his son possessed. He only saw the face of God mocking him when he looked at him or his wife. He could not endure that so he killed them. It was easy killing those he saw as substandard. He had done it a thousand times.

The bong and the marijuana and beer had been for the young prostitutes that he enticed back to his house. It was no different than what he had done in the war, only instead of a loaf of bread and some chocolate, it now cost him some marijuana and beer. But when his wife's head came rolling down onto the floor, he knew he had to kill this prostitute that called herself Jasmine. He got his son's head out of the freezer and placed it next to his wife's on the table looking at Jasmine.

It was then that he noticed the large number of flies that were in the basement and realized that his freezer must have stopped working some time ago. His son and wife's heads which had once been preserved were now rotting. He should have noticed that much earlier, but he hadn't.

He watched as the young girl on the sofa rose up and looked at him. The knife was sticking through her head and she smiled as she pulled it out.

"Here, you are going to need this in a minute," she said as she handed the bayonet to Viktor.

Without wondering what he was watching, he took the bayonet from the young woman. For the first time, he saw her eyes. They were beautiful. One was green and the other was blue and they glistened like the jewels he had taken away from some of the rich people he killed in the camp.

"I have been waiting on this moment for a long time, Viktor. You could have killed that little boy and I wouldn't have cared. Either one of them. I mean, what's one or two more after ten thousand or so? I do have to admit, that rattlesnake in the garage was genius. Could be used for anything you wanted, couldn't it? Convenient that the boy went in there and you saw him, wasn't it? You're welcome. I arranged for that to happen because I knew it was time for you and me to meet. When that freezer went out and you didn't notice it, I knew it was time.

"I just love coming to get old Nazis. Especially the extremely perverted and sadistic ones. Wait a minute. Shit. Think about what I just said. There's a lot of redundancy in that statement, isn't there? Sorry about that."

Viktor looked at the young girl speaking to him but he couldn't see her face clearly. It kept changing into other faces. The faces of young girls, young boys, young women, young men, old women, old men. It was like the face he was looking at was some television set that had lost its vertical hold as the faces rolled by over and over.

"Who are you?" Viktor asked.

"My name is Abaddon. Ich bin ein damon. Der meister damon."

"Abaddon," Viktor repeated in a monotone, almost hypnotic, manner.

"You are going to want to push that bayonet into your heart in a moment. Before the police get here. And they will be here soon. You don't want to spend the rest of your life in jail. I will make sure you spend it in a garden of roses. Doesn't that sound nice, Viktor?"

"Ja. Das gut," Viktor said as he pushed the bayonet up under his sternum and into his heart.

"Wow. You did that so easily. I guess with all that practice, it's just muscle memory, isn't it? First of all, let me say thank you. I mean what you did up here on earth was just horrific. And I knew as I kept watching you, I wanted you on my team. Using your son and wife to fertilize your garden. Wow! You certainly don't meet that person in the garden center at Lowe's every day. No, that takes a special kind of sickness that I truly appreciate. So, kudos on that.

"Anyway, once you die, let me tell you what will happen. First, we are going to cut up your body when you get to my little piece of heaven that I call hell, and then grind you up and mix your body with cow shit. Remind you of anything? But unlike your son and wife, you will still be able to feel every bit of this process, from the initial sawing off of your limbs, to each finger, hand, arm, and leg, going through the meat grinder. Even that little piece of bratwurst, and I do mean little, that you have between your legs will be cut off

166

with pruning shears and ground up. I can only imagine how painful this will be. But really, if you can't feel it, what's the point of doing it? Am I right?

"I know, I know. Sounds good, huh? Gets even better, 'cause once your flesh and bone are mixed with the cow shit, we will take you out into the garden. That's right. I did promise you a garden. Only these roses are dead. In fact, they smell kind of rotten. But you won't care, because you will just be little pieces of shit and flesh by then. And even though you will be small particles of your former self, those tiny little grains that made up Viktor Gruning will remain sentient. Being a member of the master race, you certainly know what sentient means, don't you? Yes, of course, you do, but I do love talking about this part anyway, so forgive me if I go on a bit more about it.

"For all intents and purposes, you will basically just be little pieces of shit that we will then give to the dung beetles. And those industrious little bugs will start to work with you, Viktor. They will roll you up into their little balls as they navigate across the garden and then bury you for the females to lay eggs or store you away for the delicious little shit balls that they eat. And you will smell and feel every little snap, crackle, and pop as the baby beetles and the adult beetles eat their mixture of shit and Viktor. And once you are devoured, then we will start the process all over again.

"Over and over until over and over is no longer. Sounds poetic, doesn't it? Even though it just means you will be specks of shit that bugs will eat for an eternity. But for someone who killed as many people as you did, and in such a horrible manner, I had to really think outside the flower box, so to speak, in order to find some way to reward you. What do you think? Did I knock this out of the park or what? I know you are struggling to breathe right now, so you don't need to thank me. I need to thank you because you truly inspired me."

"Fick dich," Viktor said as he fell onto the garage floor, dead.

"Ahhhhhh....Fick you too, Viktor. Enjoy the train ride. The train should look familiar to you too. It's the same type of train that you loaded up all those people in so many years ago. You can peek through the wooden slats like they did and I promise you, that you will feel the same fear they had as you took them to those Hellish camps. Your version will be a thousand times worse though, so enjoy the ride on your descent into Hell.

"By the way, you do know when I say descent into Hell, I am speaking metaphorically? Though everyone envisions Hell as being in the molten crust of earth it's not. It's just an unholy place below Heaven. It will feel like you are going downward, but that's just all special effects. The fire and heat and smell, though, those are real. It helps build your anxiety and the madness that will overcome you as you try and get out. But you won't be able to get out. Please try though - I so enjoy watching that. See you later, Viktor."

When the police arrived at Mr. Strauss's home, Sammy and I were watching with our parents from my yard as they broke into the house. The flies swarmed into the yard like a plague that Moses had created. We watched the police put up yellow tape around the entire yard and start directing traffic in and out of the house.

"Oh, my God," my mother whispered as she saw them bring out several body bags and load them into the ambulances.

"Come on," my father said as he took us back in the house. Sammy's parents did the same.

The next day, the Kingsport News-Times told the story of the deaths of Mr. Strauss and a young girl that they would only describe as a minor who had been on the missing person list for over a year. Every day for a month the paper ran

168

another story about Mr. Strauss and what had occurred at his home. Eventually, even his real name was discovered by an unknown source, the paper said, as they honored the Mossad agent's request.

After that school year ended, and as I became a young man, I learned that there were more deadly monsters in the world than I could have ever imagined. The naivety within that small rural town in southwestern Virginia was removed that year when everyone was introduced to Viktor Gruning, a Nazi war criminal; a Colonel in the SS that ordered the killing of tens of thousands of innocents. A man who also went by the name of Otto Strauss and liked to be left alone as he tended to his rose garden.

Sometimes monsters wear uniforms and pretend to be soldiers because they think the uniform gives them the authority to act upon their sadistic nature without fear of reprisal. Sometimes the monsters looked human and at times innocent, but they never understood what it meant to be human or innocent.

The real monsters we encounter in life are just as evil as anything that has ever been written about in horror books. It's those who appear to be innocent and are later described as "quiet" or "shy" and "kept to themselves" that I find most disturbing. In fact, it gives me nightmares. But I've learned that's the price I have to pay in order to recognize them and then put them away.

I wish that there was only one type of monster in this world. The kind that is slain by the knights on white horses or that only exist in myths and fairy tales. The ones that sometimes frighten you, but can never harm you because they are only present in books.

But I am afraid that will never be the way the world operates. Evil wants to make its presence known and it has the power to do so and I am afraid it always will. Anyone who believes otherwise is just fooling themselves. I don't fool myself anymore and I become highly suspicious these days whenever I see a beautiful rose garden within a neighborhood. That's when I start asking questions.

421

Many people in Bristol, Tennessee were familiar with the Burnett brothers. Most of them worked in law enforcement. The others were family members or drug dealers, all of whom would have preferred not to have known them.

Their father, Jimmy Burnett, ran a tow truck service when he was working in a legal capacity. When he wanted to pursue a more lucrative endeavor, he stripped stolen cars. He was a good tow truck driver. He made sure the cars never incurred more damage when placing them onto his trailer. But he was even better at stripping cars and getting rid of them expediently.

His coworkers and friends, who frequented the strip clubs with Jimmy, often commented that he could strip a car in the same amount of time it took a stripper to finish her pole routine. Jimmy would always smile and act like he was embarrassed by the comments. But he wasn't embarrassed. He enjoyed the notoriety, even though if you had asked him what notoriety meant, he would have probably said it was "that person that used their stamp on important papers." Jimmy didn't have "book smarts." He would be one of those people that might be described as having "street smarts" and even saying that would be a bit of a stretch at times.

Jimmy loved to show off by performing stunts that would be considered unwise and dangerous by normal people. His girlfriend and third cousin, Bobbie Louise, would tell him he shouldn't do them either, giggling while she said it. Jimmy somehow knew the giggle meant that she really wanted to see him try it. He wasn't aware that her initial denial would allow her to remain guilt-free in the eyes of justice and society should something go wrong. And considering some of the things he did, that was a smart position to take.

One night he told Bobbie Louise that he could jump from the barn roof into his uncle's truck that was parked next to the barn and was full of hay bales. He got that idea when they saw his uncle's cat make that same jump. He started talking to Bobbie Louise about what good jumpers cats were. He said that sometimes people thought he moved "like a cat." Of course, this ability that he supposedly possessed was fueled by the fact he had consumed a twelve-pack of Old Milwaukee and shared a joint of "some killer weed" with Bobbie Louise.

She told him not to say stupid things like that and elbowed him as she started to giggle. All he heard was "Show me!" as he jumped up and ran into the barn. In the next few moments, he was yelling, "Watch this!" at Bobbie Louise from the roof as he leaped from the barn onto the hay bales. Unlike a cat, Jimmy broke an ankle and a wrist trying to manage his fall. But he accomplished what he had set out to do and Bobbie Louise was duly impressed. He did make the jump and, considering the many other stupid things she had seen him do before this, she began to think he was indeed similar to a cat, seeing how they had nine lives too.

Soon after that stunt and on the very day he had his casts removed, Bobbie Louise and Jimmy got married. And seven months after getting married, Bobbie Louise and Jimmy were the proud parents of twin boys. Though Bobbie Louise argued with Jimmy regarding their names, she lost the argument and agreed to the names that Jimmy wanted for his two boys: Jimmy. Not Jimmy Jr. and Jimmy the third, just Jimmy. When Bobbie Louise asked Jimmy how they were going to be able to talk to them, since they both had the same name, Jimmy agreed that might be a problem so he said that the younger son would be named Jimmy James. So, the younger boy, the one who followed his older brother out into the world two minutes and twenty seconds later, would eventually be known as JJ. Because of the precedent set that day, JJ would follow his brother from that point forward. He would follow him faithfully and with a devoted obedience that was not subservient but simply reflective of the bond that had been established at birth and nurtured over time.

As they grew up, the brothers took on the physical characteristics and reckless behavior of their father. They suffered from so many broken bones brought on by dares from other children that the Tennessee Department of Human Resources made an investigation of Jimmy and Bobbie Louise's parenting skills and household environment. They concluded that the Burnetts were not guilty of abuse and though it was not written in their report, one of the investigators suggested to her supervisor that someone would eventually get killed. She was right.

When people talked about Jimmy's sons, they always added the words, "the acorns don't fall too far from the tree." Always. Just like their father, they were both called "nuts" by anyone who met them; another reason the acorn idiom was applicable.

They were considered incorrigible, inattentive, lazy, and slow learners by their elementary school teachers. They were considered troublemakers, truants, and incapable of graduating by every teacher that they encountered once they were 'moved on' from elementary school. Though not always the case with their assessments of other students, each teacher's evaluation regarding Jimmy and JJ was correct.

Throughout their adolescence and early teens, Jimmy and JJ were arrested for shoplifting, petty theft, and underage drinking. They were never invited to parties in high school, but they were always there anyway. The police came often, breaking up the fights between the Burnett brothers and the usual three or four other young men who were fighting them and trying to get them to leave. Oddly enough, no assault charges were ever filed - probably because all of the attendees were underage, drinking alcohol, and smoking marijuana. The affluent in Bristol didn't want their children's names sullied by association with the Burnett brothers, so all the police could do was file a report. This action further enhanced the reputation that the Burnett brothers were developing.

There was another aspect of their father that the boys acquired over time as they observed his interactions with people. If someone tried to cheat their father in a business deal, they witnessed a display of his temper and learned how effective a monkey wrench could be at inflicting pain and changing opinions. If their father was drunk and in a bad mood, they saw his temper intensify and how people became even more fearful of what he would do if they did anything to piss him off.

Unaware that they had a choice in how they would handle their interactions with people and even with their mother, the boys learned that violence helped them achieve an end. They became very good at it. They were "mean sons of bitches," as those who fell victim to their anger would say.

Fortunately, their mother was smart enough to get out of that environment before she was killed. Once she understood what her sons were becoming, she knew she needed to leave. As her fear of the boys grew, she realized her husband wouldn't be able to protect her. Not only did the boys have a reluctance to heed her advice, they ignored her actions to discipline them, demonstrating how they disliked her interference with a physical response in place of a verbal one. They never divorced, but Jimmy Burnett and Bobbie Louise Burnett were separated after fifteen years of marriage and she never saw her husband or her sons again.

He wouldn't be remembered for doing anything special with his life, but the friends and family members who knew Jimmy Burnett better than anyone else would say he did two great things. He married Bobbie Louise, and when she left, he let her go without objection or judgment. He never spoke ill of his wife even when the many beers he drank after a hard day of work would suggest he might be inclined to do so.

The Burnett sons learned how to strip cars from their father but they were not motivated to work in any capacity, whether it was legal or not. That could be attributed to the fact that they smoked a lot more marijuana and used a lot more drugs than their father. If there was an illegal drug made in the 1970s, there was better than a ninety-percent chance that the Burnett boys had tried it. And to their credit, from all of the mind-altering drugs they consumed, they were at least able to distinguish between what they liked and what would kill them if they continued to smoke, pop, or shoot the substance into their veins. Unfortunately, the boys did not understand that they were just delaying the inevitable outcome of the abusive nature of the drugs they continued to ingest when combined with their violent and reckless behavior.

After the boys turned sixteen, and after several attempts, they finally obtained their driver's licenses. Their father was able to find a car from a demolition service that was owned by a friend and he presented it to them in celebration of the occasion. It was a wrecked and rusted-out Oldsmobile 442 that only cost him a few hundred dollars, but he knew it had potential.

He showed the boys how to restore the car and though none of them realized it, that time fixing up the car would be the happiest that they ever spent together. Considering their father's easy access to original parts for all types of cars, it only took them about three months to finish the car and have it ready to paint. The boys wanted to paint the car red (or 'scarlet' as the factory color stated), but their father insisted on painting it willow gold. That was another one of those things that their father did right. Once that vintage muscle car was restored and painted in that greenish-gold color, it was beautiful.

The Burnett brothers drove that car many times along Highway 421, which was the primary road used to drive to South Holston Lake. The lake was formed in the 1940s by the TVA to generate power and provide flood control for the area. Eighty percent of the lake was in Tennessee, with the other twenty percent in Virginia. It was one of those projects that the state and federal government seldom got right, but in this particular case, they succeeded. The lake was surrounded by the Holston Mountains and regardless of the season, it was beautiful. Even if one was stoned and drunk, it was beautiful.

Jimmy and JJ loved going to the lake and drinking beer and smoking dope or hash. They often sat in their parked car on some seldom-traveled road they felt like they had discovered as if they were pioneers coming into that part of the country for the first time. There were a lot of these hidden side roads off 421 that became even smaller, more remote roads. They seemed to spread out into the countryside and woods like capillaries within the human body, and in a similar fashion, they provided a lifeline to the few homes that existed there.

Their father warned them of going out to the lake via 421 all the time because it was so well patrolled by the police, but he knew he might as well have been talking to ants. The only way he would be able to ensure they followed his advice would be to break his son's legs. At times he even considered that, especially when he was drunk and needed their help on a job he was doing. He also knew he would be risking his well-being if he tried something like that. "They'll just have to learn on their own," he told himself, and he knew that they would - one way or another.

Like many others in town who were familiar with the boys, his father wondered how they were never taught a lesson by the police. He was sure they went well over 100 miles per hour in that 442 as they sped toward the lake, and in all likelihood, they were driving with an open beer, drunk, and/or stoned. They only got a few speeding tickets but never any reckless driving charges or a DUI. The police regularly observed that stretch of road and if you asked a statistician about the odds that a deputy would catch the Burnett brothers in that car doing something illegal, he would have provided you a number that would have been on the edges of the bell curve, suggesting that the likelihood would have exceeded 99%. Unfortunately, that statistician would have understood what it felt like to be a weatherman with that prediction.

There were a lot of close calls though. Several people told their friends, and later the police, that they had run off the road rather than risk being hit by a greenish-gold car going at a high rate of speed. Even though reports were made, the police in Tennessee and Virginia were never able to find the Burnett brothers until days later, after they had plenty of time to sober up. At that point, there was little that they could do because of the lack of physical evidence, the incomplete or conflicting descriptions of the car and drivers, and the fact that they were nowhere near the scene of the incident at the time they were found.

Some of those who reported the Burnett brothers to the police were driven off the road because the boys were playing "chicken" with each other, knowing full well that neither one of them was willing to lose the game and would have run headfirst into the car in the other lane if it hadn't moved off the road. In this case, ignorance was posing as courage and it only helped further the infamy associated with the two boys. Describing them as "nuts" now had an additional qualifier: "Those boys aren't afraid of dying." The ignorant are often impressed with descriptions that they misinterpret to be praise, and the Burnett brothers were no exception.

The boys were out at the lake the day that their father was brought a restored 1959 two-door Impala. The car's exterior was the original cream and snowcrest white colors with the factory aspen green interior. "Hell, the floor mats are even the original factory green," he said as he walked around admiring the car. "Damn, original motor too," he said as he popped the hood. "335 horses."

"Do you want to fuck the car or do you want to take it apart, Jimmy? We got a lot of buyers for these parts. Make three times what the car is worth, even restored as it is," his friend Danny said.

"I don't know, man. It seems like a shame to tear this car apart seeing how someone went to all this trouble putting it back together."

"Fine, dude. We gotta go. Let us know when you're interested in making money again."

Danny got in the car and started the engine. Jimmy walked over to the driver's side and reached in to turn off the key. "I'll do it, but I want $5,000 for this one and I'll have it ready for you by tomorrow."

"$4,000 and you'll have it ready for us by tomorrow."

"Yeah, I can do that," Jimmy replied, hoping that his sons would come back in time to help him get it done. But they didn't and Jimmy worked non-stop for almost twenty hours to complete the job. He was so tired that he didn't even get to enjoy the $4,000, as he just took the money and went back home to go to sleep.

The boys didn't come home for several days. They walked into the house and immediately went to the kitchen and began making themselves bologna sandwiches before they noticed the stains on the floor.

"What the fuck is that?" JJ asked as he pointed at the dark brown droplets and bent down to smell them. He ran his finger through one of them and realized that it had a crusty feeling. He didn't notice them at first, but eventually, he saw the tiny specks of color the stain originally had when it dropped from their father's body.

"Hell, Jimmy, I think this is blood," JJ said as he stood up and started following the trail that led to their father's bedroom. When they reached it, JJ yelled and then turned around and threw up on his brother's shoes. Jimmy held his brother up as he bent over trying to throw up everything that was in his stomach. He didn't care about the vomit on his shoes or his pants as he stared at the body in his father's bed.

The only way their father was recognizable was because the killers had left his face intact. The rest of his skin had been stripped away leaving only muscle or bone, depending on how far deep they cut. The bed and floor had been covered in plastic, and though it helped minimize the blood flow that came from their father, the room was still covered in a thick layer of the brownish-looking fluid

"Who the hell did this?" JJ asked angrily.

"Don't know, but we will. And they will regret every second when we find them. Come on, let's get the fuck out of here. We'll get some more beer and go to the lake. We need to think about all of this."

Jimmy went into the kitchen and cleaned off his shoes and pants before they left for the convenience store. They finished a six-pack before they even got out of the parking lot and started on the next one as they headed toward the lake. The anger and the beer flowing through their bodies made them want to hurt something or someone and they ran several cars off the road before they encountered a truck driven by an elderly gentleman who didn't have time to get out of the way.

The 442 ran into the front of the old Chevy pick-up like an ICBM, ramming the truck engine through the man and out through the truck bed into the road. Jimmy and JJ were thrown from the car and suffered multiple fractures, internal injuries, and concussions, but they were still alive. Considering that they had just found their father murdered in such a heinous manner, and regardless of their long juvenile record, the judge had leniency and charged them both with manslaughter and fifteen years in prison. The first year was mostly spent recovering in the prison hospital.

Unlike the scholastic setting in which they struggled, the penal environment where they now found themselves was one that garnered their interest in a profound manner. Being inattentive in school only meant you didn't learn something that the teacher was saying. Being inattentive in prison meant you could lose an appendage, an organ, or even your life. Keeping all of your body parts and staying alive were strong motivators for learning and the Burnett brothers learned in a much more expedient and resolute manner than they ever did in school.

In contrast to school, the boys listened to their "teachers" in prison – otherwise known as some of the older inmates who had been locked up for a long time and did not need to belong to a gang to ensure their survival. Jimmy and JJ weren't interested in joining a gang either because they didn't relate to any of them that were organized based upon race and a desire to kill anyone that didn't look like them or agree with their simple philosophy: "Fuck with us and we will fuck you up." Simple, concise, and something that everyone understood.

Of course, Jimmy and JJ had to learn by trial and error about where they could and could not go within the common areas where the general prison population was allowed. But

180

each time they were challenged, the brothers inflicted a great deal of pain on the person who was trying to teach them they had done something wrong. When one brother was attacked, the other was there to help him. The groups learned that attacking either one of the Burnett brothers was like striking at a wasp's nest: It just wasn't worth it. Granted, the boys spent a lot of time healing in the prison hospital, but they soon developed the same reputation in prison that they held in the outside community.

The Burnett brothers were called "nuts" and "not afraid of dying," and in prison, that type of reputation was a good one to have. It helped them earn the respect of law enforcement inside the jail. The guards allowed fights in which they and the prisoners bet on the outcome. One would have thought that these fights would be subject to a great deal of fraudulent behavior, but they were not. Probably because if it was discovered that you did anything that gave you an unfair edge or that you tried to tamper with the outcome, you would end up dead. Didn't matter if you were a guard or a prisoner. The rule applied to both and was very seldom unheeded.

"If only the outside was this simple to understand," JJ said to his brother one night before a fight. "We figured this place out pretty good, didn't we Jimmy?"

"Yeah, we did, JJ. Now get in there and fuck that son of a bitch up."

The Burnett brothers won a lot of fights. Each victory not only helped them with their reputation, but it also helped them with the prison guards who made money off of their fights. They shared a small percentage of that money with Jimmy and JJ and, interestingly enough, Jimmy and JJ found it was just as easy to buy drugs in jail as it was outside the prison walls.

Each gang held distribution rights for a different kind of drug; another sort of unwritten prison law. And after a fight, regardless if they won or not, the guards would give Jimmy and JJ a twelve-pack of beer to share. Laying back on their cell cots, they drank their beer and usually smoked a joint and ignored the pain they felt. The conversations always turned to the day they would get out of prison and avenge their father.

They had been in prison for twelve years when Jimmy was smoking a joint with one of the gang members who had become a friend during the past year. As they talked, Jimmy learned that his friend was in prison for killing his family. He told Jimmy that he had been doing a lot of PCP and heroin at the time. He thought he heard the devil say that if he didn't kill his family, they would kill him.

"You heard the devil tell you that?" Jimmy asked.

"As if he was sitting right next to me, just like you," Crow replied.

"Shit, man, that's fucked up."

"Yeah, it was. Something that I will live with for the rest of my life. I try not to hear the devil anymore but I tell you I see him. I see him all the time."

"You don't see him right now, do you?"

"No, but I'll tell you if I do."

"Yeah, man. Give me a warning. I don't want to be mistaken for someone I ain't."

Crow laughed. "You're okay for a white man, Jimmy."

Jimmy smiled. "Hey, Crow," he said as he inhaled the joint and passed it over to his friend. "How in the hell do all these drugs get into the prison?"

"El Ojo Maligno."

"What the hell is yoyo magano?"

"El O-ho Ma-league-no. It means The Evil Eye. And it's spelled E-l, O-h-o, M-a-l-i-g-n-o. Oho means eye and maligno means evil in Spanish. He lives somewhere in East Tennessee. Has a very large business. Muy malo. Very bad. I heard he skinned some guy for stealing and stripping his car. Skinned the son of a bitch. That's some bad shit, man. You don't want to fuck with him."

When Jimmy heard that he skinned a man for stealing his car, he knew he had discovered who had killed his father. Now he only had to find out where he lived in East Tennessee. He knew just the people he would ask when he and JJ got out of prison and he was sure they would know all about this El O-ho fellow. But he decided not to tell his brother. Not yet. He didn't want anyone to know they were the sons of the man who was stripped of his skin. He had learned that it was best to keep something like that a secret in this type of setting, where someone could be encouraged to eliminate a threat for a carton of cigarettes. And he was certain that this "L Ma-league-no" had access to a lot of cigarettes.

"Yeah, I want to stay away from someone like that," Jimmy replied as he took another puff of the joint. And with that statement, Jimmy made the prison dean's list. That was something that the teachers in the scholastic world would have never imagined to be possible. But it was something that the "teachers" within the state penal system saw from the very first month that the Burnett brothers came to their institution.

Over the next three years, Jimmy and JJ became model prisoners. They told the prison guards that they wanted to stop fighting and the guards respected their wishes as they saw them trying to get their GEDs. Though they had indeed developed prison smarts, the guards and even some of the prisoners had a running bet that the boys wouldn't be smart enough to pass the GED exam. It took them two years, but they finally passed and the entire prison celebrated. Especially those splitting the $10,000 pot that had accumulated by that time. The following year they were released from prison and had $100 saved in their pockets.

As soon as they walked out of the last set of metal doors, they saw their father's tow truck parked across the road. JJ elbowed his brother as he pointed at it and said, "Ain't that Daddy's tow truck, Jimmy?"

"Yeah, I believe it is."

"How do you think it got here?"

"Not sure. Probably someone who knew Dad brought it by for us."

Jimmy was right. Bobbie Louise had never come to see her sons in prison but she knew when their release date was and she made sure that their father's truck was there for them, knowing that they probably had no other means of transportation. As Jimmy opened the driver's side door, he saw an envelope leaning up against the front windshield just behind the steering wheel. It was addressed to "Jimmy and JJ," so he opened it and read it to his brother.

Dear Jimmy and JJ,

I wanted to make sure you had your Daddy's truck. I have been holding onto it for you until now. I want both of you to know that I loved you dearly when you were young boys, even though you were like raising wild dogs. But you were my wild dogs and I loved you. As you grew into young men, the anger inside of you was not something that I could tolerate and I had to leave. I hope that you can look into your heart and understand that. I have put $100 in this envelope for you and, along with your father's truck, that's all I can afford to give you. I hope you will find value in your new lives as you come from prison back into society. It's a horrible way to learn about right and wrong, but for some, it is the only way they learn. Please do not try and contact me. I am afraid that part of our lives is over. But know that I will continue to pray for you and that I forgive you. Mom

Jimmy showed JJ the money and put it in his pocket.

"Do you think we should go and thank her, Jimmy?"

"No, she doesn't want us to. We were bad to her. We were bad to a lot of people and we'll just have to live with that. But, it's probably one reason why we survived in prison for fifteen years. All we can do for her right now is leave her alone and know that our mother forgives us and is praying for us. Considering what we plan to do, that's the best we can hope for. Why don't you hold onto this letter? I think we should keep it. We may want to read it again one day."

"Sure, Jimmy. I'll keep it."

They got in the tow truck and headed toward Bristol. While he drove, Jimmy didn't talk much. He was thinking about the words from his mother. It made him sad but, in his heart, he knew she was right. And at that moment, anyone who knew or had ever encountered Jimmy in any capacity could see how much he had matured.

Davis and Houston Bartholomew were brothers from a very affluent family in Bristol who loved doing drugs. Both of them were graduates of Vanderbilt with degrees in marketing and were employed by their father in his computer software business which required very little actual work from them. Their father was a brilliant computer scientist and his software solutions sold themselves, but he wanted his sons to have a job, even if in most cases it was in name only.

Davis and Houston were both handsome, well-spoken young men and their main role within their father's business was arranging for clients to have a good time when they were considering new software products. Their father rationalized the six-figure incomes they earned and allowed them to do whatever they wanted without much interference from him. He knew they used drugs; he was not aware that they also sold them.

Davis and Houston lived in a beautiful cabin on a bluff overlooking South Holston Lake. It had been built in the 1950s by a CIA agent who had chosen the property because of the many natural barriers surrounding it. There was only one way onto the property – a gated entry and enclosure at the end of a long serpentine road. Access to the house from anywhere except that road was not impossible but it was extremely difficult trying to get up that bluff. The house had a panoramic view from bulletproof glass that encircled the building. Davis and Houston had also installed security cameras in strategic areas around the property.

And even though it had been built in the '50s, the brothers didn't want to change the modern V-shape of the home. It was unique and, while they were not looking for a V-shaped house, finding it was serendipitous they thought, considering that they graduated from Vanderbilt. On the exterior, they had only done what was necessary to upgrade the security and whatever repairs would be required of purchasing a thirty-seven-year-old home that had endured harsh winters around the lake.

Inside, the solid wood floors were cleaned and covered with another coat of water-resistant polyurethane. The walls were painted and the carpet was removed and replaced with expensive marble. A new roof and septic tank were installed and a new water filtration system and pump were added. All of the appliances and furniture were updated and they added cable and a new surround sound stereo and TV system. The bedrooms were at opposite ends of the V. In the middle of the home was the great room, kitchen, and den combination that remained intact from a construction perspective and gave the home its unique look. After the upgrades, the home could have been on the cover of "Southern Homes and Gardens" had the brothers not wanted as few people as possible to know of their location.

Davis and Houston were surprised one day when they looked at the cameras and saw the tow truck drive up to the gate and beep. They immediately recognized the passengers when they saw JJ trying to use the intercom. They laughed as they watched him having trouble getting it to work, so they just opened the gate.

"Man, they haven't changed. I'm sure they're just looking for drugs," Houston said to his brother.

"But they've been gone for 15 years. Why would they think that we have drugs?"

"It's Jimmy and JJ. They don't think."

"Yeah, you've got a point."

Houston and Davis walked outside and greeted the brothers. Jimmy pressed on the accelerator as soon as he saw them and slammed on the breaks so that the truck slid toward them, making them jump out of the way. Jimmy and JJ were laughing as they got out of the truck. JJ had a case of beer in his arms and offered them one as he walked toward them.

"What the fuck, Jimmy?" Houston said as he took a beer from JJ.

"Shit, man, just having some fun with you. We used to have a lot of fun if you don't remember. Driving all around this lake, smoking weed, doing God knows what, and drinking beer. Don't tell me you don't still do that shit, 'cause I won't believe you."

Houston laughed. "Yeah, Jimmy, we still enjoy a little weed and some blow on occasion. Did you miss that in prison?"

"Hell, no! It was just as easy to find in prison as it was out here. Just had to be careful about how you bought it. You could only buy certain drugs from certain gangs, but we found out the rules and we followed them. We could get high most any day we wanted."

"Really?" Davis replied in a surprised manner. "Well, how did you boys find out where we lived?"

"We still know a few people," Jimmy replied. "Damn nice house you got. Looks as secure as our home for the past fifteen years was. Aren't you going to ask some old friends to come in?"

"Sorry, Jimmy. Of course. I'm going to need to go change my underwear though. Seeing that truck about to run me over made me pee just a little bit I think. At least I hope it's pee."

All of them laughed as they followed him into the house. Jimmy and JJ admired the great room while Houston put away the beer.

"Helluva view you got here, Houston. Helluva view. Must be nice to have money."

"I don't complain or apologize for having money, Jimmy."

"No man, you don't need to. I wasn't suggesting that you should. Just making a comment."

Houston smiled and began wondering if their dope-smoking friends were there just to reunite and get high or if maybe they had come for another reason. He knew at least half of those who got out of prison were sent back within their first year. They had often just learned new ways to become better criminals while there. Was that what Jimmy and JJ were doing? Evaluating the house or him for ways to steal what they had? He knew he had to be leery and he would make sure his brother was too. He also understood he needed to not let Jimmy or JJ know that he had concerns, but considering how he remembered them, he didn't think that would be too hard.

Davis walked back into the room with a joint and a small bag of cocaine in his hand.

"Let's get high, brothers," he said as he sat down and motioned for Jimmy and JJ to join him.

Houston grabbed some beers from the refrigerator and passed them around. He wanted them to feel as comfortable in his home as if it was fifteen years ago and they were still teenagers. He realized it was important for him to do that.

Davis lit the joint, took a hit, and handed it to JJ. He placed several lines of cocaine on a silver tray and passed it around with a rolled-up hundred-dollar bill.

"Is that a real hundred-dollar bill?" JJ asked as he took the tray and the monetary snorting device.

"Yeah. It makes the coke all that much better," Davis said, grinning.

Houston wasn't sure it was such a good idea to pull out a hundred-dollar bill to snort the coke, but there was nothing he could do now. He just needed to act as if everything was cool with them being there. He wanted the Burnetts to feel at ease around their old friends even though he was very anxious and wanted to start getting some answers.

"So, what was it like, Jimmy? Fifteen years in prison? How the hell did you get through each day?"

He didn't even say he was sorry about the death of my father. Or ask how long it took us to heal after that accident. Same old Houston. All he cares about is himself, his money, and getting high. But that's okay. I just need to know where to find that fucking Oho Maligno. But he looks a little unsure around us. Makes sense. We did just get out of prison. Need to make him feel more comfortable. Need to party some more until I start asking, thought Jimmy.

"Once we knew what we could and could not do, we were okay. We kept to ourselves for the most part, and everyone pretty much left us alone."

"That's because they were scared of our asses," JJ said as he smiled and reached over and popped Davis in the arm with his fist.

Shit, JJ, Jimmy thought. *You shouldn't have said that.*

"What JJ means," Jimmy replied, "is that we did some fighting in there. They have what's like MMA fights in there, only you're using bare knuckles. Other than that, anything

189

goes. Well, I say anything, but you can't kick people in the nuts or bite them or poke them in the eye."

"Really?" Houston replied. "I thought anything would go in prison."

"No, not at all. There are rules and if you don't play by the rules, you'll pay for it. It was much easier to learn rules in there knowing that if you didn't follow them, you would end up dead. Simple, but effective. If school had been like that, I think JJ and I would have been much better students." Jimmy smiled and everyone laughed.

"JJ and I even got our GEDs in prison. Now, who in this room would have believed that? Come on - a show of hands? But if you raise your hand and you're lying, we cut it off."

Houston and Davis stared at them with concerned looks on their faces. For a moment, Jimmy and JJ just stared back. Then JJ elbowed Jimmy and started laughing out loud.

"We had you going, man. You should have seen the look on your face when Jimmy said we would cut off your hand. Man, we ain't gonna do that to our brothers."

"JJ is right. We wouldn't do that to you guys. We had too many good times when we were younger. I know you're probably wondering what the hell we're doing here. I know we might look a little intimidating - prison is probably better than a gym in regards to getting you in shape - but you don't have anything to worry about from us."

Jimmy saw the relief wash across their faces but he could still tell they were not completely at ease. *Shit, they're dealing drugs in a much bigger way. Look around you, Jimmy. The house. The cameras. The gate. I fucking know for sure they know El Maligno now. Might as well get it out there. They might even be relieved to hear me say it.*

"I do want to know if you can help us with something, Houston," Jimmy said as he got up and retrieved another beer. He opened it up and took a swig before picking up the silver tray to snort another line of coke. He put a drop of beer on his fingertip and snorted it into his nostrils and inhaled.

"Man, that's some good shit. You guys always had good shit. Better than what we got in prison for sure. Ain't it, JJ?"

"Yeah, brother," JJ said as he snorted a couple more lines too.

"So," Jimmy said as he looked over at Houston and then his brother. "You ever heard of a drug dealer by the name of El Maligno?"

Houston smiled at his brother who seemed surprised by the question.

"Yeah, we know him. He's a competitor of ours. He's a fucking badass too. Likes to kill people just for the fun of it. And loves to kill them when he thinks they fucked over him."

"Do you know where he lives?" Jimmy asked.

"Yeah, we know. He lives out here on a little country road that goes off deep into the woods. A place no one would even notice. It's called Troublesome Hollow Road. Goes for about ten miles along a stream before you even come to a house. It's really just a trailer. Some old fucker by the name of Charlie lives there with his dogs. Looks older than dirt. Go about another mile and then you come to the home of El Ojo Maligno. Nice big log cabin. He doesn't even keep a lot of security around him because people know not to fuck with him. I think there might be two or three men walking around the property, but that's probably it."

"You know an awful lot about this fucker," Jimmy said as he moved over onto the edge of the couch and turned up his beer.

"Yeah, we do," Houston said. "We often considered paying him a visit and sort of suggesting he go into another business. Why do you want to know about him?"

"He killed our father. We would like to show him what a mistake that was."

"Ahh… just like finding our home," Houston said as he looked over at his brother. "Our friends' arrival is serendipitous."

"What the hell does 'sara and dipshit' or whatever it was you said mean?" JJ asked.

"It means the two of you coming here was meant to be. We would like to help you kill that son of a bitch that killed your father," Houston replied. "You get your revenge and we get rid of our main competitor. It's a win-win. Pass me that tray, Davis."

Houston pulled out another bag of coke from his pocket and made four very large lines. He snorted one and then passed it over to Jimmy.

"You interested in paying him a visit this evening, Jimmy?"

Jimmy snorted the large line of coke and stood up. He looked at his little brother who was nodding his head yes.

"Hang on a minute while you ponder that question," Houston said as he got up and walked into his room. He came back in a few moments with two AK-47s and placed them on the table. He went back into his room and returned this time with a rocket-propelled grenade launcher and two 10-gauge shotguns.

"Davis also has a lot of handguns in his room that we can get for you in a minute too. But based upon what you see now, what do you think?"

"I think we should drink a few more beers, do a little more coke, and go pay your friend a visit. Just as it gets dark," Jimmy answered.

"I was hoping you'd say that. I've got some PCP, too, that we can take as soon as we get out there. It'll give us all the energy we need to take care of that fucker."

JJ stood up and hugged his brother and howled and Jimmy knew he would have a hard time keeping him under control. He would tell his brother in a private moment not to take that

PCP. But for now, they would just drink more beer and do some more cocaine. And with each beer and line they did, Jimmy thought about revenge.

Davis let Jimmy and JJ pick out their handguns. They each chose a Glock 9 mm pistol. Davis said, "Good choice," just before he went to the bathroom to "drain the lizard." While he was in the bathroom, Jimmy found a small .38 with a leg holster and placed it on his leg.

"Just in case," he said and his brother nodded his head as if he understood. Though JJ did understand his brother's intent to be prepared, he didn't understand that he wasn't just trying to anticipate the worst with whom they were about to encounter. He was also trying to anticipate the worst with Houston and Davis.

After another beer, Houston announced it was time to go. He told Jimmy and JJ that they needed to make their house secure before they left and, if they didn't mind, this needed to be done privately. Jimmy said he understood and watched them go into Davis's room and close the door. Jimmy whispered to JJ to go over to the door and see if he could hear anything.

JJ could hear what sounded like several doors opening and then heard them say how glad they would be to finally get rid of this fuck. JJ couldn't make out anything else except the name of another road. He rushed back to Jimmy before they came back out and told his brother that they mentioned some other road besides Troublesome Hollow Road.

"What road?" Jimmy asked.

"Something called the Sosheo Path. You think they are telling us everything straight up?"

"No, I don't, JJ. You make sure they stay in front of you during all of this and when they offer you the PCP, just take it from them and pretend to swallow it. But don't take it. You understand me?"

193

"Yeah, I get it. We're gonna make that son of a bitch pay, aren't we Jimmy?"

"Yeah, little brother. We are."

Davis and Houston came out of the room smiling and said they were ready to go. Davis told Jimmy it would be a good idea for both of them to drive. They could park the tow truck as soon as they got to the trailer on Troublesome Hollow Road and then take his truck the rest of the way. He said when they saw his truck it wouldn't raise any suspicions since they had been out there conducting business several times before.

Jimmy said he understood and picked up a 10 gauge while JJ picked up an AK-47. They got in the truck and watched as Houston came out of the garage in a vintage 1949 F-150. He pulled up alongside Jimmy's tow truck and Davis rolled down the window and smiled.

"What do you think of the truck? Original black exterior but we put in red trim around the black leather seats with a killer stereo. Damn nice truck, don't you think?"

"Shit yeah, it's beautiful," JJ said as he leaned over, trying to see as much of the truck as possible.

"You always had good taste in cars, Houston. Always," Jimmy said. "Lead on, man, and let's get this done. I want to drink some more beer tonight."

"Hell, yeah!" Davis and JJ yelled in unison. Houston nodded his head as he led them toward a road that they had never been on before.

Jimmy looked at the stream that ran alongside Troublesome Hollow Road, which narrowed and widened as it followed the path of the water. He figured that was the reason the road twisted back and forth so much. The stream forced it too. At times, the water looked clear and had little pockets of white water as it flowed over the top of the rocks. At other places, there were pools of dirty-looking water filled with leaves and other rotting material. *Still water will do that*, he said to himself.

They soon saw the trailer up on the hill and as if on cue, Houston stopped and pointed to where they should park the tow truck. It was next to a wide dark part of the stream, where an old engine-less skiff was tied to a small dock. The dock looked like it could fall in at any time. Jimmy could smell the foul and stagnant water before he even got out of the truck. He saw a couple of tiny red flames up on the porch that looked like two old men were up there smoking cigarettes. He also heard some dogs growling as he and JJ got out and walked over to Houston.

"Don't worry about Old Charlie up there or his dogs. They've been here forever. Just stay away from their yard and you'll be okay. He doesn't like for you to get in his yard and the dogs like it even less," Houston said.

Jimmy and JJ just nodded their heads as they climbed into the truck bed and headed down the last mile of the road. As soon as they got in the back of the truck, Davis handed them the PCP and before Jimmy could stop his brother, he watched JJ swallow the pill. *Shit, he didn't remember. He's too jacked up. I'll just have to watch him*, Jimmy thought as he pretended to take the pill and then placed it in his pocket.

Houston was right about Charlie. He had lived out there in Troublesome Hollow for a very long time. There was only one other home on this road and he knew a drug dealer lived there. Charlie knew the man's name too but they didn't speak. Charlie didn't like to talk to people and he made sure Jose Malvado knew that soon after he built his house there at the end of the road.

Charlie and his dogs had heard gunfire more than once coming from the end of the road. It didn't bother him or his dogs. They weren't afraid. They watched as the tow truck stopped in front of their house and saw the two men get into the back of the other truck. He saw the guns in their hands and knew they would once again hear gunfire this evening. But he sensed something different tonight about the men that

195

were driving down this road. He sensed an evil presence within those men and knew he would have to deal with them. He looked over at his dogs and told them to be ready and heard them respond with an eager whine.

Houston parked the truck at the gate that guarded the driveway. He leaned his head out the window and told Jimmy and JJ what was going to happen next.

"In just a second, Davis is going to get out of the truck and fire the rocket launcher into the house and knock out the door. I need you to jump out and use your 10 gauge to blow open the gate and then get back in the truck and lay low. After you do that, Davis will fire another grenade into the house. I'll drive as close as I can and when I stop, get out and go for it. Look for the guards on the side of the house or on top of the house where there's a large deck. See you in the house. We'll be waiting for you beside El Ojo Maligno."

The front door and part of the wall were shattered by the grenades Davis fired and Jimmy jumped out and blew off the locking mechanism of the gate. He leaped back into the truck bed and Houston drove toward the hole that once was a door and stopped. Jimmy held onto JJ's arm as Houston and Davis ran into the house firing their weapons. Jimmy turned toward his brother. "We go in careful-like, JJ. Keep Houston and Davis in front of you. I find it kind of weird that we haven't gotten any gunfire since we drove onto the property. I'm not sure things are as Houston says, so watch yourself.'

"I will," JJ replied as he scrambled over the side of the truck and moved toward the front of the house. Jimmy was right behind him. They heard guns going off and screams but no bullets were coming toward them. At the top of the steps, they saw Houston standing over a Spanish-looking man with a beard.

"El Ojo Maligno," Houston said as he fired and all that remained was the man's beard clinging to a jaw without a face, as the body fell over onto the floor. Jimmy suddenly felt a pain in his back and fell forward as the AK-47 bullet went through his shoulder. He saw his brother JJ fall down next to him with a similar injury. Davis came into the room and picked up Jimmy and JJ's guns and took them over to Houston. He then brought in Jose's wife and children and Jimmy and JJ watched as Davis smashed their heads in with a 3-pound sledgehammer.

"Fuck," Jimmy said as he looked at the disgusting images of the dead family and the smiling faces of Houston and Davis.

"I can't stop my brother when he gets in the killing mood," Houston said. "He likes to bash people's heads in and I'm afraid if I tried to stop him, he would do it to me. Sorry about the gunshot, but we need the police to find you two here. It will help explain who killed El Ojo Maligno, seeing how he killed your father. Oh, and by the way, you'll soon have a problem breathing. That PCP was laced with cyanide. In about 10 more minutes you should be dead. See, Davis, like I said, them showing up was just serendipity, plain and simple."

Jimmy watched as Houston unloaded the guns he and his brother had into the dead bodies. He laid the guns next to the bodies and looked down at them.

"Revenge is sweet, isn't it?" Houston asked. He and Davis started laughing as they went down the steps.

Jimmy heard JJ struggling to breathe and saw the fear in his eyes.

"Don't worry, JJ, I'll get you out of here. I'll get you to that old man. I bet he has something that can help you. These old country people have all sorts of natural remedies. Even for poison, so hang in there," Jimmy said as he stood up and hurried down the steps.

He pulled out the .38 and aimed at Davis's head and shot his ear off as he fell forward. Houston looked back and saw Jimmy behind the wall and heard another bullet whiz by his head. He jumped in the truck and yelled at Davis to get in too. Jimmy shot at the tires as they drove away. Davis looked down at the blood that covered his hands and fell down his face. "Goddamn it, Houston," Davis screamed. "He shot my fucking ear off!"

"Be glad he didn't blow your goddamn head off. They'll be dead soon and we'll be out of here. Our main competition is gone now and the culprits are there for the police to find. 'Horrible thing what happened,' the paper will say. 'Revenge and everyone dead. Just doesn't pay to be a drug dealer.' We'll tow our truck out of here with Jimmy's truck and then drive it back here and park it in front of the house. They'll see multiple tire tracks but they won't be able to find us. I'll make sure of that."

They stopped in front of Charlie's home and got out of their truck. Davis was holding his hand over his ear as he watched Houston searching around for the key to the truck. He then heard the old man yelling out to him.

"If you're looking for the key to that tow truck, you ain't going to find it. I threw it in that there pond. Course I reckon you could try and find it, but you'd probably die of the shit that's in that water long before you found that key."

"What the fuck is wrong with you, old man?" Houston said as he pulled out his Glock and started walking up the hill toward him. "I'll just take your car then. And I may let my brother use his hammer on your head. He likes to hit people with that hammer of his."

"You can try and do that, shit fer brains, but you fire one shot and my dogs will be on you and that brother of yorn before you blink yore eyes. They're a special breed of Rottweilers and trained to protect and kill. Sweet as tea to me. Sir, Berry, and Bess are their names. But don't mistake those sweet names for anything but your own death. You'll hear them bones crack all over yore body and then you'll notice you have a mighty hard time breathing. Cause' them

198

dogs will rip open your throat and tear that windpipe of yorn out. Ain't a good way to die, but I guess you're a gonna do whatever you got a mind too."

"What the fuck have you been drinking, old man? Shoe polish or varnish? You crazy fuck. I'll shoot those damn dogs before they can even get near me. And if I don't shoot them, my brother has an AK-47 and I've yet to see a dog outrun an AK-47 and a Glock. Those would be mighty special dogs to be able to do that."

"They's special dogs all right. Them dogs know evil when they smell it and they been whining ever since you parked yore truck there and drove away. And though I wasn't there, I know you killed that Malvado family. And that brother of yorn did something terribly evil to his family. I knowed Malvado's a drug dealer but you ain't got no business doing that to his family. Sick sons of bitches. Hell, it might be kinda fun watching my dogs tear yore ass a new one."

Before Houston could move another step, he heard the dogs growling and saw 8 red eyes staring at him.

"Look at that shit, Houston. All those fucking red eyes. Those dogs and the old man. Their eyes are burning like charcoal. I don't like this," said Davis.

"Neither do I and we're going to fix that," Houston replied just as he heard an engine come howling down the road. He heard the loud cracking sounds of an AK-47 and saw Davis fall to the ground with half of his head gone. He started shooting back and immediately got knocked to the ground by the three Rottweilers, who looked like one huge black dog for a moment. They crushed his hand which was holding the gun and tore apart large patches of his skin and bone from his chest and legs. Houston screamed as if he had been set on fire.

Jimmy got off the ATV and as he approached Houston with the gun, he heard the old man yell out to him.

"Better put that gun away, boy, or them dogs will do the same to you that they just did to that young fella with a smart-ass mouth. There will be no guns fired around my house. Not now, not ever. You understand what you hearing, boy?"

Jimmy looked up at the old man and could see him sitting in a chair, though the night was very dark and there was no light on the porch. *Those weren't cigarettes I saw earlier,* he said to himself. *Those were his eyes.* And then he saw the red eyes of the dogs as they stood over Houston, ready to attack him if he didn't put his gun down.

Jimmy put the gun down on the ground and looked up at the old man.

"That piece of shit over there poisoned my brother and killed a family down there at the end of the road. Granted the man needed killing but they had no reason to kill the mother and her children. They had nothing to do with what their father had done. He deserved to die. But my brother doesn't. He didn't kill anyone and the only one I killed was that sick son of a bitch's brother who hit those innocents over the head with a sledgehammer. I don't apologize for that, nor the death of the drug dealer. I do wish I could've saved his family. I guess in that regard, I am just as guilty as those two pieces of shit over there because I was right there and didn't prevent it. I don't care if I have to go back to jail, but my brother shouldn't have to. And he shouldn't have to die. Can you help him, old man? Can you stop the poison from killing him? It's cyanide."

"I'm sorry, young fella, but I can't save him. I would make yore peace with him if I were you, 'cause I can feel his spirit about to leave his body."

Jimmy heard his brother gasping for breath and turned around and laid him on the ground. He held his head in his hands and whispered to him as he used his sleeve to wipe away some of the vomit he was choking on.

"Can you at least give me some water for him?"

"No, sir, I can't. You can give him some of that water from that stream if you want to ease his sufferin'. That water will kill him on the spot."

"Hang on, JJ. I'll help you, little brother. Hang on," Jimmy said as he went over to the stream. He cupped his hand and brought the water over to his brother. He let it fall into JJ's mouth and within seconds, JJ stopped breathing.

"Goodbye, JJ. I hope you find peace and forgiveness."

"Well, what do we have here?" Jimmy heard as he turned around and saw the figure of a woman walking toward them. She stepped across the water atop human heads that popped up like stepping stones. Their tormented faces screamed in silence with their jaws wide open and their eyes wincing in pain. The dogs begin to whine as the figure neared. Jimmy saw the greenish-blue aura around the woman, and he knew everything that he was seeing must be some effect of all the drugs and beer he had ingested earlier.

"The River Styx out here in the sticks. How droll, Charon. I didn't know you had such a dry sense of humor. In fact, I didn't know you had a sense of humor at all. "

"Yeah, well you don't know every goddamn thing, Abaddon."

Jimmy saw the figure bend over to look at Davis' body and then walk toward him. He felt like he had been packed in ice as she approached. His whole body shook from the cold. She paused for a minute as she looked down at JJ and then smiled as she looked up at Jimmy. At least he thought it was a smile. It was there for a second and then there was nothing but blackness. She walked by the dogs and they growled and whined and pawed at the ground. She looked down at Houston and smiled but all he saw when she smiled was a shark-like row of teeth. She then turned around toward the old man on the porch.

"Is it Charon or Charlie? What do you prefer these days?"

"I prefer for you to get the hell off my fucking property. You ain't got no business here."

"Okay, sounds like a Charlie then. So be it. Well, Charlie, your river seems to be a bit smaller than I recall. Looks more like a crick than a river."

"Things can be deceiving, Abaddon. Can't judge a book by its cover."

"Fascinating, Charlie. Such wonderful sayings now emanating from your grizzled old face. A face that only a true shapeshifter like me could enjoy. By the way, does this stream meander through Dollywood?"

"No, shitass, it don't. You've always been a smart ass. Always thinking you're better than the next being. I ain't got much use for demons like you around here, so why don't you just move on before I sic the dogs on you?"

"Ah, Cerberus. That three-headed dog you seem to like so much is just that to me. A three-headed dog. I will rip it apart in front of your eyes if it makes the slightest move toward me. I guess your mind has gotten a bit feeble since you have that old coot look going for you right now. I understand. It's better than that skeleton-like presence that is underneath your grizzled brown skin, which was always about as scary as the skeletons you see sewn onto Halloween costumes for little babies. Be careful what you say to me, Ferryman.

"I am not in the best of moods. I've already had a run-in with Tisiphone and her fucking sisters and I am not about to bargain with a fucking ferryman. I will make you piss the river Styx until you die. Oh, but I forget, you won't die, will you? You will just wish you were dead as the acid-like piss comes burning out of your little man spigot. You still have one of those, don't you Charlie?"

"You having some issues, Charlie?" an old man asked as he came around the corner of Charlie's house with a scythe.

"You have got to be fucking kidding me. Who's your friend, Charlie? I have a strong suspicion that I know him but

202

I don't know what name he is using in this neck of the woods."

"Name's Tim Farmer. Live just behind Charlie. Been living here a long time. Nice here. Quiet. Peaceful. Got about 10,000 acres. Land as far as you can see with a garden as big as seven cities. It's a very unique garden, but I have trouble with everything dying. And though it's eternally full, it doesn't ever flourish."

"Tim Farmer; the Grim Reaper. Are you shitting me?" Abaddon said as she turned around and looked at Jimmy. "Is this a fucking trip or what? I thought this was going to be just a snatch and grab and I'd be on my way, but look at the reunion that's taking place. Magical, isn't it?

"Why don't you two farm boys, if that's what you are - I don't really know and don't really care - just go back to your whittling and farming and whatever else it is you two do and let me take these serial killers and be on my way? Or, 'El Ojo Maligno,' as he likes to refer to himself and his brother, who does appear to be really dead now."

Jimmy heard the being say "Ojo Maligno" and point toward Houston and Davis. *Shit*, he said to himself. *I knew they were up to something. They just wanted me to help kill a competitor and to kill us before we killed them.*

"Fuck you, Houston. I hope that greenish-blue thing fucks you over and over in Hell with some pitchfork."

"Oh, we have much better things than pitchforks these days, Jimmy. To, as you say, 'fuck Houston' over and over. Things that will rip his body apart and stitch it back together and then rip it apart again. I thought you might like knowing that, Jimmy. Yes, that piece of shit you killed and his brother are the ones who killed your father and stripped off his skin. I can't say I don't like that kind of thing, because I do, but your father didn't deserve that, any more than that woman and her two children deserved having their head bashed in by

203

a nut job. Again, if we are being honest here, something I am not opposed to doing, but they deserved a better end.

"Those two drug dealers that you once knew have turned into quite the serial killers. Davis is fucking crazy and Houston is just plain fucking evil. And I know evil. This serene and pastoral countryside of East Tennessee has been unaware of the abhorrent presence residing here for some time. The police haven't even considered they might have a serial killer on the loose because the only people being killed were drug dealers. They just thought it had to do with drug wars. Stupid, don't you think?"

Jimmy shook his head in agreement as he heard the demon refer to someone else as stupid. Even if it was a demon and he might die a thousand horrible deaths, he liked hearing the being call Davis and Houston stupid.

"Them 'serial killers,' as you describe them are mine, Abaddon, and I'd appreciate it if you'd keep your fucking claws off of them. If they are in my presence and on my land, they's mine. You know the rules."

"Rules? I don't need no stinkin' rules," Abaddon said with a guttural Spanish accent and then laughed. "I'm glad you remember that I've got these here claws. Very sharp 'uns' that can disembowel them dogs and you and ole'slim Tim, faster than you can shake a stick at. I suggest you don't ask to see them up close and real 'personal-like' by some stupid thing either of you two geezers mite try and do,"she said with a purposeful twang.

"You can try and, I admit, you might get us both down for a minute or two but you can't kill neither one of us. And you knowed it. That scythe Tim is aholding has the ability to send whatever it cuts off into other worlds. Even things that it removes from demons. Have you forgotten that, Abaddon?"

Abaddon looked over at Jimmy. "Don't you just hate days like this? You think you are going to do one thing and then boom, shit, you end up doing something else entirely. That pisses me off."

Jimmy saw the creature walk over and pull off Houston's head and then cut off the heads of the dogs that attacked her, with long bloody claws that curved outward from her hands. He then watched as the headless forms of the dogs crawled toward each other and reformed into one big dog with three heads. He looked up and saw the man she referred to as Charlie pick up his cane which immediately became a sword and started walking toward the being he referred to as a demon. The tall man with the large scythe was walking side by side with Charlie.

Abaddon turned toward the two men and smiled.

"Charlie, I know how sharp your sword is. And yes, Tim, I am all too familiar with what your wheat cutter can do. But. boys, don't you know? That sort of thing just makes me wet. I am pain incarnate. You will lose this battle and I will win. Yet you two old death traps are too stupid to see that."

She looked over at Jimmy and then back at Charlie and Tim who were halfway down the hill with their weapons raised over their heads. Jimmy watched as the being raised her arms and saw the bloody claws transform into blue-green hands that were waving at the two men that were approaching her.

"Hey, fellows, seeing how we are old acquaintances, I just thought about something. Don't you still take heroes down the river to a resting place for them?"

Both of them stopped walking as they heard Abaddon's question.

"I do," Charlie replied. "Just helped one cross over the other day. Nice fella. A real warrior. Name was Jakub Plotniak. "

"Yes, he sounds very Greek-ish and hero-like."

"Shows you what you know, smart ass. He was of Polish descent. American, but his father was Polish and immigrated over here to these United States. Got killed in a construction accident. Was...."

"Stop with the folk tale, Aesop. I don't give a shit about all of that. I was just trying to get to a compromise. Don't you still require a gold coin for passage on your boat?"

"Yes, shore do."

Abaddon reached into Houston's pocket and pulled out a gold coin. She walked over to Davis and pulled out another one just like it. She handed them both to Jimmy.

"I'm giving you these two-and-a-half-dollar gold pieces, which these assholes kept for good luck. They are for you and your brother. I know you're not dead yet, but your brother is and the fact that you have these coins now is rather serendipitous, don't you think?"

Jimmy looked into the black face and tried to see where the voice came from but he couldn't find anything that resembled a mouth. What he saw looked like six eyes glowing and floating on a background of nothing, before they disappeared into something green and blue that moved back and forth inside of what appeared to be a dark black outline of a head.

"I recommend you give those coins to Charlie and accept his ride down the river. If you don't, I can see the possibility that I will be coming to get you one day and I don't recommend that. It will be worse than what you witnessed tonight.

"Is that acceptable to you, Charon? Jimmy and his brother have gold coins for passage on your boat. They sought revenge for the death of their father. And they knew what those piles of shit over there did was wrong. Let me take the shitless horsemen and you take Jimmy and his brother. I will even go down the road and make all of that disappear. It will be like it never existed and you will have the road to yourself once again. You and Tim there can go back to farming and waiting for the leaves to drop and have a merry old time."

"That'll work, Abaddon," Charlie replied and put his sword down. As soon as it touched the ground it changed back into an old wooden cane.

He walked over to Jimmy and helped him carry JJ onto the skiff. As soon as JJ got on the boat, he awakened and asked Jimmy where they were. Jimmy said that they were going home. JJ smiled and didn't ask anything else. Charon took the coins from Jimmy and pushed away from the shore with the pole. Jimmy watched the person Charlie called Tim and the thing he called Abaddon disappear. He wasn't sure how far they had gone when he saw a woman standing on the side of the stream. Charlie maneuvered the boat toward her.

The middle-aged woman looked sad as she handed a fifty-dollar gold piece to Charlie and got on the boat. For some reason, that gold piece looked familiar to Jimmy. He looked at the woman and smiled and suddenly remembered where he had seen a coin like that. His father used to have one.

He asked JJ for the letter from their mother and held it in his hand. "I'm sorry. What happened to cause you to be here? You look way too young to be getting on this boat," Jimmy said.

"I was killed by a drunk driver. I wasn't paying attention though. I saw the car weaving on the road and should have pulled over but I didn't for some reason. I was distracted. Thinking about something else."

"Were you thinking about your sons?" Jimmy asked as he handed the letter to the woman.

The woman unfolded the paper and read the words. She nodded her head as she looked into Jimmy's face and at the other boy who was sitting next to him. Tears ran down her face when she looked into their eyes.

"I sure hope your sons know they lost a wonderful mother," Jimmy said. "And if they didn't tell you that, I hope you can hear them say that from the afterlife."

"I think I will be able to," the woman said as she moved over and sat down between the two young men.

The Alleys

They were twins. Identical twins. An event that happens only 0.3% of the time. Science would classify them as monozygotic, meaning they developed from one fertilized egg; but they shared more than that. They were connected in a way that science could not explain. Even before they were born, what existed within the mind of one, existed within the mind of the other.

Their mother described them as a miracle. They liked being called that because they knew they were special. Time would reveal that.

Their parents were Esther and David Sutter. She was a housewife and he was an engineer. When they first married, they were very much in love. If you viewed the pregnant Esther sitting on the porch with her husband David, one would think they were looking at a reflection of American culture as interpreted by Norman Rockwell. But upon a closer look, one would see something much more abstract.

Over time, blissful banality evolved into lustful desire and a husband's affair had almost broken up the marriage. For six months they barely talked to one another but eventually, she forgave him, primarily due to his ardent desire to start a family. And like many other couples who thought a baby would be the answer to their marital problems, they were wrong. Babies are not a solution to any problem.

Their names were Ari and Ira Sutter and their influence over their parents was immediate. The cruel nature that can exist within the soul of a baby is never evident to anyone. It is impossible to see. The smiles and giggles that emerge from the rosy-cheeked cherub have a narcotic-like effect on adults. They are unable to see that smile and hear that laugh and consider it as anything but magical instead of admitting that it was simply caused by the absence of abdominal discomfort.

How could anyone look at something so innocent and ever suspect that what they held in their arms was evil? The mother's name was not Rosemary, so why would anyone be suspicious? Only in recent years has the possibility even been considered that some children are born with an inherent psychopathy that precludes them from being anything but evil. But parents and grandparents and family members and friends never imagine that when they are gazing at a beautiful little version of a human being in their arms.

We, as a population, are basically incapable of looking at any newborn animal and not feeling a desire to hold and caress the young being. Except for reptiles or amphibians. They are looked at with fear and disgust by most people. The serpent in the Garden of Eden is probably responsible for that reaction. But even it does have its followers.

They were isolated from their classmates from the time they entered kindergarten, but that didn't bother them. They preferred each other's company and enjoyed puzzles and were voracious readers. Though their peers were content with picture books, the twins were reading much more sophisticated literature. And though they couldn't read or understand their father's engineering texts, they often liked bringing them to school and looking through them.

In the first grade, a fire broke out in the classroom and Ira and Ari were left inside hiding under their desks while the other children were escorted out. They didn't leave the room until it was absolutely necessary or they would be injured by the descending smoke and the approaching flames.

"I liked the way that looked, didn't you, Ira?" Ari asked as they walked out into the playground where the rest of the children were gathered. Ira nodded his head yes. After the classroom fire, the teacher told the principal how she suspected it happened but she had no evidence to prove it. It was dismissed by the principal and because nothing else happened, eventually forgotten.

In the second grade, the teacher discovered that Whitey, the classroom rabbit, had disappeared when she checked to see that he had ample drinking water. It was then that she noticed a few drops of blood in the cage. After conducting a search for Whitey, the teacher brought the principal to the room and showed her the bloodstains along with the note she had found beside the cage. It read, "Went lookeng for Alice" and was written in red crayon. When asked, the teacher said she had her suspicions as to who did this and even went as far as saying that she knew the word "lookeng" had been purposely misspelled to divert attention from the actual culprits. Again, they found no evidence of who was responsible. The principal told the teacher what she was suggesting indicated a revolting nature that she had never seen in a child in her over forty years in the field of education.

The teacher stood her ground though and the principal finally relented and recommended a child psychologist to the parents. The evaluation was agreed to and completed and the psychologist provided a report that said: "Highly intelligent children are often loners because they can see they are not like their classmates." He also stated that he did not identify any abnormality and that, over time, these types of children learn how to adapt and become more sociable. He was wrong.

211

Their preference for being with each other as opposed to other children continued all the way through elementary school. They understood that they shared a special bond. Their love of puzzles grew as they got older and the puzzles became more sophisticated and challenging. They didn't participate in sports, although they did like playing outside. But only with each other and not their classmates.

Outside, they could set ants on fire with a magnifying glass or pick up bugs and throw them into a spider web and when they were caught doing something like that, they always blamed the other one for doing it. It was easy for one to deflect the scolding or punishment onto the other one. They both liked that aspect of being a twin. A different child psychologist said that was normal behavior too and one that would go away over time. He was also wrong.

Perhaps that would have been the right time to perform a functional MRI on the twins to examine their paralimbic system, consisting of the amygdala and pre-frontal cortex region of their brain. Perhaps they would have realized then the lack of empathy that the boys possessed. When shown horrible bloody pictures, for them, it was like looking at what they had for lunch or dinner. They would have known that interventions needed to be made immediately, because if no action was taken, whenever the twins were questioned in the future about crimes they committed, they would respond as if they were reading from a book. What could be recognized from early on in their life as a lack of empathy would become something evil because no one did anything to change the trajectory.

The signs were all there. The question becomes - why were they ignored? Parental denial and influences are very strong especially when they are confronted with defending their children in the absence of a true eyewitness to the suspected aberrant behavior. The classroom is not a court of law and circumstantial evidence is almost the same as having no evidence at all.

Parents are in denial because it's almost impossible to admit to anyone that their children are bad, much less evil. In this particular scenario, the parents could enumerate a list of positive qualities. Very intelligent. Curious. Obedient. Creative. All of these adjectives deflected any words that the teacher could use to suggest something else was going on. And Ari and Ira were smart enough to realize that. They understood what they could and could not get away with and they used that knowledge as leverage to do things that any normal person observing the behavior would describe as "very disturbing."

Perhaps if Esther and David had participated in a religion that recognized true evil within children, they might have been willing to conduct an intervention. The fact that strange behavior occurred whenever a religious environment was encountered should have suggested to them something was wrong. Vomiting, diarrhea, and/or peeing on every member of the clergy should not have been dismissed as "fussy, but normal baby behavior." But like the parents, most of those in the church are in denial, too, when confronted with the existence of true evil within a child.

After the disappearance of Whitey in the second grade, the twins realized that they needed to expand their surroundings to satisfy their curiosity. If they continued to do what they were doing in school, they knew that they would eventually be caught and punished. They resented authority but they were able to hide their feelings and manipulate the situations as they wanted. They knew what to say each time they were questioned so they could control the conversation. Most children aren't that shrewd, but these were not like most children. They were special. Their mother had told them so when they were born.

From that point forward, they expanded their actions outside the classroom. Stray dogs or cats that wandered into their neighborhood never wandered out. Trash can fires occurred more frequently than would be expected but the randomness of it never allowed anyone to isolate the cause.

As they grew, the lack of other friends never bothered Ira or Ari. They still preferred each other's company and it remained that way even through high school. It was not as easy to satisfy their unique needs when they reached high school, but chemistry class, advanced biology class, and shop class provided them with settings where planned accidents could take place. They observed these accidents with a visible lack of emotion, even though the pleasure centers in their brains were exploding like firecrackers. Severe facial burns, severed fingers, and even an explosion that burned through the safety goggles of a stoned classmate, burning his face and his eyelids off, were more than sufficient to placate their needs.

Being called weird no longer mattered to them in high school. There were enough other classmates deemed weirder and even scarier that attention on them was diluted. Because of their intelligence, significant mechanical aptitude, and the engineering influence of their father, they applied to Tennessee Tech and were offered full scholarships.

Originally founded in 1909 as the University of Dixie, Tennessee Tech was ranked the number one public university in the state of Tennessee, according to Money magazine; and its engineering program was one of the best. The twins wanted to study mechanical engineering, focusing on the use of robotics, and found Tennessee Tech ideal for that field of study. It was a natural course of study for "introverted" and highly intelligent students like Ira and Ari. What better school or work setting than one which enabled them to work with robots instead of other people who, for the most part, bored them.

The first murder occurred when they were juniors at Tennessee Tech. Ari strangled a young coed one night. He didn't know why he felt compelled to do it, but he did and he enjoyed it. He broke her neck and left her body in one of the many hiking areas around the school so that it would appear to be an accident. He was successful in creating that illusion. Even though he had killed the girl without thinking or planning it, he understood why he had done it after talking with his brother later. Ira was furious when he found out what his brother had done. "You could have gotten caught. Gone to jail. I would've never seen you again. Why would you do something like that?"

"Oh, don't tell me it's nothing you never considered, Ira. I know you. We can tell what each other is thinking. For some reason, she reminded me of Whitey. The rabbit. You remember Whitey, don't you? You're the one who broke his neck. I just felt this urge to break hers and I was surprised how easy it was to twist her head around until I heard it snap. It was very enjoyable."

Ira didn't say anything. He knew his brother was right. He had remembered what it felt like killing Whitey and like his brother had just said, it was very enjoyable.

"There are cameras all around campus, Ari. We need to be very careful about this. We must make a pact now. No one kills again without the other brother's permission and a well-planned process. We wouldn't be where we are today without understanding we have to plan things out."

Ari smiled. "That's fine, brother. I'll wait for you to take the next step."

In their senior year, Ira went to Ari and said he wanted to do one before he graduated. Ari didn't have to ask his brother what 'do one' meant. He understood. Ira also told him that he had been working on a device in the robotics lab that would detect even the smallest particle of radioactive material. Ari became excited by this news. But when he saw everything his brother had made he was even more excited.

"What do you plan to do with all of this?" Ari asked.

"I'm going to use it to get us a job at the Oak Ridge National Laboratories when we graduate. This other piece of metal will just be a distraction."

"What do you mean?"

"You'll see," Ira smiled.

Later that week, the brothers went out to another hiking trail near campus. Ari watched as Ira set up the flat circular piece of polished sterling silver on the trail at a very precarious point. "All we have to do now is sit back and wait," Ira told Ari. Just as he expected, two young hikers came up at the wrong time of the day and were blinded by the light that was reflected off the metal. In their disorientation, Ira pushed them both off the side of the mountain. They suffered broken necks and died almost instantly. Ira and Ari hiked down to check the bodies and confirmed they were both dead.

"That was amazing, Ira. Inspirational! The polished sterling silver was genius. When we graduate and get our job at the lab, as you say, you know this won't stop."

"Yes, I know. I've planned on that. But you'll have a way to go to be better than me with what I just accomplished."

Ari smiled. "Yes, I suppose I will."

They graduated at the top of their class and just as Ira predicted, they got jobs at the Oak Ridge National Laboratory working on robotic industrialization. They bought a house in Clinton, a "fixer-upper" out in the country along the Clinch River. They loved the view of the Clinch Mountains and the isolated nature of their home. Within a year of moving there, the first body was found in an alley behind Hoskins drug store in Clinton. The paper reported that a body was discovered but did not divulge the gruesome details of the murder. Ari had placed the head of the body in an old red wagon they had found in a deserted barn on their property.

"What did you do with the rest of the body?" Ira asked.

"Dissolved. It's not very hard to make solutions that will dissolve human bodies, Ira. Boiling sodium hydroxide turns the human body into sludge. We aren't much different from that anyway, don't you agree?"

"Yeah, I guess you're right. By the way, I like the image of the head in the red wagon. Very colorful. Reminds me of our childhood and the puzzles we loved putting together."

"Yes, I had to outdo you, you know. And I knew you would see that. The puzzle inside the picture. Did I impress you?"

"Yes, I suppose you did, Ari. Very much so."

Several months later, the second victim was found in an alley behind the Ace Hardware store, several blocks over from the drug store. As soon as the police found the hands in the cookie jar they knew that this was a different victim and that they were looking at a very perverted serial killer. The hands that were found in the cookie jar were male. The head in the little red wagon was a female.

"That was very good, Ira," Ari said when he saw the pictures of the hands. "Are those oatmeal cookies?"

"They are. I didn't use mother's recipe though. I made up my own. There are some extra in the cabinet if you want some."

Ari smiled, got a cookie and went outside and began to think of how he could create another puzzle that was better than the one that his brother had just made.

Over the next four years, the murders within Northeast Tennessee and Southwest Virginia became quite well-known to the local police departments and the Tennessee and Virginia Bureaus of Investigation but the public was kept largely in the dark about them. The nature of the crimes required this and the editors of the newspapers agreed. They would tell the public about the murders and identify the victims when possible, but no specific details of what they had found would be provided in their reports.

As time passed, they found a foot in the mouth of a decapitated head in a neighborhood in Lenoir City; feet in a cooler of ice in an alley in Maryville, and an arm and a leg spread out over numerous dollar bills in an alley within the small town of Gate City, Virginia. It was that murder where Ira and Ari made a misstep that led to their arrest. The police were able to trace the money back to a withdrawal that Ari had made several weeks earlier.

After the capture, the details of the gruesome murders became public and they shocked the small communities within the middle of the "Bible Belt." Past teachers and principals of the twins who could be found were reluctant to be interviewed and would only suggest that they may have been aware of some early issues. They would never admit anything definitively as they knew they would then be indicted for not taking action. The few medical professionals who were interviewed reminded everyone that theirs was not an exact science and that they had treated a myriad of sick children who became normal functioning adults. The parents maintained their denial, knowing that if they didn't they would never be able to sleep at night. Feigned or real ignorance didn't help anyone who was questioned with their sleeplessness, which only increased as each night came and went.

Ari and Ira were very proud to be the first twin serial killers in the world. They realized their work would be talked about for many, many years. Ira told Ari one night right before he fell asleep that he believed their "puzzles" would be remembered for at least several lifetimes.

"You have to consider where we are, Ari. We are in the middle of the Bible Belt. Out in the country; in communities that still speak of the Bogeyman as if he was real. All we did was give substance to the story. Yes, they will not forget us for a very, very long time."

Ari agreed with his brother and closed his eyes. Sometime before morning, he sensed a presence in the shadows of his cell and sat up on the edge of his bed. He saw something sparkling green and blue, sitting there looking at him. He could tell it was old, too. Very old but still familiar.

Ari spoke first. "You know, there have never been twin serial killers before."

"No, there hasn't. It was exquisite to watch," Abaddon replied.

Ari grinned and reached under the bed. He pulled out the razor blade that was taped to the bottom of the cot. He reached up and started cutting away the top of his forehead from his hairline. He made a cut all the way around his face and then began slowing cutting away the tissue that held the outer layer of his skin that comprised his face. When he was done, he placed the bloody but perfect eye and nose-less face next to him on the pillow and held up the small mirror that he retrieved from his pillow.

He smiled as he looked at his image. "I look much better than my brother now, don't you think?"

"Of course, you do," Abaddon replied and smiled. "I always thought you did. Your parents named you both well. Ira, the watchful and Ari, the Lion of God. Very appropriate names. It's a pity that they failed to understand which God you were named after though. Well, at least they didn't at first. I think they have a faint suspicion now. I don't think your work here is done yet, so I will be back. I suggest not shaving for a while."

"Yes, I suppose you're right," he said as he felt the presence leave and looked over at the watchful face with no eyes that lay on his pillow. He then looked back in the mirror and laughed.

They were twins. Identical twins. At least up until the very end of the third trimester, when the umbilical cord got wrapped around one of the baby's necks and strangled him before he was born.

I-75

Most people thought I-75 went north and south. They were right to a certain degree. They just didn't understand how far south it truly went. Abaddon did. The portal leading to Hell was there right outside of Atlanta. Many may have thought that when they were there stuck in traffic, but they didn't completely grasp how close they were to the truth, even though they encouraged the cars and people in front of them to visit it as soon as possible.

The exit looked like any other outlet around Atlanta because Abaddon loved to fuck with people. If they were just lucky visitors who happened onto that ramp, they would find that it led to another ramp, which led to another ramp and then brought them right back to where they started. Abaddon often disguised herself as a homeless person and sat on the grass next to the exits listening to the frustrated drivers "fuck this or that" and pound the steering wheel with their fists. It never got old.

The damned found out just how far the ramp went down and led them into a part of the world they would regret for the rest of their existence. Whatever they feared or whatever events in their past had prompted this journey always showed up somewhere along this road and they soon realized they had taken the wrong exit. But there was nothing that they could do about it at that point. Abaddon liked hearing them scream when they discovered what was happening. It never got old.

At least that's the way it used to be. As she walked along the path back toward the demonic world she inhabited at times, she didn't laugh as much as usual at the torment that the ramps or the nightmarish memories evoked among the passengers. She wasn't sure what was bothering her as she smelled the familiar sulfur and turned the corner of the dark passage.

"Abaddon! The Demon that leaves them screaming! What's up? Long-time no see!" Anzu exclaimed as he picked up the severed hand and placed it into the eternal time clock. The time stamp on the hand indicated that his shift was over.

"Hello, Anzu. Just getting off, I see. How was your day?"

"Oh hell, you know how it goes with us minor demons. Boy meets girl. Boy kills girl. Girl comes back from dead and slaughters boy's family. Boy's family haunts town. Of course, these days it could be boy meets boy and then boy kills boy and so on and so on. But all in all, just another typical day. Not like the crazy shit I hear about you doing. Dude, are all those stories I hear for real?"

Abaddon hated the word 'dude' but she liked Anzu, so she ignored his ignorance and replied with a simple, "Yes."

"The things you have done down here are fucking amazing, Abaddon. I mean the suffering and the pain and the shit. The rivers and rivers of shit that those damned fuckers swim in, live in and eat. Its priceless, dude. I love it. You know they use some of the tortures and punishments you developed in training now."

There was that word 'dude' again. If he says it one more time I'm going to reach over and disembowel him, she thought. "Yes, I was aware of that. I sit in on them sometimes. Or at least I used to. I haven't done that in a long time," she answered in a disinterested manner.

"Shit, Abaddon, what's wrong? You seem…I don't know, almost human-like."

Abaddon stretched out her arm, grabbed Anzu by his neck and threw him up against the wall. The jagged rocks tore into his scaly flesh and a greenish-yellow fluid dripped down his legs.

"Never say anything like that to me again or I will let you see just how wonderful that river of shit can be."

"My bad, my bad."

Abaddon looked at Anzu's burning eyes and saw them dim as she let go of his neck. "Sorry, Anzu. I have had a bad couple of days. I had an encounter with Tisiphone, Alecto, and Megaera that I didn't expect. How could something that looks that foul and demon-like, with snakes for hair and bleeding eyes and wings…how could something like that want to save a human? Huh? Does that make fucking sense to you?"

Anzu shook his head which floated on and off his scaly, pus-filled shoulders.

"And then I had a run-in with Charon and the fucking Grim Reaper. You're not going to believe this, but he and old Grim look like some hick farmers. Out in the middle of fucking nowhere. I mean, who in the hell even believes in that shit these days? I thought they were long gone, relegated to a forgotten book gathering dust on the shelves in a section of the library that no one goes into anymore. But no, I had to deal with those two old coots, as they would say where they currently reside, just so I could bring some nasty little fucks back here for an eternal meet and greet with that river of shit you so fondly refer to."

Anzu wasn't sure how to respond so he said nothing as he just stood there unmoving. At least as unmoving as he could

223

be considering that there were large parasites always crawling around just beneath his skin.

"But what bothers me even more is that I wasn't that interested in two little boys suffering and that they were somehow not killed by one very nasty bottom feeder. One of those old Nazis. I mean it doesn't get any better than that; to find one of those sons of bitches still alive. And this one was still killing and acting like it was 1945 when I found him. Just as crazy and malevolent as he was in the good old days when they thought they were going to conquer the world. So much for a master race, huh? Arrogant sadistic pricks. But it was a great feeling watching him die. And becoming little pieces of flesh and shit for the dung beetles."

"Dung beetles? Oh, man, Abaddon. I'm going to use that idea. Oh, hell yeah."

Abaddon heard the compliment but didn't acknowledge it. She just continued talking about what was bothering her. "And then I let Charon take two brothers on his little ferryboat ride. Granted these brothers weren't really evil and probably would have sought forgiveness for their misdeeds and been snatched away from me before I could get my hands on them, but I actually helped them. I used to not care about that type of shit at all. But I didn't want to fight with Charon and that Grim stick and so I let him take them. I did enjoy fucking up that dog of his though - Cerberus. Stupid asshole calls the dogs - now get this - Sir, Berry, and Bess. How fucking pathetic. I should have disemboweled the whole lot of them and thrown them into that river of piss and acid he calls Styx. "

"Funny, the river Styx out in the sticks."

Abaddon wanted to take Anzu's head off for saying that, but it was a moving target and it wouldn't have done anything but make her smile for a moment. And, after all, she had said the same thing when she came upon Charon. She couldn't fault Anzu for saying it so she restrained herself. And, she had someone listening to her. Someone she could relate to, so she continued to talk.

"Bashing in human heads until the skull cracks open like a walnut was something I truly enjoyed watching. Stripping the skin off a human, while they are still alive, I mean that's just a party waiting to happen. And like I said, an old Nazi killing more innocent people, I'll take two seats in the front row, every day, all day. But in each one of those scenarios, I found myself demonstrating something I have been unfamiliar with for my entire life. Empathy. Fucking empathy instead of indifference? What the hell is happening to me?"

Anzu was unsure as to what to say or do. He had never seen another demon act this way or ask these types of questions. Especially Abaddon the Destroyer. The Primo Demeno for the Boss. He knew she could make him suffer for many years if he said the wrong thing. But before he could answer, Abaddon continued talking so he stood and listened. Making sure she saw all of his eyes looking into all of her eyes as often as possible.

"Hey Anzu, you ever wonder if we are on the right team? You know the one that survives the end?"

"What are you talking about, Abaddon?" Anzu replied as he looked around the poisonous gas cavern in which they stood.

"You know, the team that comes out on top when all of mankind is destroyed. When we go hand to hand, wing to wing, sword to sword with the army of God."

"You're making me very uncomfortable with these questions."

"You know, Anzu, I don't give a shit how comfortable or uncomfortable these questions make you. Answer the goddamn question or I'll condemn your ass to working in the Vomitorium. You want to spend the next 100 years or so forcing the damned to vomit over and over? Yeah, at first, it's nice, but believe me, it gets old over time. And though we are immune to foul smells, for the most part, I promise you that place will get to you after about the eightieth year or so. Just speaking from experience, but perhaps you will find you have a greater tolerance to that chunky soup that comes out in projectile fashion from the damned than I did."

"Yes, I think that we're on the right team," Anzu said as he looked at all of the open eyes and various shapes and sizes of ears that were on the cavern walls and focused on him and Abaddon. Regardless of what Abaddon threatened doing to him, he knew he needed to say the right thing now. The one that held dominion over Hell was watching and listening to everything.

Abaddon twisted her head over to one side and then the other as she looked at Anzu. She turned her head around her entire body and she saw all of the eyes and ears too. She looked at Aznu and yawned like a baboon, demonstrating to the other one in the pack, how many teeth she had that were long and sharp.

"Without a doubt, Abaddon. We will win the war. Even says so in Revelations."

"That victory is not permanent and it's only an old story. Perhaps even a myth, considering how Neo-God had something to do with the writing of it. He has his own plan. I am sure of it, and only he knows it. Not even God knows what Neo-God's real plan is. Hell, he could let most of us die and then retreat as a subterfuge so that he could attack with a larger army at a later date when man and God become complacent. That's exactly what I would do if I were him."

"He is the supreme deceiver. And you're probably right. But I think we will win in the end."

"A lot of us will die, you know that, don't you?"

"'Better to reign in Hell than serve in Heaven,' I've always said," Anzu quoted.

"You are fucking brainwashed. Do you even know where that quote comes from?"

"From the Demon Handbook that the Demon Resource people give us in orientation. It's part of our Mission and Vision statement."

"First of all, that quote comes from "Paradise Lost," a poem written by an English poet, John Milton, in 1667. Were you even born then?"

"Of course, Abaddon. I've been around since 2559 BC."

"Then why do you go around spewing that crap without knowing its origin? Not asking what it means or where it comes from? You've been around here long enough. In fact, why are you still a demon of lesser order? You should be further along by now. Maybe it's because you still talk about the Mission and Vision statement and Demon Resources orientation after 4000 years.

"I still talk about the other part of the Mission and Vision statement, too. You know - The Game of Life? It's not just a board game anymore."

When Abaddon heard Anzu repeat the words she had written, her anger lessened, even though she knew he said it only in the hopes it would do that very thing. *It's just his submissive nature toward a more powerful demon*, she told herself. But she had to admit, she liked the fact that he knew those words and understood his submissive role in relation to her.

"Demon Resource orientation? Boy, that's a Hell within Hell, isn't it? I haven't thought about that in over 10,000 years. And even back then I thought it was way too long and that most of it was unnecessary. Does Abyzou still teach that shit?"

"Yes," was all Anzu replied. He could tell her anger had subsided somewhat but he was still afraid of saying anything that could further enrage an already ill-tempered Abaddon or what any of the ears would hear.

"Abyzou, she's a beauty, isn't she? I shapeshift into abominable things but she is just plain repugnant, don't you think? Those gills on her neck. Breath that smells like vomit and seaweed. Big old fish eyes with no eyelids, so she just stares at you constantly. I do like all the little snake fingers. Those are pretty cool. I have used them before to scare the shit out of people. At least those that don't like snakes. But she looks like a constipated boa constrictor all the fucking time. Getting rid of her in the war wouldn't be such a bad thing, now that I think about it."

Anzu didn't say anything. Again, he just stood there and allowed his head to bob up and down and side to side off his shoulders.

"I mean, don't get me wrong. I've always loved my job. I don't even consider it a job. It's a calling. Scaring the shit out of people and creating new hells for all of those fucked up beings brings a smile to my face every time. But something happened just recently. I felt empathy and had the attitude that if we just cut the heads off all of the damned and place them under a glass cover, you know, like one of those clear glass covers that they use for cakes, that would be enough. To Hell with all that other stuff. Just do it and be done with it.

"Of course, you would make them aware that would be their world for eternity. And just let them all sit there under the glass staring at all of the other heads. Seems like that would drive them fucking crazy enough, don't you think?"

Anzu knew Abaddon was seeking some sort of validation and was just crying out for help. He only hoped he wouldn't be crying out for help when he offered to her what he thought would be a constructive idea. "Have you ever considered DAP, Abaddon?"

"The Demon Assistance Program?"

"Yeah. We all know that you are the best, I mean, the Demon that leaves them screamin' and all that, but that doesn't mean you don't need help every thousand years or so. I know it's helped others."

"Is that so? And what makes you think I could benefit from it?"

"You seem a little depressed."

"Oh, and you have a psych degree, I imagine?"

"Yes, as a matter of fact, I do. Got it several years ago via DTS."

"The Demon Theological Seminary online program, huh?"

"Yes, I think a discussion with a DAP advisor and a little R & R would greatly benefit you."

"R & R? I don't think you completely understand what R & R means. It means Rip and Remove," Abaddon said as she reached over and grabbed the pus-filled shoulders of Anzu and started pulling him apart as if she was tearing a newspaper into two halves. The greenish-yellow pus oozed out of the ripped-open body and swarms of alien-looking bugs fell onto the floor trying to get back into their host before someone stepped on them.

Abaddon smiled as she looked at the two halves of Anzu on the cavern floor. She thought it looked like some giant cellular organism had just gone through asexual reproduction and was trying to coalesce into a new and larger version of itself.

"I'll be damned, Anzu. You were right. I did need a little R & R. Watching you lying there and moving all around, trying to reconnect yourself, makes me feel good. But you need to pull yourself together. You're a mess right now. "

"fisssssss issssss fffffffffnnn, prfffffuffffff……."

"What's that? I don't understand what you are saying?"

"jusssssssss a minnnnnnnnnnnet….."

Abaddon laughed as she heard Anzu trying to talk.

Anzu's body parts merged and once they did, he stood up.

"This is fine. Perfect, Abaddon. Letting go is helpful."

"If you say one more fucking self-help bullshit word, I will let you see how wonderful that dung beetle idea truly is."

Before Anzu could say anything else, Abaddon heard something calling her name from behind her.

"See…see that, Anzu. I used to love the way screams echoed within these caverns, but just hearing my name repeat itself against the walls, makes me want to leave. I'm not sure why I even came back here now."

"Abaddon. Abaddon. Hey, Abaddon!" Aesma called out.

Abaddon turned around to see the small hairy assistant to NG come running toward her. "Abaddon. Couldn't you hear me calling you?"

"They probably heard you calling my name all the way up on Peachtree."

"Peachtree?" Aesma said with a puzzled look on his face.

"It doesn't matter. What is it you want?"

"The Old Goat wants to see you. He said, 'Get Abaddon to me at once!'"

"What the fuck now?"

"Not sure," Aesma replied. "But he's in one of those moods. He's got that fire in his eyes."

"Shit, Aesma. He always has fire in his eyes. And do you know how annoying it is for you to repeat everything he tells you?"

"I do what I am instructed to do."

"Oh, I know. After thousands of years, believe me, I know."

Abaddon looked down at Aesma and Aesma could see the vile stare from her many eyes that moved around her face.

"You are a sycophant, Aesma, hoping that he will give you some cruel little task to perform. So you go running around this place doing whatever the fuck he says. Did anyone ever tell you that you look like a turd with arms and legs and a lot of hair?"

"Yes. You have told me that several times. But we need to go. Like I said he has fire shooting out of his eyes and he is one of those hellfire and damnation kind of moods. You understand that, don't you?"

"Yes, Aesma, I do," Abaddon said as she turned back toward Anzu.

"Thanks for the advice, Anzu. I found it most helpful."

Anzu didn't reply. He knew that it would be best if he just let her leave.

"And Anzu, NG told me to tell you that the pool of shit is clogged up and you need to go check it out," Aesma said just before she and Abaddon left.

"Shit."

"Yes."

Abaddon laughed. "Anzu, go into the Garden of Eden and look for the little ball of shit being rolled around by the dung beetles. Cause it to take human form. He is that Nazi I was telling you about. His name is Viktor. Take him to that pool of shit and use his body and head to remove the clog. I will enjoy thinking about that."

"Yes, Abaddon. I'll do that. Thank you for the suggestion." Anzu hoped that the words 'thank you' meant that he would not incur Abaddon's wrath again but just in case he was wrong, he would do his best to make sure that he didn't run into her the next time she entered Hell.

Abaddon followed Aesma as he walked through various dark caverns. Screams permeated the air and echoed through each chamber in which they walked.

"Don't you just love that sound?" Aesma asked.

Abaddon didn't answer. She wasn't in the mood to respond and wasn't even sure what her response would be.

Abaddon smelled a familiar smell and before she could stop Aesma from going any further, they had entered the Clown Cavern. Oni, the Master Demon waved as he saw them enter.

231

"Fuck," Abaddon said as Oni walked toward them.

Oni was a demon who scared other demons. He was blue and red in color, but the red just reflected either fresh blood or patches of red scaly skin that was always sloughing off and in some oozing state of replacement. He had three horns on his head, with the longest one in the middle. They were always being replaced, and the holes where one once was positioned, became a pool of maggots before the new horn began to form. His fingers and toes had long claws and he could rip through a human within seconds and disembowel them like birds of prey did with small mammals.

The hair that grew around his horns was bushy and full of thorns and looked like small nests of tangerine-colored hair had been glued on in random places all over his head. Blood dripped from two of his three eyes. His third eye, in the middle of his forehead, always exuded a thick sticky mucus. Abaddon doubted he could see anything from it. She was certain it was just there for effect and it was very successful in that regard.

"Aesma, we are honored that you have brought the great Abaddon into our chamber. Welcome, Abaddon. Are you interested in staying for a while to enjoy the torment or do you seek other matters?"

Abaddon knew Oni resented her and was only pretending to be gracious. She had known for a long time that Oni wanted to be known as the Destroyer, and if given a chance, he would try and crush her if he detected the slightest bit of weakness.

"She cannot stay, Oni. We seek the Master's quarters. Perhaps later," Aesma replied.

"Pity. At least look at the new clown wheel I've invented," Oni said as he took hold of Abaddon's arm and when he did, his hand went up in flames. He pulled it back, only to watch his scaly skin melt off the bones.

"Do not ever touch me, Oni. I go where I want to go when I want to go. I don't have to see your clown wheel to know what is on it. You are so predictable even though you think it's some sort of cutting-edge terror. I can see what's on your wheel in the faces of the damned that have been forced to turn it. There is a hot poker segment, probably allowing the soul to pick the site that they wish for it to enter. There are bowls and rivers of shit segments. A lava wash, railroad spikes in hands and feet, skin flaying, the vomitorium, and something that I am sure is called a stitch in time just because I see some of your servants sewing shut the eyes and mouths of those that find themselves here. How fucking amusing."

Oni smiled and brought his burnt hand up to his face and licked it. "Glad we could meet, if just for this moment, Abaddon. I will be looking forward to seeing you again," Oni said as he bowed and motioned for them to move on.

"Boy, Oni doesn't like you, does he?" Aesma asked as they walked into the golden anteroom that led to the Master's chamber.

"The feeling is mutual," Abaddon replied as she opened the door and saw the human sitting at the end of the table eating.

"Ah, Abaddon," the human said as he walked toward her. "What do you think?"

"I think you are what you are when you want to be what you are. This human form looks familiar though. Ah, yes, one of those presidents, you so like to wear."

"I'm in my politician and world leader phase. There are just so many that look good on me. Sometimes I have a hard time deciding."

"Is that why you wanted to see me, to discuss what you would be wearing for a day, a week, or a year?"

"Careful. Do not do or say something to displease me."

"You did not call me in here to threaten me. What is it you wish to discuss?"

233

The devil smiled. "There is something wrong with you. I hear and see all. You know that. The souls you have brought to me are delicious. But your volume is down and I sense ennui."

"Ennui. I haven't heard that word in a long time. It's not used enough. I love your use of words. I learn from you."

"Yes, I know, Abaddon. You are my favorite within my entire kingdom. But do not avoid the context of the statement."

"Quality over quantity. I have embraced that philosophy."

"Do not mock me."

"If I do not speak the truth to you, who will?"

"I allow your cynical comments, but you have yet to speak the truth to me. That is why I give you some latitude. But do not cross the line."

"Fuck you. You move the line to suit you."

"You are wise, Abaddon. Too wise at times."

"I'm not sure what is wrong with me."

"You have encountered Tisiphone and her sisters. And Charon and Grim. Did that anger you?"

"Yeah. That damn Tisiphone really pissed me off. And if Charon and Grim weren't so pathetic I would have destroyed them."

"And with that, you begin to demonstrate the candor in which I seek."

Abaddon found that comment unsettling and insulting. "Why do you still have demons walking on the ceilings or twisting their heads all around their body and then have them walk backward on thin legs and arms. Shit, every fucking horror movie that has demonic possession as the subject matter does something like that."

"You don't always need to reinvent the wheel with humans. They must be confronted with images that overwhelm their senses and when they hear the bones pop and crack and see the head turn around and the hands and feet turn backward and start walking toward them, it frightens them. We use terror to our advantage," the Devil explained.

"Have you seen 'America's Got Talent?' They have contortionists on there that can do the same thing. And they aren't possessed. And don't say you don't know that, because I know you are very aware. I just don't think that image is terrifying to most of them. And I'm not even sure we need so much terror anymore. I think being more subtle, more seductive, would be wiser."

"She who speaks to the Master of Seduction. Seduction and terror are both tools we use and you know that. You are merely trying to change the subject. But it won't work, Abaddon. Come, next to the fire and sit down. Would you like some green tea?"

"No, I hate that shit. I don't know why in Hell you still drink it. Give me a Jack and Coke. Fuck it. Just give me the Jack."

Abaddon saw the bottle of Jack on the table with a glass as they walked over to the sofas in front of the fire. A large cup of green tea sat across from it. She picked up the bottle and drank half of it before putting it down.

"What do you think of the new leather sofas? Can you tell what it is?"

Abaddon looked at NG as she brushed the skin with her hands. "Scientologists?"

"That's what most people think, but it's not. It's religious zealots; false prophets who blew themselves up. It takes a little longer to make because of the little pieces that remain of them, but it's worth it, don't you think?"

"It's nice, NG. Very nice."

Abaddon's boss picked up his cup of green tea and took several long sips before setting it back down on the table. He leaned over and looked into Abaddon's face and focused on each eye that she made present for the moment.

"Look, Abaddon, our overall soul conversion rate is down for the year. Way down. I didn't call you in here for a damn job interview. I want fucking results and if you cannot produce them, I will find someone that can. Now, are you going to tell me what the hell is wrong with you or should we just end this conversation and let me put your entire body under one of those clear cake covers you mentioned to Anzu? Perhaps a thousand or so years under that will make you more willing to talk."

"I think I'm just having one of those years. Nothing other than that."

"Oh, come on! Don't try and fool me. It cannot be done," NG said as he finished his green tea.

Abaddon sat and looked at the devil across from her. She picked up the bottle of Jack and drained it.

"Where is the old Abaddon that I use as an example to others within this realm? The one that came up with "Neo-God." Still love that name, by the way. The one who took the words "shit storm" and turned them into an actual shit storm down here. I love that room. Watching the damned in there is still one of my favorite things to do. They don't know what to cover first: their mouth, nose, eyes, ears. It's hilarious.

"Why don't you go and take a vacation over in the Middle East? Finding lost souls over there is like shooting fish in a barrel. I love it when they show up and we give them the dead and rotting virgins that were promised them. Drives the necrophiliacs crazy, since we remove their genitalia and make them sit and watch. Which as you know, was another one of your great ideas," NG said as he leaned back and laughed.

The laughter resulted in a geyser emitting hot steam and sulfur within the famous park in Wyoming.

"Are you ever going to blow up that damn park?" Abaddon asked. "I can't believe people continue to go there."

"Humans are ignorant, Abaddon. They condemn some behavior as reckless only to ignore their own behavior which is just as damning. I am just waiting on the right day."

"From what I read in the papers, that day could be any time now. Or hell, just listen to the news every night. Every fucking headline or story starts with some disaster."

"Since when do you give a shit about what you see in the papers? Your ability to see the future is better than that."

"But I cannot see the end. You don't allow any of us to see the end. Only you know that."

"There is a plan, Abaddon."

"You do realize that you drive a lot of people to church with all of these disasters that are occurring now? And now with all the terrorism, they are flocking to God in record numbers."

"You mistake their fear for reverence and deference to the All-mighty. Most of them are just hiding there for a moment while the riots and violence begin to happen. The innocent and the rioters both profess that they understand right and wrong, but they don't, because they do not understand their enemy is their friend.

"Accepting the differences of another is not one of man's strengths. It is a crevice within their composition that I can exploit. Inciting violence is easy. Their bigotry and victim mentality lends itself to it. It allows those that have been wronged in the past to remain wrong in the present and their stupidity and hatred are an aphrodisiac to me. I love listening to them weep and worry and scream about all that is happening to them, and when they are doing that, they are not paying attention to Him or me. And so it goes on for a little longer."

"Do demons go crazy, NG?"

"Of course, they do. The crazier the better. "

"That's not the crazy I am talking about."

"Yes, I know. You demonstrated empathy and you think that is the beginning of the end for you."

Abaddon didn't say anything as she focused on the human form across from her.

"You forget, Abaddon. I, too, understand empathy. Do you not remember that I was once an angel? Empathy is a weak emotion that I abhor but it does not mean that you cannot experience it. You are part of me, Abaddon, and as such, it would not be unusual for you to have encountered this feeling. But, after ten thousand years, do you really think it matters?

"Look at all the sadistic and horrible things you have done to humans. There is no equal, excluding me of course, that can inflict such pain. You understand seduction and how to use it to your advantage. And you understand terror. Terror that is awe-inspiring and grand in its scope and its attention to the smallest of details. You are not weakening, Abaddon. You are only getting stronger. The fact you are here tells me that."

Before she could ask for another one, the bottle of Jack appeared on the table. Abaddon smiled exposing her many rows of sharp teeth as she picked it up, took a drink, and then looked over at NG.

"You said vacation in the Middle East, but I think I would prefer to go down south. There are so many crazy sons of bitches out there in the country. And though most of them are pious, I much more enjoy converting the pious than just providing strength to those that are already evil."

NG nodded his head in agreement.

"All of them are there; awaiting you to help them fulfill their destiny. And I agree with you. Seducing hope and love into evil is much more enjoyable than escorting what is already evil into the world of the damned. I love the south too. Lots of hellfire and damnation down there. They do call it the Bible Belt for a reason," NG said as he smiled and the fire within his eyes blazed.

Abaddon took another drink and rubbed her left hand across the sofa.

"Maybe I can get you a new sofa in a month or two?"

"If anyone can, it would be you."

"Thanks, NG. I have regained my passion."

"Yes, I see that."

"You ever wonder why all the alien sightings are out in some godforsaken part of the country that no one has ever heard of?"

"Because they need a way to describe something that has been done to them in a hurtful manner by a loved one or because they are ignored and want some attention. Either way, they are both opportunities. Humans love sci-fi. They always will. It helps explain away a lot of things."

Abaddon picked up the bottle and stood up. She started to turn it up when NG spoke.

"Take it with you. I find it helps to have it with me when I go through the clown cavern."

Abaddon laughed. NG walked her to the gold doors which opened up as they approached. "Hate groups, religious zealots, false prophets, psychopaths, sociopaths, Scientologists, they are all there waiting for you, Abaddon. As well as the virtuous that stumble and ask for the wrong helping hand. They are all looking for you to come and show them the way."

Abaddon smiled and then realized something that still bothered her. "But what about the squirrels?

"Oh, I almost forgot! That's why I had these made for you," NG said as a pair of boots appeared in his hands. "Squirrel boots. Made up of seven thousand layers of human skin. That's at least one of every ethnicity. The squirrels won't be able to get through these boots should they try and bite you. I even got you this special bottle of perfume. Just spray it on when you're walking around down there in the woods and you'll be protected."

Abaddon took the boots and the bottle and left. As she walked away, she took another drink of Jack and wondered just what was so special about that perfume and how it would keep squirrels away. "Of course." she thought, as she looked at the label on the bottle NG had handed her and began to laugh. "He thinks of everything. Politician piss."

Acknowledgments

"The Evil Dead" – written and directed by Sam Raimi, 1981

"Snoopy" – fictional character created by Charles Schulz, debut October 4, 1950

"The Joker" – fictional character created by Bill Finger, Bob Kane, and Jerry Robinson for Batman DC comic book, debut April 25, 1940

"The Conjuring" – Written by Chad Hayes and Carey Hayes, directed by James Wan, 2013

"Insidious" – Written by Leigh Whannell, directed by James Wan, 2010

"The Alien" – Written by Dan O'Bannon, directed by Ridley Scott, 1979

"The Wizard of Oz" – Adaptation of L. Frank Baum's 1900 book *"The Wonderful Wizard of Oz."* Screenplay by Noel Longley, Florence Ryerson and Edgar Allan Woolf, directed by Victor Fleming, 1939

"Better the devil you know…" - Irish proverb in use since 1300s, often attributed to Robert Taverner

"Ghostbusters" – Written by Dan Ackroyd and Harold Ramis, directed by Ivan Reitman, 1984

"Nancy Drew" – created by Edward Stratemeyer, published under pseudonym Carolyn Keene, debut 1930

"Hardy Boys" – created by Edward Stratemeyer, published under pseudonym Franklin Dixon, debut 1927

"Three Stooges" - American vaudeville and comedy team active from 1922 until 1970, Columbia Pictures

"The Sound of Music" – Screenplay by Ernest Lehman (based on the memoir by Maria Von Trapp, *"The Story of the Trapp Family Singers"*), directed by Robert Wise, 1965

"Batman" – TV show based on DC comic book of same name, produced by William Dozier, 1966.

"F Troop" – TV show created by Seaman Jacobs, Ed James and Jim Barnett, 1965.